"Is this a joke?"

Rothwakes, to his credit, looked about as amused by all this as Lawrence.

That is to say, in no way whatsoever.

"No, Hayes, this is not a joke. Bobby will be racing in my stead."

"This is preposterous."

"Please do enlighten us," Bobby mumbled dryly.

"This wager, this *business*," he said, rising to his feet and encroaching into the woman's space—not that she seemed to mind, not moving a hair except to look up at him. He silently thanked the Lord for the blessing that was his height, a head more than hers. "Was meant to be executed by two people of similar talent and position. Therefore, *you*, racing, is preposterous."

"Don't worry yourself, your lordship," Bobby said drolly, a wicked smile tilting her lips up. "You can still make a show of it, perhaps train a little so the deficiencies in your talents and *position* are not so glaringly obvious."

"Your tongue is quick, girl, but words will not save you when you're ten miles out and crying to return home."

"Oh, we'll see who's crying, *boy*..."

Author Note

This book has been with me for a very long time, born, as so many are, of a single image. This time, the lone rider on the beach, racing toward an unknown future just beyond the finish line.

And, as I've come to realize with every other book I've written thus far, I feel this one was written when it needed to be written. When I was ready to meet Bobby and Lawrence and tell their story properly. When I was ready to truly delve into what makes them who they are.

With *The Viscount's Daring Miss*, I wanted to write a tale full of joy, love and adventure, as always, but mostly, full of warm, fuzzy feelings. Of summer nights under the stars and long fireside talks. As much as I love my Gothic romance, I did feel the need for a bit of a departure, and I hope you enjoy this book as much as I did writing it.

On a historical note, equine endurance racing did not become an official, organized sport in the West until the twentieth century. Naturally, that does not mean there was no such thing before then. Throughout history, humans and horses have traveled the length and breadth of continents together. And throughout history, there have been tales of people racing, breaking records and wagering on their own talents.

Above all, I sought to represent that spirit in these pages. The spirit of collaboration, and respect, between man and animal. The spirit of breaking barriers.

And most of all, the spirit of endurance.

LOTTE R. JAMES

———

The Viscount's Daring Miss

HARLEQUIN®
HISTORICAL™

Recycling programs for this product may not exist in your area.

ISBN-13: 978-1-335-72386-4

The Viscount's Daring Miss

Copyright © 2023 by Victorine Brown-Cattelain

For questions and comments about the quality of this book, please contact us at CustomerService@Harlequin.com.

Harlequin Enterprises ULC
22 Adelaide St. West, 41st Floor
Toronto, Ontario M5H 4E3, Canada
www.Harlequin.com

Printed in U.S.A.

Lotte R. James trained as an actor and theater director, but spent most of her life working day jobs crunching numbers while dreaming up stories of love and adventure. She's thrilled to finally be writing those stories, and when she's not scribbling on tiny pieces of paper, she can usually be found wandering the countryside for inspiration or nestling with coffee and a book.

Books by Lotte R. James

Harlequin Historical

The Viscount's Daring Miss

Gentlemen of Mystery

The Housekeeper of Thornhallow Hall
The Marquess of Yew Park House
The Gentleman of Holly Street

Look out for more books from Lotte R. James coming soon.

Visit the Author Profile page
at Harlequin.com.

To the One & Only Christina for her enduring friendship. A special thank-you to her and her secret source for all their help with this book.

To anyone unsure of where they fit in the world.

And always, to my mother, Brigitte.

Chapter One

Race Rules

1. *The race will be between the horses Beowulf (belonging to His Lordship the Right Honourable Lawrence Hathaway, Viscount Hayes), and Arion (belonging to His Lordship the Right Honourable Julian Overday, Baron Rothwakes), and will begin at Land's End, Cornwall, on July the 14th, 1838, ending at Jocelyn Bay, Kent, on July the 23rd, 1838.*

2. *There will be eight sections to the race. Each rider will begin at the same time and place, and end at a set marker (exact locations listed herein). Upon arrival at the end of day to the agreed upon location, each rider will provide the contest supervisors with their planned route for the following day.*

3. *These planned routes should be of similar difficulty, though exact distances may vary. At each evening meeting, the standings of the riders will be measured, and should a winner be proven categorically at any stage, the contract will go into*

full effect (including settlement of debt), though the race will continue until the end. Only in case of disbarment or forfeiture due to injury will the race be suspended.

4. *The only section not planned by riders will be the final portion of the race (a test of speed, to be raced bareback) through Little Gate town, finishing at the northern end of the beach in Jocelyn Bay, on the 23rd of July, 1838.*

5. *Participants will be required to participate in an event in London on July 20th, 1838, and will be allowed a night indoors following said event.*

6. *Participants will be responsible for their own victuals, and those of their horses, to be prepared and taken with them, with the exception of the stop on the 17th of July, where riders will be allowed to spend the night at an inn, (details listed herein), and refresh their supplies.*

7. *No aid to be given to another rider in distress and no allowances made for a rider or horse's injury or distress. Any incapacitation will result in automatic forfeiture.*

8. *No delays, rescheduling or timetable changes will be allowed once the race has begun.*

9. *Any disregard for these rules, any further rules made in addendum, or of the overall contract, will result in immediate forfeiture.*

Rothwakes Estate, Sussex,
July 7th, 1838

If Lady Rothwakes had been here to witness her eaves-dropping, Bobby would've had to write a lengthy and thorough dissertation on the importance of good manners. Only, Her Ladyship was not here to witness such vulgar, ill-mannered behaviour. She had been gone a long time now, so this, like so much else Bobby did that the lady might've objected to, would go unpunished.

Not that it felt that way to Bobby. Twelve years since the best woman in the world had died, and still, it felt as if she was there, waiting around a corner to call her to tea, or reprimand her for things like eavesdropping. Feeling her presence constantly, particularly in the house, was something which was both reassuring, and painful. Reassuring, for it felt as if all those preachers actually had it right, and that loved ones remained with you, always, looking out for you from Heaven, painful, for it reminded her of the gaping loss, the hole in her heart which would never heal.

Shaking her head, Bobby pushed away thoughts of Lady Rothwakes, and focused instead on her son Julian's voice, leaning closer, until her ear was actually pressed upon the wood of Lord Rothwakes' door.

'Goddammit,' Julian screamed, frustration, sadness, and a touch of fear obvious in his voice, even from here. A crash quickly followed, along with more cursing. 'I don't have two months! What part of that did you not understand the last time you attended me?'

'My lord—'

'Get out! Just get out!'

Bobby had just enough time to make herself scarce by leaping down the corridor ahead, before the doctor emerged from the room, huffing and mumbling, and slamming doors as he went.

Leaning her back against the wall, taking in a deep breath, Bobby gnawed on her lip, and asked forgiveness for the elation currently filling her breast. Being glad of others' misfortunes was another sin Lady Rothwakes would not have withstood.

Only, Bobby *did* feel bad for Julian, truly. He was her best friend, the truest *human* friend she had, all the family she had left, even if it was only in spirit and not in blood. So of course she felt bad for him. Of course she'd been utterly terrified when she'd heard of his accident. He wouldn't have been the first lord to trip and fall down a set of stairs, and not survive it. As it was, he'd escaped with a nasty bump on his head—and the rather gnarly broken leg which, if the doctor was to be believed, would take a solid two months to heal. Up until a day or so ago, they'd all still been scared to death the wound might fester, so no, she didn't take his injury lightly. If she lost anyone else…

Well, there was a good chance she might become truly *feral*, as people were already wont to call her.

So no, Bobby hadn't taken anything about his injury lightly, nor in other circumstances would she have felt any sort of excitement at the prospect of her friend being injured. Only today, she couldn't help it.

Because although circumstances were dire—some might say, even more dire than they had been *because* of Julian's injury—it felt as if Fate, or God, or whoever, or whatever, had given *her* a chance. A chance, to seize her own destiny. To show the world who she truly was. To prove her worth, and perhaps even, pay back the Rothwakes family in some way, for all they'd done for her.

For taking her in, giving her not only a good life,

but a family, a *home*, and a future far beyond that she might've had if their paths had never crossed.

I can do this. I know I can.

So... Get in there.

Right.

And don't take no for an answer.

Right.

Glancing out the small window across from her, Bobby reminded herself of all that was at stake.

Rothwakes. Julian's reputation. The land. The stables. The rest of the staff. My family.

My life.

Julian would see right by her if all was lost—Bobby knew that—but the life she wanted, craved, dreamt of, would remain just that. Glittering fairy dust on the wind.

I can do this.

In that moment, staring out across the Downs that had seen every step since her first, Bobby felt the truth of that reassurance. It was as if the lush green of the hills, the rustling of the silver beech leaves in the wind, and the dance of light and shadows as clouds moved across the pale blue canvas, were reminding her of who she was. Of what her life up until now had been, of all she'd done that seemingly led to this moment.

This very moment.

Yes. She could do this.

Now, to convince Julian. Not that he has better options.

Other options, surely, but none better. Bobby at least knew one thing with absolute certainty: her worth.

Smoothing the errant strands from her queue, brushing the last few blades of grass from her jacket, Bobby returned to Julian's door, only this time, she knocked.

'Julian? It's Bobby.'

'Come in,' he said, the sigh which the words came on, heavy, and full of despair.

I can do this. I can fix this, Julian.

If only you'll let me.

Letting herself into his rooms, Bobby glanced around until she spotted him, slouched in one of the armchairs by the window, his leg up on a footstool that his mother and she had embroidered together, the remnants of a tea set—silver, luckily, so bruised, not broken—a few yards away.

Bobby busied herself picking it up best she could, before setting it on a table by the door, far from his reach. She took a moment once she turned back to him, before striding over there, and explaining her purpose. Not that he seemed in a hurry to discover it.

It had been a while since she'd been in this room, not because of propriety—the servants all knew better than to think anything of the two of them spending time alone, in *any* room—but rather because it had been a long time since they'd had reason to meet here. Since his last illness, a chest cold some two or three years ago, when she'd attended to him despite his protestations that it wasn't her place, nor her duty. Except that it was—family, no matter how high up on the social ladder they be, was meant to take care of each other. Or so Lady Rothwakes decreed.

Which is what you're doing now. Taking care of family.

Coming back to the room, Bobby realised it hadn't really changed in all the years Julian had had it—twenty-five or so. It was all still pale blue silk walls and rugs, strewn strangely over each other on wooden floorboards, dark navy-and-white-striped upholstery, and very little of anything else. A few pictures on the walls, a watercolour of his mother, and a stack of books on his bedside table. Nothing more.

Not that any more was needed to make it his; his family, his blood, was in the very walls of this house. In every leaf of every book, every chair, and every piece of silverware. It always had been, and always should be.

Which is why you're here.

Glancing at Julian now, Bobby could see the weight of it all, the weight of his decisions, weighing him down, sinking him further into the plushness of the chair. He seemed...*dishevelled* today, when normally, even at his worst, any unkemptness, or tiredness, or rumpling, merely appeared purposeful. Added to his handsomeness, his presence, his stature.

Julian was one of those men who had been blessed with all the world could offer. Money, a respectable barony, a good family, good health, and yes, good looks. With his mop of hair neither blond nor brown, neither curly nor straight, rounded but delicate features typical of Englishmen, piercing blue eyes, and tall, lithe, but well-defined form, Julian was undeniably handsome. Charming, to boot. He could make anyone blush, with merely a wink and a smile. His kindness, and goodness, those were what set him apart from many others who could lay such claims.

Bobby wasn't immune to him, or at least, hadn't been once upon a time. Their closeness had become something more for a time, when they'd both felt the shift from childhood to adulthood, and in a perfect world, they might've found what their hearts truly sought in the other. Lord and Lady Rothwakes had sensed the *rapprochement*, and though they might've wished for a more illustrious daughter-in-law, they had done noth-

ing but encourage the match. To them, it would've all
been the work of Providence.

Except that the world wasn't perfect, and Providence was apparently not at work then, so Bobby and
Julian both had to accept that friendship was all they
would ever have. Not that it was a bad thing. Quite
the contrary. Julian was the only person in the world
Bobby could truly say she loved now. The bonds of their
friendship were stronger than anything man could ever
forge; though admittedly, the past few years, they had
grown…apart, somewhat, as life led them down slightly
different paths.

Nonetheless, he would always be her friend, her family.

Which is why those new lines on his face, worry
lines, worried *her*. Hurt her. Why the pain, not born
of his injury, but of the dreadful future now looming
ahead for them all *because of* his injury, was her own.

I can make it go away.

Steeling herself, Bobby strode back over to Julian,
and, crossing her arms, planting her feet, she uttered
the words she knew would seal all their fates.

'Let me take your place,' she said, steadily, with as
much conviction as was in her heart. Julian looked up
at her, startled, but she forged on. 'Let me race in your
stead. I can do it, Julian. I can win, and I can save Rothwakes.'

'You're mad,' Julian said flatly after a painfully long
moment, the surprise in his eyes gone, replaced with
harshness and dismissal, the likes of which she'd not
seen in a long time, and which cut to the quick. 'I should
call Dr Morris back. Honestly, Bobby. It's impossible.'

Shaking his head now, he turned back to the window.

Something about it, the ease of his dismissal perhaps, chafed against that part of Bobby that was always
ready for a fight.

'Explain to me how it is impossible.'

'You know very well, Bobby,' he sighed, massaging
his forehead before dropping his head into his hand.
'Even if you weren't a woman, the bet was between
Hayes and I.'

'No, it wasn't.' Julian frowned, and looked up at
her, and that little glimmer of doubt in his eyes gave
her hope, and the courage to press on. *You knew this
wouldn't be easy.* 'As I recall the terms of your wager,
the bet was over the talents of the horses. That you each
would be racing them was implied, however, considering the circumstances, were you to inform Viscount
Hayes that someone would be racing Arion in your
stead, I fail to see him crying off the chance to win
Rothwakes.'

And all that implies, loathsome wretch.

Not that she'd ever met him, neighbour though he
was. Grooms like her—no matter that for all intents and
purposes she was family—did not attend tea, dinners,
parties, or any other social gathering for that matter.
Well, once upon a time she did. Before Bobby made it
clear she had no true desire to be part of a world she'd
not even been born into.

Before the only reason she'd ever tried to fit into such
society, left this world.

Not that Hayes attended many dinners, teas, or parties himself from what she'd heard, certainly none here,
considering their families had been rivals for as long
as Hayes Manor and Rothwakes Estate existed. Bobby
never attended church anymore, and neither was she to
be found often in the nearby villages, other than for a

night at the pub—somewhere *viscounts* were not typically encountered. But she didn't need to meet the viscount—she'd heard enough to form an opinion.

Arrogant know-it-all, friendless, and doggedly ambitious spoilsport.

Even if she hadn't heard all those things, well, only *loathsome wretches* believed untainted bloodlines to be the determining factor of a horse's or a man's worth.

Tearing her thoughts away from the infuriating, pompous, grasping excuse for a peer, Bobby focused on winning the battle at hand. Holding Julian's gaze, she waited as her words permeated his mind.

Finally, she saw him arrive at her conclusion, then saw him remind himself of his first objection, which would surely be Hayes' own.

'He'll never go for it,' Julian said, speaking more to himself than her. 'A woman, racing in a gentleman's bet? It's unseemly, dishonourable—'

'It is neither of those things,' Bobby exclaimed, and Julian had the decency to look slightly abashed.

'Over four hundred miles, Bobby,' he said, gentler, as if she were one of his mares. Oh, how she hated it when he treated her as though she were of *a weaker sex. With kid gloves—as though we are infants.* As if she hadn't done enough to prove she was his equal. As if a woman sitting on the throne of the kingdom wasn't enough to prove women were *bloody capable.* 'Surviving, on only your wits, your skills…'

'You cannot be using that as an excuse,' she retorted, letting the mockery, and disgust, be heard in her tone. 'I'm a better rider, a better hunter, and have spent more nights under the stars than you. You know I can do this.'

'Hayes won't go for it. He'll have the solicitors in here within seconds.'

'Let him, then! There is nothing in the contract that would exclude me,' she told him, not that he didn't know that perfectly well.

Months, this gentleman's race had been in the works.

Months they had spent organising it into a proper event, rather than some hurried wager over a glass too many.

One of the primary reasons why Julian couldn't delay it, as it happened. That, and debts needed to be paid— before the end of the summer.

No delays—only forfeiting now.

'If you stand strong, champion *me*, Julian, Hayes will have no choice but to relent.'

He turned back to the window, and Bobby could see him mulling it over, *properly*.

She waited, not moving an inch lest he take that as some excuse to dismiss her again.

'You really believe you can win it?' he breathed, after a time.

'You know I can. At the very least, I'm your best option. And you know it.'

Julian nodded, and Bobby's heart skipped a beat.

When he turned back to her, she felt it skip another when she noticed some of those worry lines seemed to have been smoothed away.

'Very well then. I can't wait to see Hayes' face when I tell him,' he said, an encouraging, wry smile on his lips.

Neither can I.

On top of everything, teaching the ass a lesson would be utterly priceless.

'Thank you, Julian.'

'Thank me by winning.'

'I will,' she smiled, her heart full yet again, of hope, and excitement.

Perhaps, as it had never been before.

I will, she promised, launching herself into Julian's arms for a hug.

I can do it.

Chapter Two

From atop his favourite everyday mount, Chester, Lawrence Hathaway, third Viscount Hayes, surveyed the hilly pastures bordering the gardens of Rothwakes Estate, as he crossed over the boundary from his family's land, into that of the swindlers and cheats. It had been a while since he'd passed this way, because he had no reason to, and because these pastures, verdant, fertile, and lush, were a bitter thorn in his side. Only today, he was glad to see them, survey them again.

For soon they will be mine.

Returned to the Hathaway family—finally.

His grandfather had been cheated out of them because of a bet, made while the old man was well into his cups and unable to fathom anything from the wager to the damn cards in his hand, but soon, they would belong to a Hathaway once again—thanks to another bet. There was a poetic irony in there somewhere, not that poetry, Fate, or anything other than Lawrence himself was to thank for this boon.

And at least this wager could be called a *gentleman's bet*—not that he considered anyone in the Overday family, particularly those carrying the Rothwakes title, to be a gentleman, but at least his own conscience was clear, for there could be no debate about the propriety of the circumstances surrounding this one. Neither party had been in their cups, they'd negotiated the terms in full consciousness, and with enough time to baulk—should either of them have cared to do so.

All in all, it was more of a business proposal than a wager.

A deal, between two parties who required something from the other that the other refused to give.

If by some insane miracle Rothwakes won, he would win enough to save his estate from financial ruin, and himself from dishonour, et cetera, et cetera, et cetera. How the Rothwakes had even allowed matters to become so terrible—for it wasn't only the newest little baron to blame—Lawrence wondered. Well, he didn't care, so he didn't wonder, but he did agree that it was, if not repugnant and dishonourable, then at the very least reprehensible.

If Lawrence won...

Well, these pastures, and everything marked within the boundaries of Rothwakes Estate, would be his. Including the stables—for all Lawrence could tell, the only dependable, and true source of sizable income for the sad little baron and his barony. Whatever the other man was—something else Lawrence didn't give too much thought to because he didn't really have to deal much with the man, and so his original summation of a spoiled young brat with too much pride for his own good remained—Lawrence did have to say, he had some of the best stables in the land. Rothwakes had become in the past decade or so, one of the best breeders in the country—his horses regularly won every race imaginable.

Lawrence hoped that if—*when*—he won, those who worked the stables would choose to remain. In fact, he rather hoped *all* the staff would remain—they would have the choice to if he won, according to the contract—and not solely because it would avoid having to hire new people. No, it would be…rather satisfying to see Rothwakes lose the loyalty of his staff too.

First, you have to win.

Carts, and chickens, and eggs, and horses and all that proverbial nonsense.

Yes, quite. Only, Lawrence wasn't…worried.

Because good stables notwithstanding—it isn't solely about the horse this time.

No, for this race, it would be about the horse, but equally, about the rider.

And Lawrence knew for almost a fact, that though Rothwakes may be an accomplished horseman—credit where credit was due and all that—he was not one to suffer the trials and vicissitudes of a four-hundred-mile journey all on his own well.

But I am.

Because though Lawrence may appear to be merely an eminently dull and bookish viscount, he was actually also a dull, bookish viscount who enjoyed the solitude and quiet nature offered. Before this whole affair, he'd been known to disappear for days at a time, having a natural talent—which he supplemented with books— for *living off the land.* So, he hadn't much experience racing four hundred miles either. But he'd set a proper training regimen up for himself and Beowulf, and he felt he had a slight edge in this race.

Spurring his mount to a healthy gallop, leaping fencing and obstacles as though they were nothing at all but pebbles on the ground, Lawrence let himself feel…

good, for once. Though he laughed all the way there, he at least had the decency to stop himself when he finally reached the house's front door.

The smile on his lips, and the feeling of utter excitement, lingered nonetheless.

At least, they lingered until Lawrence entered Rothwakes' study, and spotted the man himself, not at his desk—the usual position of power he took on the few occasions they'd met—but rather, in one of the armchairs by the unlit hearth, his leg bandaged, splinted, and raised on a footstool. At once, all that was good within him floated away like dust on the wind.

No.

This couldn't be happening. This wouldn't happen. He wouldn't let some excuse like this ruin what he'd set up, so very carefully. He wouldn't let this ruin his future, all those plans he had for this place, for his name, for his legacy. He'd lost one future—he wouldn't lose another.

I won't.

And actually, it couldn't happen, Lawrence reassured himself, as he shook his head in response to the offer of refreshments he saw come from Rothwakes' lips, rather than heard.

He can't get out of this.

Unless Rothwakes forfeited—there could be no delays. Not only because it was spelled out in the agreement, but because they both knew Rothwakes' debts were to be paid before the end of summer.

Reassured, certain perhaps that the man's pride was pushing him to forfeit in the quiet, comfortable privacy of his own home, Lawrence strode over, and offered the man his hand.

'You'll forgive me for not greeting you properly, Hayes,' Rothwakes said, grimly, but wryly, as he took Lawrence's hand, and shook it with a strength that belied everything he thought of the man. 'As you can see, it's not so easy a job to be upstanding nowadays.'

'Of course,' Lawrence said, seating himself across from the little baron. 'I admit, not quite what I expected from today's meeting.'

'Me either.'

'May I ask as to the nature of your injury and its origin?'

'"*An exceptionally well broken leg,*" as Dr Morris so aptly phrased it.' Rothwakes grimaced, and continued. 'As for its origin, it pains me to say it was all rather boring. I fell down the bloody stairs.'

Lawrence couldn't help it—a laugh escaped him, though he was gentleman enough to attempt and conceal it under a cough.

Rothwakes didn't seem offended, merely exasperated, nodding.

'I know. I shall of course put rumours about I was attempting something dashing and dangerous, but there you are.'

'I appreciate your candour, Rothwakes.' And Lawrence did. Not many men would openly admit to such an accident—particularly not one so prideful and concerned with people's opinions as this one. 'And I am sorry for what it has cost you.'

Rothwakes frowned, but then, a smile appeared on his lips, as did a glint of mischief in his eyes.

Lawrence liked neither.

Not one bit.

'Well, that's the thing, isn't it Hayes? It may have cost

me racing for my own honour and estate, but nothing more than that.'

'I... What?'

Now, Lawrence was not typically the type of man one could throw off guard.

When you trusted no one, or at least, trusted them to only do their worst, you were rarely surprised when they obliged.

And neither was he a man to be made speechless.

That simply wasn't the way of a proper gentleman.

Yet, here he was, caught off guard and speechless.

Rothwakes stared at him, torturing him with that childish grin and impish glint in his eyes, for a moment longer, before something softened, and hardened all at once.

'Someone else will be racing in my stead, of course.'

'Unacceptable. The terms—'

'Of our agreement clearly state which horses shall race,' Rothwakes cut in, silencing Lawrence.

He clenched his jaw, and forced himself to remember that shouting, and pummelling already injured lords, was not the way to go. Tamping down the anger brewing inside like a hot summer storm, he forced himself to listen. If only so as not to let his anger run away with him.

'Not which riders.'

'It was implied,' Lawrence pointed out, patting himself on the back for remaining civilised.

'But not spelled out in our contract. And given the circumstances, you can be damn sure I will exploit this loophole rather than simply lay down and let you take my family's heritage from me, along with all I have built.'

Measuring his breathing, Lawrence bit back a thousand cuts against the Rothwakes name, and forced the baron's words to permeate his brain.

Fact was, the man was right. They hadn't put who must ride in the contract, and that was Lawrence's own fault. But in the end, it didn't matter who he raced. He would win.

Too much was at stake for him not to.

'And who is it, may I ask, that I shall be competing against, then?'

If possible, the smile on the little baron's face returned, ten-fold more self-satisfied.

While the glint in his eye turned to *anticipated amusement*.

Something inside Lawrence told him he was not going to like the answer to his own question.

He waited with bated breath, but feigned boredom as only a lord could perfect, while Rothwakes rang the bell, and instructed the attending footman to show *Bobby* in.

Lawrence expected a surprise, perhaps a world-renowned rider—not that he could remember one by the name of Bobby—or an old adversary, but what he didn't expect, not in a million years, was what Bobby turned out to be.

A groom.

It was insulting was what it was. The idea that some young country groom would be worthy enough to compete against *him*. Was Rothwakes truly so desperate?

And wait one moment, now that he examined the interloper properly—beyond the *somewhat* clean and tidy brown jacket and trousers done up in the most lamentable excuse for cloth, white linen shirt, and boots—he realised something else.

That rounded face, those full lips, that straight and somewhat blunt nose, and even those thick silken raven strands pulled back tightly, were not those of just *any* groom.

'A woman?'

Nearly onyx-brown eyes turned even darker, as her hooded eyes narrowed.

Looking down at him, she gave him a look of utmost disdain and disgust, and what bothered him most about that was that *he* should be the one looking at *her* thus.

He examined her from the tip of her head to the toes of her boots again, properly this time, noting that nothing of her femininity stood out—not a curve, not a roundness, not even a smidgen of softness. She was strong, solid, and something about the tension she held told him immediately she was extremely agile. How, well, Devil take him he had no clue.

A thick black eyebrow raised, and Lawrence shook himself back to the room.

'I shudder to imagine what inanity will leave your lips next,' Bobby the Groom said, with fierce mocking.

He might've responded quicker had he not been so turned around by the well-bred tone, and choice words.

Covering for the lapse, he turned to Rothwakes.

'Is this a joke?'

Rothwakes, to his credit, looked about as amused by all this as Lawrence.

That is to say, in no way whatsoever.

'No, Hayes, this is not a joke. Bobby will be racing in my stead.'

'This is preposterous.'

'Please do enlighten us,' Bobby mumbled dryly.

'This wager, this *business*,' he said, rising to his feet, and encroaching into the woman's space, not that she seemed to mind, not moving a hair, but to look up at him. He silently thanked the Lord for the blessing that was his height, a head more than hers. 'Was meant to be executed by two people of similar talent and position. Therefore, *you*, racing, is preposterous.'

'Don't worry yourself, Your Lordship,' Bobby said drolly, a wicked smile tilting her lips up. 'You can still make a show of it, perhaps train a little so the deficiencies in your talents and *position* are not so glaringly obvious.'

'Your tongue is quick, girl, but words will not save you when you're ten miles out and crying to return home.'

'Oh, we'll see who's crying, *boy*—'

'Bobby!'

Clenching her teeth so hard he could hear them grind, even over the sound of his own pounding heart, and clicking jaw, Bobby forced her mouth shut, and so did Lawrence.

The audacity, of the two of them…

'I refuse to engage in this race with someone whose worthiness remains undetermined,' Lawrence said finally, as lordly, measuredly, and *finally* as he could. 'I demand to see some sort of demonstration of your supposed prowess before I waste my time.'

'No,' the woman said simply, in a tone matching his own and which she had no right to use.

'Bobby, perhaps His Lordship deserves some reassurance—'

Raising her hand, turning to glare at the little baron, she cut him off.

He wasn't entirely sure *what* the relationship was between these two, but Lord help him should he ever be ordered around in his own home by a *groom*.

'His Lordship has no right to demand anything of me,' Bobby told him, before turning her chilling gaze back on Lawrence. 'I'll not prance around before you, and assent to the notion that *you* could determine my worth. You'd have raced Julian, and you've never seen him ride.'

Julian? Christian names? They must be close.

Not that it bloody well matters.

'Rothwakes has a reputation. You,' he pointed out, inching a little closer, not that the infuriating wretch did anything but hold his gaze. 'Have no reputation.'

'Well then Julian's reputation should be enough, when he says I can, and will race in his stead.'

Their gazes held for an uncomfortably long moment.

Until Lawrence realised his breath had come into time with hers, and that her scent—*horses, grass, life, and lemons*—was really rather pleasant, and so he straightened, moving away from the strange creature.

'It's your funeral, Rothwakes,' he said, straightening his lapels, and removing some particles of invisible dust from the edges of his sleeves. 'I'll not hear any argument when your rider here fails to prove she's up to such a challenge.' Bobby looked about ready to leap, and pummel him, but Lawrence gave her no chance to, slipping past her to make his way to the door. 'Until next week. Good day, Rothwakes,' he said, bowing his head. 'Harpy,' he added, dismissing the insufferable woman, and letting himself out.

He was quite sure he heard the words '*Good day, toad,*' and funnily enough, he was smiling again as he stepped out of Rothwakes' front door.

Chapter Three

Land's End, Cornwall,
July 14th, 1838

Pale blue, silver, wisps of white, and metallic greys
erased the line between sea and sky, so that it was
merely one enormous canvas of hues, stark against
the edge of dark grey boulders, and yellowish green
of the grasses, where land ended, and the rest of the
world waited on. The sun would be rising soon—not
that Bobby would be here to see it, see how it shifted
the painted colours to pink, red, oranges even perhaps.

Somehow, it made her heart twinge a little, to know
she'd have been here, at the edge of the great isle she
called home, and not seen that sunrise.

There will be plenty of incredible sights and sunrises.
No time to be wasted today.

Indeed, no time at all.

Arion nudged her shoulder, as if reminding her of
that, and all that lay ahead. Smiling, she turned back
from the horizonless expanse, took his head in her hands,
and gently stroking him, lay her forehead against his.
Closing her eyes, inhaling deeply, she let the briny breeze

and sound of gulls wash over her, focusing on the task at hand.

Not even on what lay ahead—merely this moment. This day.

'Nearly time to get started, my friend,' she whispered, continuing her stroking, but looking him in the eye as she spoke to him. 'What do you say we go for a nice ride?' Arion whinnied, answering her, and she grinned, wider. 'That's what I thought.'

'Riders!' called a voice, the shrill commanding of it belonging to Julian's solicitor, Watkins, she knew.

Bobby turned towards it, Arion following her without a single command, and she took in those around her properly.

It had all been a whirlwind since Julian had told Hayes she would be racing for him. After that meeting with the vainglorious viscount—*honestly the nerve of the man*—she and Julian had spent a few minutes talking, well, laughing about said viscount's face when he'd seen her, and then, it had all become a blur.

Meetings with Watkins, preparations, travel… Not that there were many *new* plans to be made—most of everything being already in place—merely adjustments for Julian's condition, as the stubborn idiot refused to stay at home until the race neared Rothwakes. The doctor had had a fit when Julian had told him he'd be travelling, but had nonetheless ceded, and helped organise travel so as to avoid Julian's condition worsening.

Bobby hadn't been part of much of it, too busy continuing Arion's training, and ensuring the preparations she'd already made for horse and rider were fulfilled, making only minor changes for her own comfort as opposed to what she would've done for Julian. And then, before she knew it, they'd been on their way here. There had been little conversation, at least between her and Julian. Just miles, and miles of road, tending to the horses, mud, rain, sunshine, dirt, inns, and now...

We're here.

Taking a breath, Bobby glanced around at their small, motley band. Watkins, the small, severe man, Matthews, Hayes' solicitor, tall, spindly, and grave as he was. Julian, who'd been insistent on making it here from the small inn they'd stayed at last night, leaning on his crutches, visibly in pain, his valet beside him. And Hayes, next to his—undoubtedly breathtaking—black thoroughbred. Luscious coat, which shimmered in the light. Seventeen hands high, lean, with long strands of slightly curled hair. The beast was magnificent—even if he did not hold a candle to Arion in Bobby's eyes, though her own mount was, to everyone else, but a mixed animal of no true value.

Too much draught for racing.

Too much spirit for farm work.

What do they know...

No, Arion was magnificent to her too. His speckled grey coat, beige hair, and fifteen hands of muscle didn't make him less—they made him special. As did his eyes, which held so much.

Kindred spirits.

She'd known that from the first. It was why this whole thing was meant to be. Arion and her, they shared something...*unique.* And for all his breeding, and bloodlines, and training regimes, that was something Hayes could never understand. Nor replicate.

It's why he won't win.

This is what it's all about.

Quite right.

Looking over at the man again, she did have to concede that it wasn't just his beast that was magnificent. Not that she hadn't noticed the longish mop of slicked back brown hair, speckled with threads of copper. The fine-featured sharp symmetry of his features, even covered by a not-quite beard as half of it was. The almond-shaped eyes, the colour of coffee. The straight dark brows, the rather oddly blunt long nose. The thin lips, except maybe the bottom one wasn't so thin—especially when the clod *pouted*. What kind of grown man pouted?

What kind of ninny finds it attractive?

One like her, she supposed. One who also noticed his lean height, the grace and gentleness of his hands. The adorable nature of his rather large ears, poking out from his head. Noticing he was handsome, attractive, that he smelled rather nice—*of horse, wild daisies, and summer sins*—didn't take away from the fact that he was an entitled oaf. If she'd had the smallest doubt that she'd change her initial assumptions upon meeting him, *well*. He'd gone and proved there was nothing to be reassessed, hadn't he?

Demanding that I prove my worth to him.

Contemptible toad.

So no, it didn't matter that he was attractive. Bobby knew well that meant absolutely nothing. Attraction had nothing to do with a person's worth, or even if you liked them. It was merely… A natural reaction to something pleasing. And just because the…the…*poltroon* looked nothing like one, standing there on the cliffs, his coat, and hair, flapping in the wind, like some vagabond pirate you'd read about in some lurid novel, didn't mean he *wasn't* one.

A poltroon.

Or a vagabond pirate.

Why did people romanticise them so—

'Riders!'

Shaking her head, Bobby brought herself back to the present, stroking Arion as she led him towards the group gathered ahead, Hayes doing so as well.

Keeping her gaze on Watkins and Matthews, Bobby stood tall, determined not to let her competitor get to her. In any way. He was merely an obstacle for her to overcome. Like so much else.

A stiff, unyielding, prideful—

'We all know why we are here,' Matthews announced with bored gravitas. 'We shall count the riders down, and then you will be off. We shall meet you this evening at the Hare's Gully,' he sighed, flinching at the inn's name as though it personally offended him. 'There, we will make the suitable notes of times, and take your plans for tomorrow's routes,' he droned on, as if they didn't already know how this would all go.

Meeting every night to determine who had won the day.

Giving their planned routes for the following one, before the riders went off on their own to spend the night at a place of their choosing—save for three days from now, when they were allowed to spend the night at an inn, and another, three days after that, in London, where there was to be a party. One which Bobby was surprisingly...*excited* about.

Those supervising the race, times, and rules would travel the main roads, whilst the riders faced the countryside in all its splendour and trials.

All in all—they knew the rules.

And if there was one thing Bobby trusted, it was that Hayes would follow them. This race was all about honour, and reputation, and she knew he would never do anything to risk either of those. A small reassurance, but a reassurance nonetheless.

A gentleman's bet. A gentleman's race.

'Very well,' Watkins said, taking off. 'Riders, mount up.'

Bobby and Hayes both made final checks of their saddles, and bags, and slipped on their hats.

'Be careful, Bobby,' Julian said, and she turned to find he'd hobbled over to her.

'I will be,' she smiled reassuringly. 'I won't let you down.'

'You never have,' he shrugged. 'You never could,' he whispered, his eyes misting somewhat, as the words his mother had always said to them both passed his lips. Bobby hugged him, tightly, but carefully, ignoring the slight stab those bittersweet words brought, and he pressed a kiss to her temple. 'Godspeed.'

Nodding, her throat tight, Bobby released him, and in one swift motion, tossed the reins up, and swung onto Arion's back.

Patting his neck, she walked him to where Hayes waited, and lined up the horses.

'On my count!' Watkins exclaimed.

Glancing over at Hayes, Bobby saw the same determination in his eyes as was in her heart.

She also saw how stiffly he sat—and she grinned.

'Something amusing, shrew?' he asked, raising a brow but not looking directly at her.

'Your rather stiff seat, my lord,' she quipped back, his insult not close to original enough to wound. 'I wonder whether perhaps you might've removed the broomstick you usually sport up your backside before beginning this.'

'Five!'

'At the end of the day, we'll see whose seat needs improvement.'

'Four!'

'Care to wager on that?'

'Yes, carper.'

'Three!'

'Loser cooks dinner, my lord.'

'Two!' Watkins continued, and Bobby noticed he seemed put off by the competitor's inattention, and petty squabbling.

Apologies, Watkins. Only, it's ever so fun.

'Loser is obliged to cease with name-calling.'

'One!'

'Deal, your stiffness.'

'Go!' Watkins screamed, exasperated.

With a sharp whistle, and a slight tightening of her thighs, she and Arion were off.

A quick run, to start the morning off—they would slow shortly, and take a more sedate pace, but for now, off they went. She could see Hayes out of the corner of her eye, keeping in time with her, and as they raced together away from where land supposedly ended, Bobby couldn't help but laugh.

The wind rushing past them, Arion beneath her, England before them—well.

Bobby felt more herself—almost *happier*—than she had in a very long time.

This day, this race—are mine.

Lawrence may have been many things, however, he was not one who would refuse to recognise when he'd been wrong, or beaten. As he led Beowulf through the thick brush of the moors, the craggy outline of the landscape stark in the light of a dimming, but eagerly colourful, afternoon sun, he shook his head, and chastised himself for having allowed himself to be schooled by a country groom.

An hour—that had been her lead today, despite having taken a slightly trickier route through the Cornish countryside than he had, as he'd been trying to be clever, and not overtax Beowulf on the first day. What had it got him?

An hour behind her.

He'd underestimated Bobby—not that he would admit it to her though it would be plain for all to see, *especially* her—and now, he would eat some humble pie as he'd heard said.

I'll have to cook it along with the rest, he mused, the scent of fire drawing him nearer to his destination.

He didn't exactly relish the fact he'd have to cook her dinner—indeed, that they'd likely spend the evening together, but then again, perhaps he didn't mind so much. He typically wasn't one to seek out company when he wasn't obliged to keep it, preferring solitude, however the thought of having to spend one evening in the woman's company surprisingly wasn't entirely loathsome.

Unlike her employer.

The little baron had had that mischievous glint in his eye again when Lawrence had arrived at the inn of the nearby village, smug in the knowledge that his rider had won the day. Not that Lawrence could blame the man—he'd probably have been crowing if the day had gone his way. He'd not underestimate Bobby again—that much was certain.

A simple miscalculation. These happen all the time. We shall simply recalculate. Nothing is lost yet.

His pride and ego had taken a hit—that was certain.

But the prize at the end of the race—that was neither lost nor won yet.

'I hadn't thought it possible for you to be stiffer,' Bobby's voice drawled as he reached the edge of the clearing, and his eyes were drawn across the rather inviting fire she'd built, to where she herself sat, the satisfied smirk on her face infuriating and charming all at once. 'Seems you're not used to a good day's ride, Your Lordship.'

Over fifty miles—a good day's ride indeed.

Something else Lawrence wouldn't admit was that she was right again.

He was stiff—despite the vigorous training he'd put himself through for this. Something about the excitement of it all, the sheer amount of all it had taken to even get here, the heat, all of it, had put him in less than top form. Not that he was making excuses.

Straightening a little, he led Beowulf to a small tree, tied him, and began the long business of getting him ready for the evening.

Rothwakes' horse, he noted, was looking mightily relaxed and content across the way, almost as relaxed and content as the woman lounging—if it was possible to do so considering the conditions—on a log, watching him.

Termagant.

So, he might've agreed not to call her names—that didn't mean he couldn't still do it in his mind.

'And here I was going to congratulate you on a well done first day.'

'No, you weren't,' she scoffed, and he found himself grinning back at her as he removed his packs and Beowulf's saddle.

'Fine. I wasn't.'

'You'd better hurry up with that, Your Lordship,' she

added a moment later, and he realised he'd been staring at her. *No, gazing.* Unacceptable, whatever it was. 'There's some hares here that needs cooking.'

'Don't worry, Miss…' Lawrence frowned, realising he didn't even know her last name. 'Miss what, come to think of it?'

'Kingsley—but don't you be calling me Miss Kingsley,' she warned, pointing a rather sharp looking knife at him. *Is she whittling?* 'I'm no miss, you and I both know that. I'm just Bobby.'

'Well, just Bobby,' he said, trying to focus on what he was doing. *Brushing Beowulf. Feeding him. Fetching water. Cooking Bobby dinner.* 'I'm just Lawrence. Or toad, if you prefer. It seems we are truly well in this together now, no matter our feelings, so I venture we can at least be civil. Hell, perhaps even cordial if that wouldn't offend your need to be so antagonistic.'

The word *harrumph* came to mind with the sound Bobby made in response.

Lawrence finished his work with Beowulf, grabbing the watering bag from his pack.

'There's a river back there,' Bobby said, intently focused on what she was doing—*skinning a hare, delightful and so unthreateningly to boot*—though he knew instinctively she'd been watching his every move.

He found somehow that the idea didn't bother him.

He wandered over towards her, spotting the brace of clean hares already beside her.

'That was nice of you, Bobby,' he noted, leaning down to take them.

'I'm hungry,' she said pointedly, finally meeting his eyes again. He smiled, because well, there was no reason. He simply, *did.* Something flashed in her eyes, and as she continued to rant, he let his eyes examine her again. 'Wasn't sure when you'd decide to join me, so I made myself useful.'

The firelight flattered most—particularly when coupled with the shadows and warmth of late afternoon—softening otherwise harsh features with its glow, even as shadows lengthened grooves and lines, and it was true of Bobby as well, though there was nothing harsh about her he realised.

She wasn't soft, but beneath the strength, the solid nature of her, she was...*soft*.

In a fashion.

He'd noticed it this morning too, as she stood and spoke to her horse. Along with a beauty he'd *not* noticed before. He noticed it now, as he did the appeal of the figure not so hidden tonight beneath a tighter fitting shirt, and trousers. Even those bare feet of hers were...

Notable.

Blinking, he forced away the unwelcome thoughts and indeed, *stirrings* of his body. Entangling himself with the competition was a dreadful idea—an idea which couldn't even exist, for the competition in question he was quite certain detested him rather thoroughly.

Why—he neither knew nor cared.

Well, maybe he cared a little.

He didn't trust anyone—but there were reasons for that. Simple, logical reasons, born of years of observation and experience. The woman before him had no reason to detest him as she seemed to—beyond that of a mere competitor.

Lawrence quirked his head and Bobby's eyes narrowed as she watched him closely.

'Perhaps you should have a wash too, while you're down there,' she said after a moment, turning back to the hare in her hands, the heat he'd thought he spied, obviously an illusion. 'But water your horse, first. And put the hares on. Then, you can wash.'

'As madam orders,' he grinned. 'And his name is Beowulf.'

'I know,' she said, as if he were a complete dolt, grimacing like a child. He grinned wider, something warming inside him. 'Good name for him,' she added, softer.

Clearing his throat, Lawrence strode off, at a loss of anything to add.

It was a good name.

So is Bobby. Though I am curious...

Chapter Four

'Is Bobby short for Roberta?' His Dunceness—*Lawrence*—asked. They had finished eating some time ago, though in the end Bobby had done most of the cooking, since his mountebankness had taken so long washing. Not that she was complaining about the end result of that—not that he actually smelled or looked horrible to begin with either.

They'd sat in silence for a while now as the sun continued its descent, having eaten their fill, and packing the rest, making sure both Beowulf and Arion were well settled for the night.

It had felt strangely comfortable, sitting next to—*rather closely*—him, listening to the sounds of the surrounding beasts, great and small. Watching the colours of the sky, and landscape change, then the stars make an appearance, watching the fire crackle and burn down. The *comfortableness* of it bothered her—hence the continued name-calling, at least in her mind. It bothered her, because she wanted to grasp onto her initial impressions of him, hold them tight, lest she…

Start to like him.

Bobby wasn't entirely sure why that would be such a

terrible thing, other than they were competitors in this strange tale, and that…and that…

That's all we are, and can ever be.

Not that she wanted anything more. It wasn't something that she'd ever really wanted—a companion, a partner, a husband. Even as everyone told her it was unnatural not to; though sometimes not in so many words. As Lord and Lady Rothwakes had—merely by asking every few months or so once she'd emerged from childhood, if really, she was certain she did not wish for such things. If really, she was certain she wished to *work* with horses, and not have them find her a good husband. The only time they'd stopped making such comments had been when Julian and she had become more than friends.

Bobby had thought then, when she and Julian had tried at intimacy, that perhaps, *that could be nice*—a friend, to travel life through with, someone who understood her, and let her live as she pleased, but when it had ended, she'd still had their friendship, so she hadn't felt as if she'd missed out on anything.

Since then, she'd had her fun, *sewed her wild oats*, though she wasn't entirely sure that analogy worked in her case. She'd had many a good time, and that's all it had ever been. Her plans for the future, her work, those were the things that mattered. Not whether she had someone to warm her bed long-term.

Because that was the thing, wasn't it? With Julian, it might've been different—she could've lived as she pleased still, not relinquished her freedom—but then again, thinking on it now, perhaps not. Perhaps he would've wanted, *needed*, a baroness. Regardless. The point was, long-term and marriage and all that—

required what she wasn't ready to give. Loss of freedom; loss of self.

Not entirely sure why you're thinking of all this just now.

'Yes,' Bobby said, clearing her throat, and stretching a bit before leaning forward, forearms on her thighs.

'How long have you worked for Rothwakes?'

Bobby glanced over, trying to determine what Lawrence was after.

But studying him, she found no malice, no ill-will, no judgement.

Merely, an open curiosity, to get to know her.

Very odd.

What was even odder was that she had this strange urge to get to know him.

That would merely be your attraction speaking.

'Since I was about fourteen or so,' she shrugged, turning back to the fire.

'That's young,' he said, and she could hear him frowning. 'How did you come to work for the family? Surely, it must've been the father who took you on, he was still alive then, wasn't he?'

'They both were,' Bobby said, before she could stop herself, or the emotion she revealed when she did. 'It's a long story, and not one I care to tell tonight.'

Or any other night.

The past was past. And Lord knew she dwelled upon it enough herself without having to recount the sad, sorriness of it all to some viscount who was only here because he was after some land, and had a fondness for upholding old family squabbles.

No, I do not.

'Fair enough.' Bobby thought for a moment he'd leave it there, but no, he was determined to have an actual *conversation* apparently. 'Will you murder me in my sleep if I ask what's in this for you?'

'No. But that doesn't mean I won't murder you in your sleep regardless,' Bobby said, throwing him a mischievous grin over her shoulder.

He laughed, deep, and hearty, his whole face lighting up, his entire demeanour relaxing.

He *was* stiff—but now she saw it was one of the affectations of great lords. Or perhaps, merely a defensive wall, built up against the world, much as she had. Underneath, out here, without the rest of the world looking on, they were both freer.

Something about woods, and masks, and Shakespeare flashed through her mind, but she forced herself to dismiss it when she recalled thoughts of lovers.

'Indulge me,' he said, and the word *indulgence* brought other thoughts with it.

Lovers, echoed in her mind, carried on the breeze, and she decided to answer his question.

Far safer than anything else.

'A chance to buy my own farm,' she said, and what little playfulness had been in him, for the slightest second, disappeared.

'Horses, if I were to guess?'

'Yes,' she told him. Then, without wanting to, she filled the silence which followed. 'A sanctuary. Not to breed them and win races and foolish prizes, but a place where I can raise them, and heal them, and yes, sell them, to worthy owners if they are good work horses, or riding horses. But mainly, a place where they can live in peace.'

Where I can live in peace.

'You're not just his groom, are you?' Lawrence said, and there was a measure of both awe, and mockery at his own presumptions. 'Ten years his stables have been winning every prize imaginable—when mine are not. I would say you would've been…early twenties,' he guessed rather aptly, after appraising her. 'Long enough to have gone from…apprentice to something more.'

'I'm impressed. Think you're the first one to figure it out—at least so quickly.'

'You're the reason Rothwakes' stables are nigh on the best in the country.' Bobby nodded—pleased by the compliment though it wasn't the first time she'd heard it. Somehow, coming from him… Made it, *different*. 'What's your secret?'

'I notice you didn't ask why more people don't know about me.'

Lawrence flinched, and nodded, turning to the fire.

'Does it bother you?' he asked finally, turning his warm gaze, the colour of the earth, back on her.

'Some days,' she admitted quietly, unwilling to lie completely.

The truth, the *whole* truth, was that it didn't bother her that Julian told no one about her—though some guessed eventually, those who cared to look, few and far between.

It didn't bother her to live in the shadows. It bothered her that *not* doing so would result in insults, and losses of reputation, and cuts, and put-downs, all because this supposedly progressive society they lived in couldn't see past the surface of things.

Even with a new age coming.

'Why haven't you gone off on your own before now?'

'It's…'

'Complicated? A long story?'

'Both,' she chuckled.

It was strange—she couldn't quite remember the last time she'd chuckled.

Not unless she was…*out for an evening.*

'And what if you lose?' Bobby shot him a glare, chuckles long forgotten, and the man had the temerity to merely *smile*. 'I said *what if*, Bobby. Surely, you must have a plan. Or would you remain with the estate?'

'You would enjoy having me work for you, wouldn't you?' The man's temerity continued—this time with the injury in his eyes. A sense of having misjudged him, and guilt for that, invaded her heart, and Bobby sighed. 'I wouldn't stay. My place…wouldn't be there anymore. I would find work where I could, likely in London as Julian would only have the townhouse left. We'd rebuild, together. He would see me right.'

'I wouldn't imagine London would suit you.'

'What about you?' Bobby asked, deflecting from that very insightful comment. She wished she could convince herself it was meant as others might've said—against her being suited for such a grand place—but really, she knew he merely understood she was not meant for city life. That quick way of seeing her, it added to the list of things *bothering* her just now. 'Why are you doing this? What's one small piece of land to you, when you have a brace of grand estates and acreages the length and breadth of the country?'

'Have you been researching my lineage, Bobby?' Lawrence smirked, and she swatted him lightly on the arm.

He stared down at the place she'd touched him, as if shocked that she'd dared.

Or perhaps he too had felt the flash of warmth that had travelled through her own fingers.

'I have not,' she said proudly.

Lies.

'To answer your question,' he said, clearing his throat, and tossing some twigs into the dwindling flames. 'That land was in my family for generations, before we were even given the Hayes title. That scoundrel of a Roth-wakes stole it from us. I mean to restore what was ours. And I mean to make something of it.'

'The farmers who make their living off it aren't enough of a *something* to you?' Bobby asked, a warning sparking along with anger in her breast. *Just when I was beginning to like you.* 'What will you do with it?'

'Progress is coming, Bobby,' he said harshly. 'I intend to be at the forefront of it. We need to build, to grow, to advance. Do you think I've merely plucked my grand estates and acreages from thin air? No, I've *worked* for them. Worked to build a legacy.'

'What will you do with it?' she asked again, rising to her feet, to tower over *him* for once.

'I'll keep the house, and the stables. As for the rest… I intend to connect us to the rest of this country. To the world,' he ground out, rising, and taking away her advantage.

'You'll force the people who've lived, born, died, and bled, in that soil, to leave, so you can have *the railway* come through?'

God, what had she been thinking, *liking him* for even a second.

'I'll compensate them and find them good places elsewhere!'

'Oh, bravo,' she sneered, clapping her hands. 'You'll *compensate* them. Pay them off to assuage your guilt. I cannot believe you. I was right to think you were nothing but a high-born, insolent, prideful, loathsome, self-centred *prig*.'

'We're done racing for the day, so you can get off your high horse, you judgemental, stubborn, shielded, and ignorant country bumpkin!'

The two stood there, staring daggers at each other, faces inches from the other's, their breaths mingling as they breathed hard, anger, annoyance, lightning, and loathing flowing between them.

Until it turned, as swiftly as a storm from the sea, into something *very* different.

Until Bobby's heart was racing for a completely different reason, blood rushing through her veins, the tightening of her belly asking for something other than a fight.

Until the lightning between them crackled, electricity and heat filling the space between them.

Perhaps it was a terrible idea. Only, in the end, Bobby thought that maybe it was the best idea she'd had in a while. After all, attraction meant nought but that there was an attraction, right?

And just because she was furious with the man before her, just because she wanted to bash him over the head with one of the nearby boulders for suggesting compensation could be enough to assuage people whose land was being taken from them, well, that didn't mean she couldn't still, *indulge*.

So she grabbed hold of his shirt, and hauled him towards her until the final inches of distance between them were no more.

Lawrence hadn't missed the tidal wave of lust, and heat that had swirled between them, rising higher and higher from the crackling electricity of their argument. It was so thick, so palpable, that even he, who hadn't been with anyone in a *very* long time—and even then, hadn't really ever felt true, unbridled, incandescent passion before—could recognise it for what it was. Only, he hadn't expected anything to be *done* about it.

He was a gentleman, for starters, and also he had no need for any of this. Any hint of entanglement or anything of the sort. He suspected the woman before him didn't either. They were competitors. He'd offered cordiality—a peace, or rather a truce of sorts—not…passion.

He for one didn't need it in his life; never had, never would. Same went for love, even marriage. He'd tried it, it was his duty, and it had been a business contract. Nothing more. One which had been violated, but he wouldn't linger on that. Regardless, he'd done it, and been satisfied that even marriage for duty wasn't necessary for him to function, to thrive, to build a legacy for his family's name.

And he didn't know much about Bobby, but she seemed—for all her bluster, quick temper, and insults—to have a good head on her shoulders, a plan for her future, and *complications* between them would serve no purpose. Beyond that, he'd seen the ease between her and Rothwakes, heard how she spoke of him, seen that intimate moment they'd shared just before the race, and for one thing, he wasn't one to get entangled with other people's lovers.

All that to say, that when Bobby grabbed his shirt, and hauled him so their lips could meet, he was eminently surprised. His eyes remained open as their lips first came together, his mind telling him that was a very lovely resting place indeed, but also that he wasn't entirely sure what to do. Until he met her own gaze, and the desire in her eyes—*for him*—the promise of illogical, unfathomable, unthinkable passion, so stark and vivid, he couldn't resist it. For once in his life, he realised, he didn't want to be correct, or logical, or rational, even. He just wanted to feel, only maybe for a moment, a kiss, and then he could move on.

Focus again.

So he let his eyes drift closed, and he let his body do what it wished, what it craved, what it *needed* just then. His mind turned from reason, to processing sensation. His lips moved against the soft pillows of flesh against them, capturing them, releasing them, sliding against them to feel every ridge, every valley. Bobby stepped in closer to him, the heat of her body radiating against his even though they weren't quite touching. He remedied that, his hands finally remembering they could move, raising to her hips and bringing them against the top of his thighs.

Teeth scraped across his bottom lip, and so he opened, swiping the tip of his tongue along the inside of her upper lip, before delving in to meet her, even as she thrust out to seek him. At first the pace was frantic, that first taste setting off something in them both—the need to remember, to drink it all in—but beyond the initial sample—of their dinner, of sweet toffee, and something richer, like pepper perhaps—he couldn't seem to identify all the notes, all the complexities of what he was being offered, so he tightened his hold on her, one hand sliding up her back to tangle in the queue at her neck, so he could move her, just that way, and slow the pace, so he could truly savour everything she offered him.

Bobby didn't seem to mind, quite the contrary, her tongue sliding and swiping along his, seeking out everything he was, as her free hand slid around his neck. He dipped further down at her silent request, but then he thought better of it, and moved his hands to her thighs, gripping tightly before hauling her up so she could wrap around him.

Better.

Yes, much better. Now, he could feel, *see*, everything he hadn't been able to before. Soft hard thighs, clenching against his waist. Warm, supple muscles, along her back and waist; against his chest, the most wonderful fleshy globes. All of her seeping warmth into him as they held each other tight, still seeking, teasing, playing with each other's lips, tongues, teeth.

He hadn't thought he'd been cold before, until he'd had her like this, and then he realised he had been. Not his flesh, his skin, despite the frigid water and night's breeze. But inside, in his belly, in the cavity of his chest, *there*, at the back of his neck, right below his ears, where deft, callused little fingers toyed with his hair.

Bobby undulated against him, and he felt his ardour rising, she must have to, but it didn't make her baulk, pause, or even slow. If anything, her movements became more deliberate, as she sought him out, coaxing him to higher pleasures.

Beowulf snorted, the sound cutting through the lust-filled haze, and he tore his lips from hers, his nose bumping alongside hers as he fought to catch his breath, and make her open her eyes and look at him.

Finally, she did, inhaling deep gulps, her tongue flicking out occasionally as if seeking what remained of him on her flesh.

Damn.

'We shouldn't do this,' he breathed, loosening his hold to signal he would release her.

'Do you want to do this?' Bobby asked, no hesitation, no dimming of desire in her gaze.

He pondered the question, with as much solemnity as she'd asked it.

Did he want this?

At first, he'd succumbed to the passion, the setting aside of reason, for a moment.

A kiss.

Did he want more than that?

Or did he want to stop here, perhaps steal more kisses, some touches, and then end it?

Want.

Such complexity hidden beneath such obvious simplicity.

As he watched her, the quick rise and fall of her eyelashes, the occasional flaring of her nostrils as she inhaled, the shimmer of freckles he hadn't noticed before on her nose in the glow of red embers, he seriously pondered the word *want.*

When was the last time he had wanted something—for himself?

He couldn't quite recall.

But perhaps the better question was, did he want *this* for himself?

Did he want to live with the potential consequences?

'You, and Rothwakes...?' he asked, because somehow that would be the worst of it, if he did as others had to him.

'I'm not his,' Bobby told him, and he saw no lie. 'I'm no one's.'

Want.

'I want this,' he said after a long moment, quietly, but with infallible certainty.

Bobby nodded slightly.

'I don't have a French letter,' she told him, somewhat

catching him off guard with the starkness. 'Though I would normally employ one.'

In other circumstances, perhaps he might've minded what she was telling him.

Only he didn't, because she was being nothing but honest, and that was the most precious thing anyone could ever give him.

'I haven't been with anyone in a long time,' he admitted, and one of her eyes narrowed slightly at that, as though it didn't quite make sense with what she'd made of him in her mind. 'Healthy, as far as I'm aware. I won't get you into trouble,' he promised, though his mind knew he could only promise now, in this context, trouble, it seemed, was something he inherently knew he could let himself get into with her if he wasn't careful.

Another slight nod.

And then she was leaning in again, peppering gentle kisses along the outline of his lips, and he let his eyes close yet again.

He let himself fall into sensation, becoming in that moment, some version of himself he'd never known before; nor was likely to ever know again.

This was a very good idea, Bobby congratulated herself as her lips met Lawrence's again. Really, a supremely *excellent* idea.

Attraction as flowed between them—not that she could quite recall another instance of it being quite as intoxicating—was best explored, rather than pushed away. She didn't care—never had—that people believed passion to be immoral, or wrong, or even, best ignored. If partners were willing, if there was desire, it was the most natural thing in the world.

And it did wonders to clear the cobwebs in one's mind, even to work out the kinks in a sore body.

So she was eminently glad that Lawrence had agreed to continue down the path they had started on. For one, it would be a good release for all the turmoil, the concern, the fear, that had lived within her since... Well, she would say since Julian had been injured.

It would also avoid her mind getting all fanciful on her about Lawrence—thinking that she actually *liked* the numbskull, when really, it was only her body that did.

And oh, did it like him.

As their tongues swirled together, his taste—*wild mint, winter fires, ripe peaches*—flowed through her, awakening what little specks of flesh and blood within her hadn't yet been. Inhaling sharply against his cheek, she detected the salt of his skin mingling with it, underscoring and amplifying it, and she clutched to him a little tighter, feeling his manhood right where she needed to as she shifted against him slightly.

Her brain was swirling, she was tumbling, but then again maybe that was merely because he was moving, laying her down in the small gap of earth between their woody seat and the dying fire, which still warmed the side of her. Not as thoroughly as he did, covering her with his body, his weight reassuring and enveloping.

And then he was pulling away from her, but she knew what came next, and so she simply opened her eyes, watching greedily as his half-shadowed form rose to his knees between her thighs, tearing off the shirt he'd donned after his river bath. He was all sinew and muscle—lean, not sharp, nor hard—but with an agile softness that belied his typical stiffness. She watched as he unfastened his trousers, not removing them, pausing for a moment, looking down at her, waiting.

She didn't keep him, nor wait for him to do it, she disposed of her own clothes, him assisting to peel off her trousers, before he set the pile of their things on the log beside them. He looked around, as if seeking something, a blanket, she gauged, so she merely held out a hand, asking him to return to what they'd been doing.

A little dirt didn't hurt anyone—they could wash in the river again later—and the earth was actually rather inviting, and not so strewn with hard dirt or sticks to make it unbearable. He nodded, a lock of his now mussed locks, curlier than they had been up until now, released as they had been from constraints, and slid up her body, his gaze looking, feasting, enjoying, but not pausing until he was perched above her again.

She was glad of it—the lack of attention. It felt as if any more attention, *lavishing*, might give the impression this was something other than what it was.

A rut in the wilderness.

Dropping to one forearm, he trailed fingers down to her slick nest of curls, testing her readiness for him, and when he found her eager and waiting, he took himself in hand, and lined himself up. In instinctual concert, he thrust, and she rose to meet him, her legs opening further, her body opening for him.

It was deep, and long, and it felt…

Glorious.

The tightening inside her, the need to be full of another being, the fire that had been raging inside her since she'd kissed him, exploded, and yet calmed all at once. Her head lolled back, as her thighs clenched against his hips, and her fingers took hold of the flesh above them. Together, they found their stride, the slick slide of him as he moved within her, growing it seemed with every stroke, igniting the fuse of something far greater than she'd felt up until now.

Looking up at him, she found his mane loose around his head, sweat and lines across his face, and it spurred her on, the visceral beauty of his unkempt wildness, so at odds with everything she'd thought he was.

And then, shifting his hips slightly, he hit a spot inside her that forced her eyes closed again, and she followed that thread of pleasure as it grew, drifting it felt, into the earth. The sounds, the scents of them together, filled her ears, her nostrils, every pore.

When his fingers found her curls, and the small nub inside them, slicking against it with the honey of their meeting, Bobby knew it was time. Her breath stilted, a cry dying at the back of her throat, as she rode the cresting wave, all thoughts and cares melting into the soil at her back.

As her spasms, and tightening around him, in every sense, ended, he pulled himself from her with a groan, and a moment later she felt the hot stickiness of him on her belly.

Finally, she opened her eyes again, watching his face contort in beautiful ecstatic bliss. She watched him, until he too returned from his primal journey, and when he met her eyes again, the surprise, the wonder, and the question lingering in the crystalline amber depths stole her breath.

Perhaps this was not so clever an idea after all.

Chapter Five

'Wake up, wastrel,' Bobby's voice called, piercing through the deep, dark, potentially most restful slumber he'd ever engaged in. Groaning, he blinked open his eyes, finding the grey-purple light of morning above him. The scent of firewood and tea met him, as did the cold dampness of the ground, despite the blanket he'd spread beneath him last night, after they'd taken their turns washing themselves—*in utter silence*—checking their horses before making their own sleeping spots then drifting off to sleep nowhere even close to the other. 'I won't be responsible if you are late to this morning's meeting.'

Rolling his eyes, then himself, slowly, groaning all the while, because *dash it all to Hell* he was sore, and smarting, in places he'd not even known existed, he rose to sitting, and rubbing his face, he glanced around to find Bobby casually sipping some tea as she petted Arion.

Not stroked—*petted*—as if he were some fashionable new companion about her home.

'Good morning,' he growled, not meanly, but a little frustrated, he wasn't going to lie.

And sore.

Why am I so sore?

It wasn't as if he wasn't used to such exertion—well perhaps not the final kind he'd engaged in last night, but the riding, at least—and yes, he was getting old, his fortieth birthday nearly half a year behind him, but still. Feeling as he did now—another fifty miles to ride today—he felt for the first time a little out of his depth, and Bobby lounging around having *tea* as if nothing at all was unusual, well, it chafed somewhat.

Or maybe it was simply being awoken from a very restful slumber. Typically, he woke up well before pinks even began to chase away the summer twilights, but well, nothing was typical about this day.

Or last night.

'There's some water on the fire, if you want some,' Bobby added, less prickly than before, and he nodded.

'Thank you.'

Rising to his feet, he went about his routine, taking care of Beowulf before relieving himself, and getting out his necessities for a sharp and small breakfast.

Preparing himself some chicory, and munching on some leftover hare, he tried his best to fully wake his mind and body, intently ignoring Bobby, who he felt watching him occasionally, and who he heard, busying herself with Lord only knew what as from what little he'd seen already, she and Arion were nearly ready to be on the road. But then, they always seemed that way, he realised. As if they belonged there. Always.

Once he felt slightly more prepared, he rinsed out his cup, and set about extinguishing the fire.

'We should talk, don't you think?' he asked, his eyes on the smoking heap, unable to quite look at her in the soft light of morning.

'About…?'

Lawrence turned, an eyebrow quirking, wondering if she was being intentionally dim, or serious.

Serious.

'What passed between us,' he specified, and she shrugged, turning to pack her cup away.

'It was only coition, Lawrence,' she said, and though yes, he knew that, that it was *supposed* to be just that, the idea somehow didn't sit right.

He stared at her, and she turned back to him, closing some of the distance between them.

Her hair had been done in tight tresses, she sported a tight waistcoat that somehow revealed none of the generous flesh he knew was under it, and she seemed all in all fresh as this damned fine summer morn.

He studied her, searching for any sign of game playing, but found none.

'Right,' he choked out.

'It was good, Lawrence,' she smiled faintly, not mocking, but somewhat patronising, as if he was *indulging* him. 'And if you're asking if I'd be open for a repeat performance at another time, the answer is yes. Beyond that… There were no feelings involved. It was merely a strong inherent connection, and we enjoyed it. We ensured there would be no consequences, and if you're somehow worrying about my reputation or something equally as farcical like the gentleman you are, well, you need only head to the Queen Mary on any given evening, and you'll see that if anything, you merely added to my reputation.'

Yes, they had enjoyed it.

It had been perhaps the best experience of his life— no expectations, merely freedom—and despite some lingering doubts as to his own ability given his general lack of experience, and also, his previous *marital* experiences, he'd been able to make her reach her peak, and that had been about as satisfying, if not more, as his own release.

But to say there were no feelings... He didn't want there to be, and there weren't any on his part, naturally not, except perhaps gratitude, for her trust, and for being able to trust her. With what they'd done, at least. He'd been free because he trusted her to tell him if something wasn't right, because he trusted her to know it was only *coition*, as she put it, and yet now when she said it...

It feels like an unsatisfactory definition.

Because hadn't there been that desire, to take it slow, to savour all of her, to lavish those dusky pink nipples with attention, and trace the contours of her body with his tongue? Hadn't he *not* done so because it had felt as if there lay danger, and they'd both known it, so they'd kept it... Simple.

Yet coming undone with her still had felt far from *simple.*

And did he want a repeat performance? No obligations, no rules, no consequences?

It was what he'd sought in the past—before his vows, and once or twice after. It would be no different to those times—so why not allow himself...the pleasure?

He'd have to ponder that.

That, and the woman who threw him off balance in every way.

Speaking as casually, almost harshly, as she did, of what they'd done; of herself, and her supposed *reputation.*

'You think me cold, and callous, don't you?' she asked, and he pondered that too for a moment.

'Perhaps.'

'I'm merely realistic, Lawrence,' she said gently, and he nodded, turning his attention to the smoking heap of ashes before him. 'You should know—though I'd have thought you'd realised by now—I don't play coy. I say what I mean. I'm sorry if I hurt you, I don't mean to. I know you haven't been with anyone for a while, but I thought you understood the limits of what this was.'

So, she thought him the one to have thought more of it all than it had been?

Hogwash. Merely tired, and not used to speaking so plainly of such things.

'I understand very well the limits,' he told her in his best flat tone, meeting her gaze unflinchingly, and her eyes narrowed, little slits of onyx peering through him. 'I only hoped to ensure we were both in agreement on them. That you knew this changed nothing. I suppose I was put off by your candour, I admit I am not so used to such blunt talk.' Now that he said it, it felt true enough, so likely that's all his earlier *confusion* was about. 'I'm still going to win this race.'

'You can try,' she said slyly a moment later, a grin lifting the corners of her lips, seemingly satisfied by his words.

'Same deal today, then,' he said, a smile threatening, even though he was still, a bit, well, troubled by everything. 'Last one in cooks dinner?'

'You'll have to provide it too, when I thrash you,' Bobby said, pointing a finger at him. 'What was it last night? At least an hour behind me?' she laughed, turning back to Arion, launching herself up into the saddle with a grace he'd never witnessed before. 'Must've been at least that.'

'I'll never tell,' he shot back, glancing at the remnants of the fire one last time, before following suit, and mounting Beowulf.

With a bright laugh, Bobby tore off down the path, and Lawrence followed through the rocky brush, back towards civilisation.

Back towards the final goal.

Slowing Arion as the lights of Bellworthy's inn— The Black Dog—indeed, as the rest of the tiny town came into view, Bobby patted his neck, and twisted her own, trying to relax the knots and tension that had been in it all day, not that at this point, a little stretching would help. Acknowledging their true origin might— only she wouldn't, as she'd done splendidly all day *not* doing so, purporting instead that it was a night on damp cold ground, a long ride, and the pressure of the race.

None of those things are new for you, so rather odd...

How many nights had she spent sleeping on harsher ground, staring into the unknown void of glittering stars above? How many trial runs had she and Arion made in the months before this very race—preparing him before Julian took over to train himself, and then when he could not, engaged elsewhere as he'd often been? Those runs had been longer even than these distances. How many nights and days had she spent worrying about this race—Arion, Julian, and then finally herself?

Too many for that to be the source of a sore neck.

Go away, she instructed the voice, as they came into the quiet yard.

Waving away a waiting stable hand, she led Arion to the trough, and tied him to a post. She'd take care of him properly when they settled for the evening. The lack of a giant black beast nearby told her Beowulf and

Lawrence had either come and gone—or were later than her—though her gut told her it was definitely the former.

I have a feeling I'll be cooking tonight.

Not that I didn't last night, despite thrashing him.

Pushing open the inn's door, she took the opportunity to push away the twinge of excitement she felt at sharing a meal with Lawrence again. An evening with him.

It was just a bet.

And as you told him—last night and any which follow are solely a means to scratch an itch.

Right. Just because she enjoyed his *company* didn't mean she enjoyed his company.

He was still a…a…

'Bobby!'

She'd think of the proper insult for the man later.

Turning to her right, she spotted Julian sitting with the solicitors and Hayes' valet at a small wooden table by the hearth, two of them in comfortable armchairs, whilst the others took up stools. Oddly enough—the solicitors were the ones on the stools.

Striding over, she noticed Julian looked a bit pale, his hair a bit limp from what must've been a tiresome journey.

'Gentlemen,' she greeted, doffing her hat and smoothing back her own gnarly strands.

She waited, standing beside Julian, studying him, as the solicitors checked their watches and made notes.

Narrowing her eyes enquiringly, Julian shrugged.

'He was here about twenty minutes ago,' he said flatly.

'Indeed,' Matthews agreed, setting down his pen and closing his ledger. 'Your lead stands at thirty-nine minutes, Miss Kingsley.'

'I had a feeling he'd made it first,' she agreed, gritting her teeth. She was annoyed by his win, and by that name, but she knew she still had a fair margin; and that these official gentlemen would never agree to call her Bobby so she'd have to live with it for now. 'Are you well, Julian?' she asked, quieter, and Hayes' man was clever enough to engage the solicitors in a quick chat. 'You look…worn.'

'I'm fine,' he assured her with a feigned smile—his *Society smile*. 'Long day. And the leg is smarting, I won't lie. Mostly I'm just bored of sitting in a stuffy carriage all day, then sitting in an inn, then lying in bed.'

'I understand,' she smiled. 'Perhaps you should take some time—'

'This is the least I can do,' he bit back. 'Please, Bobby. You're the one doing all the work. Let me have this.' She nodded. 'Now get out of here. Rest, and for the love of the Almighty find a river,' he added with a laugh and exaggerated wrinkling of his nose.

'At least I have an excuse for my lack of hygiene,' she retorted, sticking out her tongue before lunging out of the way of his crutch.

Laughing, she waved to the little group, slipped her hat back on, and strode out.

Hayes' man caught up with her just as she was going to ride away in search of Lawrence.

'Miss Kingsley!'

'Bobby,' she corrected, and the valet nodded, though only time would tell if he heeded her request. 'And you're… Barnes?'

'Yes, Miss—Bobby. His Lordship left this for you,' he said, passing her a note before disappearing back inside.

There was a little map drawn—ending in a smiling

stick figure man and horse exclaiming how famished they were. Bobby laughed, shaking her head at it, and the little note beneath it.

> *I'll starve before I let you renege on your promise. There is a river here, and some rather delectable fish swimming about therein. And don't forget—no more insulting monikers—not even in your head. L.*

Bobby grinned, stowing the note in her inside pocket, and giving Arion a nudge onwards.

Never promised not to call you names in my head you smug demanding butcher of an artist.

There.

Much better.

Chapter Six

'Took you long enough,' Lawrence smirked when she and Arion arrived at the camp he'd set up on the river-bank, beneath the shadow of mighty pines that seemed to be colouring the sky above a deeper blue with every second they touched it. Sliding off Arion, she led him to the opposite side of where Lawrence had settled Beowulf—though there was no sign the two wouldn't get along—because perhaps it made her feel better to make sure no one became *too cosy*. 'Thought I might have to go back on my word and start dinner myself.'

'Ha. Ha. Ha. So amusing,' she mocked, rolling her eyes as she took to unsaddling Arion. She'd do as Lawrence had the night before, get some dinner cooking before she properly settled him for the night. 'I was barely twenty minutes behind you, and still have a wide lead, so I wouldn't get too comfortable in your revelling, you—'

'Ah-ah-ah,' Lawrence warned, raising a brow, enjoying himself too much, the *wretch*.

'Paragon of English nobility,' Bobby said, biting the other insults back. Not that these words were meant as a compliment—and not that Lawrence didn't know that. She forced a blatantly saccharin smile on her face, and he laughed. 'Besides, I might've made it here earlier had your map been legible,' she commented, feeding Arion an oat patty before grabbing his water bag, and her pack, and striding to the fire where Lawrence waited, like the lazy lord he was.

Except that he isn't.

Bobby knew that much. Had to give him that much. Not that she wished to.

Because any reluctance to be blindly annoyed by him, would lead to liking.

More than his body.

Dumping her things beside him, shooting him a look of pure annoyance, she took out her fishing necessaries, and Arion's water bag, then strode down to the river, set up a line, and returned to give Arion water, all while intently ignoring Lawrence.

She did pass by Beowulf on her way, and said hello, but only because the horse had no say in his owner.

'And you are a rather gorgeous fellow, aren't you?' she muttered gently, and the stallion preened for her.

Grinning, she gave him a scratch, and returned to take care of Arion.

By the time she had returned, she'd caught a fish, so she reset the line, and prepared the first, staunchly keeping her eyes on her tasks, and not on the man across the fire. Was it childish?

Perhaps.

Only, she didn't feel... Quite ready to *properly* look over at him. Sitting there, basking in the warm glow, looking as if he was a man from the past—or perhaps the only man on earth—all free, and wild, and inviting.

Won't do. Not one bit.

Because... And well, this was where it all got a bit

hazy in her mind. Where her stream of thought ended, because there was no true answer. She'd wrestled with this all day, actually, and though she wouldn't admit it, it was the source of her sore neck.

Last night… Last night had been good. In so many ways. And she'd meant everything she said this morning. Words she'd spoken, well, *many* times before.

Only a physical connection.

Nothing more.

Only coition.

Still, even as she'd spoken them, thought them, reassured herself with them as one would a warm wool blanket in the cold of a winter's night, they felt… Imperfect. Unsatisfactory. *Wrong*, even. All day, she'd attempted to find out why, as she rode through magnificent countryside without barely seeing any of it.

Perhaps it was that their physical compatibility was stronger than any she'd felt before. That could be…unnerving. Or perhaps it was that she was in an unfamiliar situation, and that she was merely worried about Julian, Rothwakes, everyone who depended on the estate, herself, Arion… The list went on. Then, Lawrence's comfort became… *More*, than what it actually was.

Only, the thing was, those hypotheses, and the myriad of others she'd toyed with, could not hold a candle to the explanation which kept popping into her head without her consent.

I like him.

There'd been hints of that last night, before he'd gone and ruined it all with talks of kicking out tenants should he win, but even reminding herself of that was not enough to prevent her from thinking there was…

A potential to truly like him.

There was an ease to their conversation, despite its

stiltedness. An ease to being in his company. As if they were merely, Bobby and Lawrence. It was disconcerting, and very, very dangerous. Why?

She wasn't quite sure how she knew it was, only that it was.

Right.

'I think the poor fellow is well and truly dead now,' Lawrence said, bringing her sharply back to the time and place at hand.

Blinking, she stared down at the fish over the fire— indeed, well and truly dead considering it was now charred.

Oops.

Quickly, she took it from the flames, blowing on it slightly, before sliding it from the remnants of the spit, onto a plate. Handing it over to Lawrence, she pasted on an evil smile.

No need for him to know that was not done on purpose.

'*Bon appétit*,' she grinned.

'You spoil me,' Lawrence said with gracious seriousness, poking at the black lump with a fork before abandoning that technique in favour of his fingers. 'Delicious,' he moaned theatrically, and she laughed.

She couldn't have stopped herself from doing so if she'd wanted to—she knew, because she *had* wanted to.

Only, sitting there, stooped over his plate of nearly inedible food, devouring it as he was with fervour and delicacy all at once, complimenting her as a husband might a well-meaning but untalented chef of a wife… He was charming.

And you can find him charming as long as you don't get lost in it.

Right.

'Well, now that I know your preference, I shall be sure to make them all as you like them,' she smiled sweetly, nearly adding *dear* at the end—for effect only.

The look of panic in his eyes made her laugh again, and as she let him stew in fear for a short while, heading back to see if she could in fact, provide more fish, she thought that actually, being charmed, *liking* him, to an extent, was all fine, and nothing to worry about.

It did not preclude her being realistic about everything.

It did not preclude her focusing on the race.

Trying to deny it all—that might.

She'd simply…

Enjoy it all, as she had many times before.

No reason she couldn't do that—and mind herself at the same time.

She was a grown woman, who knew how things stood in the world.

Who she was, and what she wanted.

So no reason at all she couldn't do as she had before. *No reason at all*.

Bobby Kingsley was fascinating. He didn't use that word lightly. In fact, Lawrence liked to think that usually, he didn't use any words lightly. He chose them carefully, for whatever purpose he required them to serve. Explain. Define. Destroy even, sometimes. Precision, and care, were two factors in success, and two very important parts of who Lawrence was. So no, he didn't use the word *fascinate* lightly.

He used it, because he meant it. He meant that he found Bobby Kingsley enchanting. Spellbinding. Bewitching. He meant that he felt as if he was under some witch's spell when she was around—actually, he'd felt like that all day. The countryside he and Beowulf had traversed today had been fascinating. The land was fascinating.

And he'd never noticed before.

It was all very sudden—and very unexpected. One minute he was merely racing on ahead in the bright cool of dawn, and the next, he was in the middle of a country lane, in the shade of great oaks and shimmering beeches, the light flickering against the leaves forming a tunnel of shade over his head, and he'd been transported somewhere else.

Or actually, nowhere at all, but *into* life. Into his own life, as he'd never lived it before. Not even during his previous solitary escapes in nature—which was a rather terrible realisation.

The beauty of that one moment, of the streams of sunlight pouring in through the gaps, glancing off pieces of rock and spider-webs, had made him breathless. He'd slowed Beowulf, and stopped, stared at the scene in wonder for a good five—very precious—minutes.

Awestruck.

Another perfectly apt word for what he'd been. He wasn't quite sure what had happened to wake him from the state of living he'd been in…for as long as he could remember—even as a child—but he didn't actually care. Because…it was monumental. Life-changing, really. He couldn't explain it, and he didn't want to—a first for him.

All his life, he'd thought he'd been living, for he'd been alive. He breathed, he ate, he laughed, yes, he wasn't *that* bad. He loved—his parents at least. He felt pleasure, and he felt pain. But looking back on his life, as he had all day since that moment in the lane this morning, he realised, he'd passed through it somewhat...*mechanically.* Functionally. Even the more pleasant bits.

That lane this morning had been no different, he was sure, from a hundred others he'd traversed over the years. On horseback, on foot, in carriages... Except that, he'd never *seen* them before. He felt as if he'd never seen anything before. Never quite realised the length and breadth—the variety, the possibilities—of what was out there in the world. And for all his so-called living—how much of it had he actually seen?

None, really.

He'd never left these shores—not even to go to the Continent. So close, and yet, so far. The only places he'd ever been had been for functional purposes. His estates. Others' estates. London. Edinburgh. Yes, there had been parties, and dinners, and the like, but those had all been functional too. Making connections. Fostering connections. On, and on...

No wonder she left me.

Something twisted in his gut then, the bitterness of the past resurging. Taking a deep breath, he pushed all those thoughts—*regrets*—away, and focused instead on the good he'd just been waxing poetic about.

This land.

Bobby.

Bobby, who he barely knew, and yet, who he felt so...*comfortable* with. Bobby, who was beautiful, inside and out. Bobby, with her fearsome stomping, and unmatchable grace. Bobby, who was open, and honest, and yet guarded and vulnerable. Bobby who made him smile as he never had, and who burned fish, and who muttered compliments to his horse, and moved with a strangely seductive efficiency, and who now, lying as she was against the log he'd set up so they could sit by the fire, as they had last night, lying there, staring up at the hole in the canopy above them, up at the stars, looking absolutely beguiling, and enchanting, and spell-binding, yes.

Perhaps she was a witch, or a fae, born of the land and returned to her true home now.

Strange thought—stranger even because he'd never really given much thought to myths, and superstitions, and magical creatures. They weren't part of the world— of his world.

But then, as he'd recently realised, not much was, was it?

'An old man at the inn told me to beware tonight,' Lawrence said, sliding down to settle himself so he was lying as Bobby was, right beside her. In her orbit, in her world. 'The waning moon is apparently a time of high activity for all the ghosts who walk these moors in search of souls to take.'

Bobby snorted—and he smiled, remembering how he'd scoffed at the old man, very, *very* serious in his warnings.

Naturally, he didn't believe in ghostly nonsense, but he'd wanted to speak of something with Bobby, find an excuse to engage her in conversation—sorely lacking all through the evening so far—because...

Because.

'You believe in ghosts now, Lawrence?' Bobby asked, laughter in her own voice.

And it felt good—to know he could amuse her.

It felt good to return to...

Comfortable.

Not awkward, not cold, not...

Anything but free.

'No,' he admitted. 'But then, the old man was steadfast in his warnings. And though I have never seen one myself, nor seen any proof as to their existence, well. I am a fair-minded individual.' Another snort. He would allow that. 'I will not discount it altogether. If there were ever a place in the world... Well, I think perhaps, this might be a place for such things to roam.'

Craggy rocks, windswept moors, tall, groaning, creaking pines, fog to cover the earth in white—or so he'd heard.

Prisons, and tombs, and hidden valleys.

Yes, if ever there was a place spirits would roam, Lawrence thought it would be someplace like this.

'What kind of visitation do you think we might have here?' she asked, not mockingly, but rather...*invitingly*.

As if she wanted him to continue.

To use his imagination.

Can I?

'Hm,' he hummed, forcing his mind to conjure up *something* to satisfy the lady. He'd heard tales of wild beasts, and headless horsemen. None of those quite fit however. 'Here, in this forest of ours, I think, we might encounter... A druid,' he said, almost too excitedly, enthralled by his own creativity. 'A fearsome remnant of ages past...'

'But why is he here? What does he want from us?'

'He... Was not always a druid.'

'No?'

'No. Once... Once he was merely a young man,' Lawrence said, letting his voice become soft, and appropriately *storytelling*. He tried to recall stories from his youth, and what all good stories held within them. *A tale of love.* 'A young man who loved. Did you see that high crop of rocks on the hill across the bank?'

'Yes…'

'Well, that was their marker. So they could always find this place. Hidden from the world… They could be together.'

'Why couldn't they always be together?' Bobby whispered, seemingly entranced by his story.

It made him…*happy*.

And he lost himself a little more in his own tale, seeing it play before his eyes as if a vision of the past, not something he'd conjured out of thin air.

'Warring villages,' he told her. *Two families at war— always a classic.* Even he knew that much. Hopefully Shakespeare wouldn't mind him borrowing some, considering the man had done a fair share himself. 'The druid's love, she was promised to the son of a nearby village elder, who promised warriors to her village. So she and the druid, they made a plan to run away.'

'They didn't make it, did they?'

'No. The night they planned to leave, the moon was as it is now. Mists rolled in, blanketing it all so his love couldn't find her way. Or so the druid thought. For in the morning, he found her. There, at the bottom of the rocks, on the other side of the river. Consumed by grief, he vowed to get her back. That is how he became a druid. He learned the ways of the old gods, and of the earth, convinced he could bring her back. That is why he roams to this day. He still searches for her—for a way to bring her back—or perhaps, for another, who might share her spirit.'

Silence washed over them, only the sounds of the world, and of their breathing, echoing in the dark night.

Lawrence wasn't sure where that had all come from, only that it had come from somewhere. He'd been inspired, by the landscape, by Bobby, by his need to…

Make her dream.

After a long moment, he chanced glancing over at her, the tranquil peace of her face before somehow more profound now. The emotions in her eyes, glittering jewels in the night, were different though. She seemed… affected. By his tale. Sadness, wonder, thoughtfulness, they all mingled in the seemingly placid depths that were anything but.

As he said, fascinating.

'You tell a good story,' she said finally, and so seriously as she turned. 'You definitely paint pictures better with words than you do with a pen,' she teased, a grin appearing, but only visible because of the tiny line at the corner of her lips.

'I've never told a story before,' he admitted, and the smile vanished instantly.

There was a question in her eyes now, and he knew for a fact neither of them wished for him to answer it.

As they had the night before, they teetered on the edge of something *else*, and he knew it was his duty, to them both, to drag them away from that edge. So he did the best he could, leaned forward, and took her mouth. And then he lay her down on the earth, by the fire, as he had the night before, only not quite *just* as he had before, and he gave her as much pleasure as he could, before she took his own.

After, they lay there together again, staring up at the canopy, and when he finally drifted off to sleep, his dreams brought to life the story he'd told.

Bewitching.

Chapter Seven

Before her eyes had even opened, Bobby knew she
was not the first to rise. She was *always* the first to rise.
Her body never failed her. At any sound, it woke her.
Only today, it had not. It *had* failed her. In fact, it felt
as if she had entirely failed herself in every way possible. Grumpiness, and irrational irritation bloomed in
her chest as she lay there for a moment, needing a little
time to get herself ready before opening her eyes and
facing the day.

Last night... Last night she'd slept with a man. *Slept*,
all night, curled up next to him. At the time, it had felt
so nice—to feel his body against hers dispelling the
discomfort of cold ground that had never bothered her
before—that she'd told herself a little while like that
wouldn't be so bad. It didn't mean anything—despite
the fact that surely there was a reason she'd never slept
the night through with a man before; not even Julian.
She'd dismissed that notion because really, it was silly,
to accord so much importance to something so functional as a warm cosy sleep.

This morning, it was not so easily dismissed.

Nothing was.

This morning, it felt as if *sleeping* with Lawrence was so much more than functional.

Their entire evening had felt more than just functional, with his tales of ghosts and lost love. At first, she'd needled him into a story thinking *why not*. She remembered those childhood nights with Julian, and sometimes others from the farms or village, sitting around a fire, telling each other ghostly tales of bloodshed and horror. She'd remembered the strange fun of it, and somehow, been tempted to…if not relive it, then perhaps, experience it again.

Except that it had been nothing like her youth. It had been fun, yes, but not for long. Things had taken a turn. Lawrence's story had not been the monstrous thing it was supposed to be. It had been a tale of longing, and heartache, so familiar and yet…personal somehow. It had stirred strange feelings within her, and though she'd pushed them away, refusing to acknowledge or examine them, they left a trace on her heart. A mark.

And she didn't like it.

Just as she didn't like the intimacy that had followed. It had been too intimate, with his confession that he'd never *told* a story before—*what the Hell was that about?*—and the way he'd touched her, pleasured her… Despite her attempts to remind herself it really only was coition, and *very nice* coition at that….

Something had shifted between them without her consent, and this went beyond *liking* him. Liking him, she could deal with. She'd previously established that. Whatever this was…

Makes me anxious.

And she didn't need that. She needed to focus, and do her job.

Secure her future, and Julian's. And Arion's. And so many others.

Right.

Opening her eyes, she turned to find a plate of food and a cup of tea, still steaming, waiting beside her.

No.

Glancing around as she rose to sitting, she found Lawrence standing at the edge of the trees, staring out at the landscape across the river. Even though his back was to her, she could feel the peacefulness, the settledness about him she inherently knew were new for him. Even with his back to her, in the dim twilight of fading night, he was...

Magnificent.

No.

Rubbing her hands over her face, she shook herself out of the moment and got to work washing herself, changing, and seeing to Arion, intently ignoring the breakfast laid out for her, and the man who had done so.

Focusing hard on thinking only about the next move—*pack the blanket* or *button waistcoat*—she found as she went through it that she was slowly feeling overall worse about it all, rather than better.

'I admit I had forgotten just how many wonders England has to offer,' Lawrence sighed contentedly as he strode back up from the riverbank. As if he'd waited for her to be decent, or ready, before coming back to her. *Not to me. And I'm not ready. I'll never be.* 'It's so easy, to travel from place to place, locked in a coach, determined merely to get there, and forget to stop, and breathe, and soak in the vistas.'

Bobby made the mistake of turning, and *Goddammit he is magnificent and so in awe of simple pleasures and I...*

Lawrence glanced down as he reached the fire, frowning slightly when he noticed she hadn't touched her food or tea.

And then he was looking at her, a little hurt, a little questioning, and…

I can't.

'You'd better enjoy them,' Bobby said coldly. 'Before someone just like you comes along, and destroys it all in the name of progress, when really, it's about commerce, and man's eternal hubris.'

'Is this about my railway projects again?'

Yes.

No.

'I might've known you couldn't simply let it lie and agree to disagree,' Lawrence scoffed, shaking his head as he bent down to deal with her untouched breakfast. 'Even though I doubt you're doing so for any other reason than you seem to delight in being contrarian and pigheaded.'

'Oh, so anyone who disagrees with the Great Viscount Hayes must merely be doing so for the sake of argument, it couldn't possibly be because he actually doesn't know all.'

'I never said I know everything,' he seethed, throwing up his hands, before realising he still held the crockery, and stomping off to dispose of it. 'And you're merely disagreeing because you seem to be hell-bent against progress!'

'I'm hell-bent against the notion that men should be able to cite *progress* whenever they seek to destroy something of value, merely because it doesn't make them enough money,' Bobby countered, because no, she wasn't opposed to progress. Progress *could* make the world better. In fact, she longed for progress. 'And

I'm not hell-bent against your damn railway, because I too, believe in progress, but I do find fault with *you*.'

Raising a brow, she made a face that could be deemed *petulant*, but decided not to think on it, and instead went about dousing the fire, preparing it for their departure.

Lawrence made it worse by helping.

Ugh.

'Oh, please, do enlighten me,' he said as he did so, with such dripping sarcasm Bobby thought perhaps he could use *that* to quench the fire. 'Miss *I'm-So-Perfect*.'

'You're using this railway project as an excuse to do something you *know* would just destroy all the Roth-wakes have tried to do with the land, because you're petty, and want revenge against some forefather long dead, for what they did to your forefather, also long dead!' she accused, and yes, that's right, that's what she was angry about. Opposed to. *Yes, indeed.* 'And you've not given a second thought to the people who actually *live* on it *right now*, beyond what you can *pay* them so they'll leave because they're mere pawns, little simple folk, in the way of your great plans of vengeance.'

'What spectacular powers of insight you have, to know a person, and every one of their plans, and thoughts, and motives. Perhaps you should rethink your choice of occupation, and turn to fortune-telling instead!'

'I notice you haven't outright denied the accusation!'

'Why should I, when your mind is already made up! I would have better chance of arguing with a brick wall, but then a brick wall might actually have some knowledge of the subject it was debating!'

An affronted noise escaped her, and in that slight moment of pause, Bobby felt the pure, white-hot anger that had been coursing through her properly.

Oh, she'd been angry, worked up, combative, aggressive, but she hadn't quite *noticed* how quickly it had come into her body, coursing through it, powering her forth, pushing all the rest of the troubling feelings away.

Good.

'Are you questioning my intelligence, or merely my knowledge in relation to railways?' she retorted, stopping him before he could end this, and walk away, for if he did end it here, and walk away...

It will be as before. We'll end up... Finding a way to the nicer things.

And that wasn't good.

'Either way, not that you'd have any experience to the contrary, set upon your lofty, high, unreachable seat as you are, I'd like to inform you that merely because someone does not share your title, your sex, or your education, does not mean they cannot comprehend such things, or have *some* manner of intelligence.'

'And not that you'd have any experience, set behind the walls of your great fortress of summary judgement as you are, but not everyone's intentions are impure, solely because they make choices you don't like.'

How dare he?

Bobby didn't judge—the world judged her.

'Your intentions may not be *impure*,' she conceded, because she supposed fair was fair. 'But I have no doubt you think your position means that even the most harebrained idea in your head is a gift to humanity.'

'Your righteousness is astounding!'

Lawrence took a step forward, and it was too much like the other night.

Something was shifting, and...she couldn't have that.

So she drew from every nasty word she'd heard whispered about him, and attacked.

'And your pompous arrogance truly knows no bounds! It's no surprise you are alone,' she spat, and thankfully he stopped. 'Friendless, detested by your fellows, and unmarried. Any woman tasked with such an insufferable chore as enduring the likes of you every day would surely pack up and risk dishonour rather than remain in your loathsome company!'

Oh, no.

He'd flinched, as if she'd physically struck him. The hurt that flashed across his face, the pain in his eyes, chilled her blood, quenching her anger as though that fire had been doused with ice water.

A sick feeling churned in her gut—*regret, shame, hurt for him*—and she knew she'd gone too far.

How was she to have known her cruel taunts weren't merely taunts, but laced with truth?

'Lawrence…'

'Oh, please, do not stop,' he challenged, his voice hollow, and a vicious sneer on his lips. 'You seem to have plenty more to share.'

'You were married? Your wife left you?' she asked quietly, though from his reaction she knew the answer already.

'Died, actually,' he corrected nonchalantly, except that it was there, plain to see in his eyes, that he was deeply affected by this part of his past. *You're a right snipe, Bobby.* 'But I suppose if we are being technical, she had left the marriage long before that.'

'I—'

'Save your pity and empty apologies for someone else, I care for neither.'

With that, he strode away, jumped on Beowulf, and rode off, leaving her to deal with the rest of the mess.

That of their camp, and the other, larger, more complicated one she'd made herself.

That was not how any of this was meant to go.

None of it should matter. Not the fight itself, nor the words they'd spat at each other. That Bobby had spat at him. Not her sudden switch of temper this morning; nor even what that temper revealed she thought of him. None of it should spoil his own mood, turn what had begun as a glorious, promising morning, where he'd actually been able to simply *be* for the shortest moment, rediscover lost beauty and pleasure, into something foul, dark, and unpleasant.

He could barely see the landscape around him, what miniscule portion of his mind available not consumed by cutting words, accusations, and anger, able to just navigate today's path. The rest of his mind was consumed with Bobby, their fight, and yes, he was not so dull as to not recognise it, the hurt in his breast.

Rationally, he knew he shouldn't be hurt by it—just as none of it altogether should affect him—because that meant he cared about what Bobby thought, and considering he'd just met her, *properly*, two days ago, and that at the end of this race, they would return to being strangers, *caring* about her was positively ludicrous.

Caring about what she thought. Not her.

Indeed.

Come to think of it, maybe he didn't actually care what she thought.

Perhaps, what really bothered him, was that she was correct about the *petty vengeance*. In some measure—and no, he hadn't denied the accusation because he hadn't had it in him to tell her a bald-faced lie, not when honesty was so rare and precious to him. Truth was, the railway had been a plan of his for a while now, and he'd investigated many possibilities. But when this whole bet with Rothwakes had come up, he'd thought, well, what better use to make of the returned land than to properly mark it. As his. As his legacy. The only one he might have that truly stood the test of time, come to think of it.

Actually, he had come to think of that a lot since his wife had in essence, left him. Even before. The title he wore, the name he bore, had as good a reputation as any could. Not unblemished—marred by some indiscreet or fanciful ancestors here and there—but not unworthy. The lands and assets which came with it had always been well-maintained, profitable, and rather than dwindling with the centuries, grew. He himself was well-respected by his peers, or at least so he believed. They might not like him, for his *progressive* thoughts and political leanings, but he'd thought they respected him. For all he did, for his own title, his own heritage, and for the country. So he was somewhat aloof, and had no problem telling a man he was being an arse if he was in fact, being an arse.

It wasn't as if he was entirely loathsome, and it certainly didn't make him friends. But then Bobby was right—he didn't really have friends. Acquaintances, people he could share a meal or an evening with, but no one that would stop by on their way past his house for a chat, or anything like that. He didn't really see the use. Never had, never would. And he'd never felt the lack.

Perhaps, as a young boy, but then there had been books, and learning, then school *chums*; even his parents, and grandparents, who, though they couldn't be deemed overly affectionate—treating him more like an heir than a child—raised him in a comfortable home where he lacked for nothing. What more could a man ask for?

Not much.

Only, he had had more. Success, in school, in life. In business, and, well, not in his personal life, however that could happen to anyone. Bobby wasn't the first to say such about the reasons behind the disintegration of his marriage, though unlike anyone else he'd heard it from, she didn't know the rumours or even that he'd been married at all. At least that much had been plain in her instant shock and regret at striking *that* particular nerve.

Small consolation.

Over the years, he'd let every insult, every jibe, every rumour about what had happened between Milicent and him roll off him like the proverbial water on a duck's back. Innately, he knew people merely liked to gossip, found pleasure in others' failures, and used it as a reason to disagree with him on other matters. As if his supposed shortcomings as a husband represented just how wrong he was about this political view, or that. He begrudged them none of it, even when that attitude seemed to confirm their summation that he was cold, aloof, and uncaring.

So, *objectively*, he shouldn't mind it when Bobby posited that his wife left him because of who he was. Because of his own lacks. Only she had *posited* it. She didn't know him, his past, or the rumours, apparently. She merely looked at him, evaluated him, and found him wanting. Found him incapable of being in such a relationship as marriage, because of his *loathsome company* as she'd put it. Therefore, the likelihood was... She was right.

They'd all been.

Even Milicent herself.

Had his wife not accused him of being cold? Unable to give her the passion, the fun, the excitement, the emotional bread of life she so desperately required? Told him as she'd packed her trunks to go and live her own life, that she'd shrivel and die if she remained one more moment in his rigid world? That she would suffer eternal damnation before suffering another day in a house without love?

Lord knows, he'd tried before that. The first time she'd strayed, and they'd made their pact, he'd *tried*. To give her what she craved, needed, to live. Still, it hadn't been enough, and so by the time those trunks were being packed, and they'd made yet another pact, he'd chalked it all up to insurmountable incompatibility.

Oil and water.

Fire and ice.

Now… Those feelings of inadequacy returned full force. The idea that perhaps he might've done more, if only he'd known how…

Things might've been so different.

Regrets weren't something he truly had many of. Again, good life, all around, for the most part. He couldn't change the past, so he moved on, and worked to changing the future. He'd tried his best at the time, to be a good, caring, husband; to give Milicent what she required, but one couldn't be forced to truly love another could they? He was far from an expert on love—particularly the romantic kind as he'd never experienced it and though that was quite sad, had resigned himself to his fate—but he did know love was not something you could force. He'd tried to marry to begin with, tried to do as duty required—*produce an heir*—and when that had all failed miserably, he'd worked towards finding another way to create a proper legacy for the country, and the next Viscount Hayes.

Yet somehow, accepting past mistakes, moving on and making new plans…it felt a little harder to do today. Felt a little harder to live with Bobby's opinion of him and move on. Bothered him more than he cared to admit.

Why?

It felt like the question to change a life. His life.

Because…

I like her.

Beyond the passion between them—that he'd never known until her—a passion he'd never quite believed *could* exist other than in insipid poetry. Beyond liking how she looked, how she tasted, he liked *her*. In the few moments they weren't fighting, like last night, around that fire, he felt an ease. An understanding even though he didn't understand her very much at all—because he didn't know her. She was prickly, and stubborn, and ill-tempered, and had a mouth on her that would have a saint running for cover. She annoyed him, infuriated him, picked at every sore on his soul, but at the same time, he *bloody well liked her.*

Being with her, around her, in her world.

It didn't feel like he had to try and be anything, that he had to be on guard, waiting for the next lie, nor that he himself was lacking anything—despite her harsh words. He felt as if he could just *be*, and that was enough.

Was he secretly desperately lonely? Was his lack of personal relationships now coming to the forefront of his heart and soul, so much so that he'd latch onto her as a rare chance to have a friend?

He doubted it. Because it wasn't a general lack he

felt—it was a lack of *her*. And he still didn't give a damn about others' opinions, but he did give a damn about hers—if he didn't, her jibe about wives wouldn't have cut so deeply. He knew that much.

Where the Hell does this leave me?

Sighing, he slowed Beowulf to a stop—a moment's pause wouldn't hurt. The surrounding patchwork of pastures, hills, and valleys, cow-studded expanses of bright green, and thick copses of trees, seemed familiar, and foreign, all at once. This was England, how many saw her, in all her picturesque natural idyll. So similar to his own lands, and yet, a world away.

Ride. That is what you do.

Yes. Ride, and enjoy this chapter in his life. Full of adventure and wonder for once, as he'd realised last night. Ride, and enjoy the novelty of it all. Ride, and think. Ride and plan.

Ride, and find a way to put into words what he wished to say to Bobby.

I like you.

I don't mind fighting with you, but I don't want to be at odds with you.

I...

Hm. Needs work.

Grimacing, he gave Beowulf a slight tap of his heels, and they were off again.

Chapter Eight

Bobby wasn't stupid. At least, when her emotions were at an even enough keel for her to think straight. When the fires that often raged within her, urging her to *fight, fight, fight*, lessened—she could see plainly the damage, the destruction they had wrought. If she was lucky, the flames burned down what she'd intended them to do— vicious people, prejudices, unfair obstacles. If she was unlucky, which, to her regret, happened often enough, then, she scorched things, *people*, she didn't mean to.

The problem with her current situation was that although she'd meant to destroy anything remotely *nice* between Lawrence and her, she hadn't meant to hurt him. So badly.

At all.

Bobby wasn't stupid. Once her anger had simmered down, once she'd chased Lawrence away yesterday, she'd known *why* she'd done it. Initiated an argument to begin with.

So we could return to antagonism.

So I could return to safety.

Her wan sigh was carried away on a mighty gust of wind that swept in from the ocean, and up the cliffs to her. The trees to her left shook and hissed, and to her right, the roiling sea was peppered with more white-caps and higher waves. Above it, the sky was darkness, the incoming rain merely miles away robbing her of a clear horizon.

The storm is nearly here.

By the time she'd realised one was on its way this morning, it had been too late to change her route for the day, so she would have to make do with this one. Perhaps the need to be even more careful, once the storm hit—turning the clifftop path into a muddy, slippery, dangerous mess—would help her keep her mind on the race, and not on regret and useless guilt.

It should've had enough by now. After all, her mind had spent all of the day yesterday, from Dartmoor to East Devon, and last night, alone by her own sad tiny fire as she'd been, save for Arion, mulling over it all. It should've been done with the *whys*, the *wherefores*, the explanations, and the conclusions.

Apparently, it is not.

At least the sky seems to share my grim mood.

Nudging Arion on a little faster, hoping to make it nearer to the end of the cliff path before the storm truly hit, Bobby summed up all she'd examined yesterday; all her seemingly fruitful conclusions.

Firstly, that as explained, she'd pushed Lawrence away—*fine, started a fight*—because she hadn't felt comfortable with the way intimacy, almost friendship, had bloomed from what was supposed to be merely animal attraction. When she was with him... Things felt simpler than they ever had before. With other humans. With her horses, with animals, things were always simple. And safe. Only the safety she felt, lying by a fire, looking up at the stars, felt anything but *safe* and *simple* by the sheer fact that they did in fact. She knew it made no sense, but then, well, it didn't have to. It was the only way she could explain it.

Secondly, she did feel bad for the turn things had taken. Really, she did. She'd meant to remind herself, to remind them *both*, that when they weren't...*copulating*, they didn't like each other. They didn't fit. They agreed on nothing. They were highly incompatible in any other respect than physically. And that was important to remember because...otherwise they might get fanciful, silly notions into their heads. Neither of them wanted, nor needed such ideas in their heads. Because the world was as the world was, and their lives were as their lives were, and that was that.

But really, she hadn't meant to hurt him.

Not that she ever meant to hurt anyone. She didn't like hurting people. What she'd said to Lawrence... It had been cruel, and cutting, and she'd meant it to be mean, and cold, but not...

Pouring salt in old wounds.

She'd gone for a weak spot, yes, because she'd heard Julian and others talking about how so many despised Lawrence for his haughtiness, his pride, often enough to know it was likely a sore spot. She'd heard them joke about his lack of friends. As for a wife... She'd never heard anything about him being married. Widowed. She'd thought that because she'd never heard of a wife, that he didn't have one. She'd thought...

Well, she wasn't sure what she'd thought.

You didn't. As usual, you just attacked.

And...it worked.

She'd got what she wanted. Regardless of her intentions, the end result had been the same. She'd got rid of Lawrence, choked out whatever whisper of *more* there had been. Stifled the fire before it could grow. And because of that, she'd been able to focus again. This morning Julian had told her she'd had an hour's lead on Lawrence again last night.

So well done there.

Yes, well done indeed.

Another bracing gust of shockingly cold wind swept over her, and seconds later, it was as if the light went out, as a deluge poured from the heavens, big fat drops of rain drenching her and Arion, thumping against the brim of her hat with grim efficiency.

Slowing him, she tried, and failed, to ignore the pang in her heart at her own words to herself. *Well done*, felt like a lie. Nothing felt as if it had been *well done*. Not last night when she'd sat staring at the fire alone for hours, Arion nudging her more than he usually did, sensing her turmoil, and certainly not now.

What she'd done—no matter the result, *Lawrence gone, another hour lead*—felt wrong. Perhaps somewhat because of the result, but though she'd reached that conclusion before, she still was reluctant to accept it as truth.

What does it matter anyway?

Even if she wanted to apologise, which she *did*, she had tried, Lawrence wouldn't hear it. Maybe he didn't care that much. After all, what was she to him—

A piercing crack of thunder flashed against the sky to her right, lighting the landscape in stark, brutal relief for the briefest second. A rumbling growl of thunder seemed to shake the earth, and Arion neighed, prancing nervously.

Shit.

'Calm down, boy, calm down,' Bobby urged, patting

his neck, while tightening her hold on the reins, ever so slightly.

He settled, and Bobby surveyed the scene, cursing herself for not managing this properly.

Damn it.

'We need to make a run for it,' she told Arion, nerves colouring her voice. 'Not too fast, carefully now, but we're sitting ducks up here…'

Neighing, Arion pawed at the ground, agreeing, and Bobby released her hold on the reins, letting him take the lead.

Together, they navigated the increasingly tricky road with measured speed and caution, and when they made it to the path she'd chosen inland, Bobby felt a wave of relief that they'd done it.

The worst is over.

Only, it wasn't.

Only a thin line of pinkish light remained above the line of tree-topped hills outside the inn's window, the lanterns in the yard brighter with every passing minute in the slowly darkening pale blue light that was cast over the world, and Lawrence's drumming fingers increased their pace, as did his bouncing leg.

Where the Hell is she?

It was too late. Something was wrong. It didn't take someone who had thrashed him by an hour on similar runs—albeit slightly easier—nearly three hours more than him to complete today's section of the race. Storm, or no storm.

At first, he'd been gleeful.

A bit smug, yes, no point in denying it, at having redeemed himself. At having beaten her again. Yesterday's defeat had stuck in his craw, no denying that either. He'd told himself to ride, to enjoy the adventure, to cast away Bobby's words, his own remorse, all of it, for the sake of enjoying what he was doing—the moment—for once in his life. And he'd mostly succeeded—he had enjoyed the day—up until he'd realised she'd beaten him by an hour again. When he realised…

She wouldn't give him the chance to make things right, because everything was seemingly right in her world. She'd come and gone from the meet point, and yes, he might've been able to find her if he'd tried, but she obviously had no urge to see him, to apologise, not that he wanted to hear it, because he didn't—*liar*—and really, he had no urge to see her, and have a repeat performance of that horrible morning.

So he'd gone and found his own place to camp, and spent a very fine evening with Beowulf, thank you very much. He'd not missed her company one bit; not regretted that things would end before they'd even begun. She'd done them a favour really, showing her true colours as she had. Vicious, and cruel, and stubborn, and…

And…

Fine, so I missed her company.

I missed having her around, and I don't want it to end as ugly as it did.

He'd mostly realised that this morning, and he'd mostly enjoyed his ride today, except for that short stretch where he'd been able to see the sea, and he'd started to think about the blasted Continent again. The Continent, where Milicent had gone to live her life, find her happiness, that love, and warmth, and passion she'd craved so, and that Lawrence had been unable to give her. The Continent, where she'd died, and where what was left of her would stay for ever.

The Continent, which had lain just beyond the horizon to his right. Beyond the collection of ominous clouds gathering at the horizon, slowly nearing, seemingly mirroring his own mood in that moment. He'd thought about all the places he'd never been, never seen, never experienced, and then he'd reassured himself that there was no reason to be grim about that. He still had time.

Just as he still had time to make it better with Bobby, though God help him, he knew it wouldn't be easy. He wasn't sure why he needed to make it better, only that he did. And for once, that was enough for him. No true logic, no reason, merely...emotion.

Only, he couldn't very well make it better if the woman never showed.

Something is wrong.

Springing to his feet, he strode over to the table where Rothwakes and the solicitors waited. He hadn't wanted to seem like he was waiting for Bobby, so he'd gone off on his own, to stare out the window like some forlorn lover—which he categorically *was not*—nursing an ale for the entire time he'd sat there. None of the men noticed him coming, too busy whispering to each other, but Lawrence was relieved to notice that at least Rothwakes had the decency to look about as worried as he felt.

But then Rothwakes had an excuse to be worried. Why should Lawrence be worried anyway? Bobby was...nothing to him. Even if she was, she was capable, and she was strong, and he was sure she could handle herself, so really there was no use in worrying.

Still...

'We should go and look for her,' Lawrence announced firmly when he arrived before their table, and the three men moved their heads away from each other, and ceased susurrating like little misses, and looked up at him. 'Something must've gone wrong.'

Rothwakes' jaw clenched, as his eyes shot to the window, and he looked to be considering it.

But then his solicitor decided to open his mouth.

'*No aid shall be given to riders*,' he reminded them all pompously. 'Should we go after Miss Kingsley, the race will be forfeit—'

'That doesn't matter if she's not alive to race the rest of it!'

Lawrence didn't realise he'd shouted until he felt the eyes of the numerous patrons keeping the inn respectably busy on him.

Taking a breath, he reminded himself he was a gentleman, typically cool, calm, and collected, even though at no point in this entire endeavour had he felt to be any of those things.

'Yes, well, you wouldn't bloody well care if we were forced to forfeit, would you?' Julian sneered, and Lawrence reminded himself he wasn't the type to lay a fellow out for being disrespectful either. 'Nor if she were dead, so why don't you go back to your cosy window seat, and let me deal with my rider!'

'I bloody well do—'

Care.

He was about to say *care*; about Bobby. He was about to say they didn't need to *give aid*, merely find her, and be reassured she was all right, and not injured, lying in a ditch somewhere, and *that*, he certainly *did* care about.

Only he didn't get the chance because the door flew open with a bang behind them, and then all eyes were on it, and the bedraggled figure standing on the threshold.

Thank God.

The relief that washed over Lawrence when he saw her paralysed him momentarily, and it was lucky too, because if not he might've rushed over there, and done something foolish like take her in his arms and ravish her mouth like some piratical hero, and that sort of public spectacle was not something either of them would be happy about in the aftermath.

And really, it was entirely out of character.

But then, he was realising, so much of his character wasn't really...his.

'Bobby!' Rothwakes cried, tottering to his feet, as Bobby strode to them, shooting murderous glares at the many onlookers. 'Thank God! What happened!'

'You going to write the time, or what?' she asked mutinously, staring down at the two solicitors who were staring, wide-eyed at her.

Drenched, muddy, with dark circles under her eyes, and a sunken air about her body and movements, she was a sight.

A sight for sore eyes.

A sight, who wouldn't look his way. Matthews recovered first, clearing his throat, and hastily scribbling down a note of her time.

Satisfied, she turned to Rothwakes.

'Arion twisted something in his haunch,' she stated flatly. 'Slipped on a rock. He's fine,' she added quickly, before Rothwakes could open his mouth. 'I'll make him a poultice up in a moment. Had to walk the rest of the way, carrying the pack though. Couldn't risk it. I'm sorry, Julian.'

'I'm just glad you're all right,' Rothwakes said gently, and the relief in his voice mirrored that which Lawrence felt. He wasn't jealous, and yet he was, because Bobby was speaking to Rothwakes, *looking* at him, and meanwhile Lawrence was nothing at all to her. *As it should be.* And wasn't he meant to be angry with her? Perhaps, but now it felt as if that anger were trivial at best, when compared with the potential loss of Bobby. To the world. Not to him, certainly. 'I'm relieved you're both all right. I'll show you where the supplies you requested are, and I have a room for you—'

'I'll find it all,' she said sharply. 'And you know I'll settle in the stables.'

'Bobby…' The woman in question shot him a glare, and he relented. 'As you wish. Take the key anyway, they can prepare you a proper bath if you like,' he added, pulling said key out of his pocket, and offering it out to her.

She took it, begrudgingly, but aware of the audience, and apparently not keen to make a scene.

Or she does want a proper warm bath.

Lord knew, Lawrence could do with one, and he hadn't *walked.*

'How far did you walk?' he asked, and Bobby *still* refused to meet his eye.

'Fifteen miles, give or take,' she did deign to tell him, before knocking on the table. 'I'll get tomorrow's route to you once I've taken care of Arion.'

And with that, she strode back out as determinately, challengingly, as she had entered.

They all stared after her, admiration flowing along with relief in Lawrence's veins.

Fifteen miles.

Christ.

No wonder the woman was late. Fifteen miles, carrying, he posited, more than she rightly could, all so she would not risk hurting her horse further. Some would argue she'd done it knowing the horse still had two hundred miles to go, but somehow Lawrence knew that wasn't why.

Smiling a bit to himself, he quite forgot he was just standing there like a useless ninny until Rothwakes cleared his throat.

'Did you need something further?'

'No,' Lawrence said flatly, as if he'd meant to still be standing there, staring at the closed door. 'Gentlemen,' he added with a nod of his head, before returning to his table.

Oh, he still had a thing or two he wished to discuss with Bobby, but he would wait, give her some time to settle herself and Arion.

Then, he would find her, and...

Well, he wasn't quite certain.

Make it better.

Chapter Nine

Worse than smelling and feeling like death, was the bitter pain of having disappointed Julian; and herself. Leaning on the door to Arion's stall, Bobby watched him avail himself of all the nice treats she'd got him, looking none the worse for wear, which was a relief. She'd done as she'd said, made up a poultice for him, packed and prepared the new supplies Julian had furnished her with, including some nice *sainfoin*, and made sure Arion was settled for the night.

Now, it was her turn, and despite otherwise being keen on *not* having anything to do with the room they'd secured for her, she had to be honest, and admit that a good warm bath would be more than welcome. Her entire body was smarting, but her shoulders and legs were the worst; though with a good soaking, she'd be right as rain and ready to go tomorrow.

Tomorrow.

When she'd have to try and make up for the dismal disaster of today. She couldn't be certain, she hadn't had the heart to ask, but she imagined she was somewhere around three to four hours behind Lawrence today. Even with the lead she already had, that was a lot to make up.

But not impossible.

It would be tight, until the end now. It could still be done, yes, but it didn't lessen the disappointment at having thoroughly failed today. Failed Julian, failed the Rothwakes name. Failed every person who depended on the estate. Failed herself.

Arion, sensing her melancholy, came over and nudged her, snorting a wet breath into her ear. Unable to help herself, she laughed, and stroked his nose.

'I know,' she muttered, annoyed. 'I made the right choice for us both. Still feels like failure,' she shrugged.

Another snort, and Arion went back to munching on his treats.

Rationally, she knew she *had* made the right choice for them both.

Rationally, she knew not all was lost.

But her heart still twisted with doubt, and guilt. What if everyone had been right? Her entire life? What if she couldn't do this? What if she was meant to be safe at home, cooking, and carrying babes?

No.

Her heart screamed that one out, reassuring her that she hadn't made the wrong choice. She forced herself to remember all those who had believed in her, in her dreams, in her work. Even old Lord Rothwakes, grumpy, staunch preserver of honour and duty and propriety that he was. *He'd* been the one to see where her true talents lay—where her true love lay—and given her a position in the stables, though he'd also requested she continue her education as a proper young lady. And he'd merely given her one of the lowest positions in the stables—as any other new lad would've had. It had been up to her to work her way up. And so, she had.

Old Lord Rothwakes hadn't been wrong in that first

show of confidence. He couldn't be. He was never wrong; or so he said.

Smiling slightly at the memories, Bobby kept that thought close.

He wasn't wrong.

This whole…dreadful melancholy was merely born of the fact that she was tired—*exhausted*—emotionally and physically.

Pushing away from the stable door, promising Arion to return later, Bobby grabbed up the bowl she'd borrowed from the kitchens for the poultice, and made her way out of the stables, raking her fingers through her hair.

A bath would help perk her up. Refreshed, and clean, she'd be able to shake herself of this mood for good, and maybe even do as she'd promised herself during those fifteen excruciating miles.

Apologise to Lawrence properly.

It didn't matter if she was nothing to him, she'd hurt him, and been cruel, and that shame had stopped her from even looking him in the eye tonight. It wasn't sustainable, that sort of behaviour, or relationship. So, she'd have to pull up her bootstraps, and grit her teeth, and get it done.

Right.

Bobby returned the bowl to the kitchens, thanking them, then made her way around to the main entrance of the inn. Still lost in her thoughts and sullen mood, she barely saw nor heard anything as she went in, and requested a bath. Once the arrangements had been made—the innkeeper saying it might be a while—she finally lifted her eyes, and surveyed the room, raking back some strands fallen loose from her queue.

It was as busy as a place such as this should be, but

among the many faces, Bobby spotted no familiar ones save for Matthews. Reminded of her duties, she strode over, wordlessly gave him her route for the following day, then watched as he too disappeared.

It shouldn't have been a surprise, that no one of her *party* as she supposed it should be called, remained, the days were long for all of them involved in this, and once she'd arrived, and now delivered her route, they had no real reason to remain down here when a warm bed and an early start awaited them all. She might not have been so disappointed had one specific person remained.

Not that she really wanted to make her apology down here, in the middle of the public rooms. Or perhaps she did. It would make it simpler. No going into detail. Just a quick *I'm sorry*, and then, she'd be gone.

Coward.

Probably. Undecided on whether the lack of Lawrence was a blessing or a curse, Bobby pushed through the small groups of people, and made her way up the stairs. Wandering down the first floor's low, beam-strewn corridor, Bobby wondered vaguely which room might be Lawrence's. Surely, he'd got a room on this floor too—the best rooms were likely here considering the floor above looked to be stuffed beneath the eaves—same as the rest of them. Not that it mattered whether or not she knew. It's not like she would walk up to his door, and knock, and…

No matter at all.

At the end of the corridor, she found her room on the left. Opening the door, she glanced in to find a fire already raging, and what looked to be a small, but comfortable, inviting, fluffy bed.

Only a bath.

Then back to the stables.

It wasn't that she denied herself comfort. It was merely that she usually felt more comfortable on a bed of hay with Arion, than sleeping alone in tiny boxes like these. Why... Well, Bobby wasn't in the mood to go down that particular road.

Already too many travelled today.

Sighing, she was about to turn tail, go and wait downstairs for her bath to be ready, when the door behind her opened. Glancing back, she found Lawrence standing in the doorway, in only his trousers and rolled up shirtsleeves, the firelight behind him casting him in a breathtakingly ethereal glow. She didn't mean to stare, really she didn't, only, the look of him, it hurt her heart somehow. Its grace, its...beauty, she supposed. And it only hurt all the more when she made the utter mistake of meeting his gaze. There was...an eager hopefulness, a relief, that made her momentarily forget...everything. Herself. Where they were.

Everything but him.

'Bobby...'

Shaking her head, she cast away the pleasant reverie she'd been caught in.

Apologise.

This is your chance.

Taking a deep breath, she steeled herself, but Lawrence spoke before she could.

'I was going to come find you,' he told her, and her eyes shot up to his, questioning. Raking his fingers through his own hair, he did nothing more than give the long strands falling on his forehead more...luscious bounce. She'd never really thought of the luscious bounce of a man's hair before. *Hm.* 'I thought maybe you'd decided to forego a bath after all,' he said, not answering her unspoken question.

Not that she minded.

'I...um... Need one,' she shrugged weakly, latching onto this talk of baths because it was eminently better—*safer*—than anything else. 'They said it might be a while though.'

'Likely my fault,' he grinned, gesturing over his shoulder, where Bobby now noticed a steaming hip bath waited for him. 'I...' He hesitated, and they both stood there awkwardly for what seemed an eternity until finally he put her out of her misery. God, she hadn't noticed until he did, how fast her heart was beating. Fluttering like a bird's. 'I could share it. So you need not wait. I would wait in your room,' he added hastily.

Heavy footsteps and laboured breathing caught both of their attentions, and they turned to find two young lads holding a hip bath between them, a maid in their wake sploshing hot water from a bucket.

They all stared at each other for a moment, all uncertain as to what the next move was meant to be.

Until Bobby made the decision for them.

'I'll not be needing that after all,' she told the young men with the tub. 'Though I thank you. I will take that bucket if you don't mind,' she told the maid.

If anyone had any thoughts on that proclamation, they said nor revealed nothing.

Bobby did catch some muttering as the lads navigated the tub back down the stairs, and the maid brought her the bucket, before disappearing after them, her eyes cast to the floor, only the blush on her cheeks signalling any understanding of the situation at hand.

Once they had gone, Bobby turned back to Lawrence, and was snared again by him, the heat in his gaze, and the sweet smile on his lips utterly spellbinding.

'Don't wait in my room,' she said, though she knew it sounded like begging.

She didn't care.

This wasn't what she had planned, but wasn't there a saying about gods and plans and laughing at men who made them?

Lawrence stepped aside, and she sidled in.

The door snicked closed behind her, and she took another deep breath, readying herself for what came next.

This wasn't exactly what Lawrence had planned when he'd promised himself to *make it better* with Bobby. His original plan had included a calm, private discussion. Not…offers to share a bath. Not inviting her into his room—though he had to admit it was probably the best place for a private discussion.

He'd come up here because he'd driven himself mad downstairs, staring out the window again, waiting for her to come back in. He'd heard Rothwakes and the others go upstairs, and he'd told himself that was a good idea. He'd feel like he was doing something other than waiting, so he'd dismissed Barnes, told the man to get some rest himself, then sat on his bed as the inn's people set up his bath. As he'd sat there, he'd tried to understand why precisely he was still so… Fidgety. Apprehensive.

He knew Bobby was safe. And that had been why he was so…on edge earlier, wasn't it? If so, why wasn't he…settling?

And then, as silence and tranquillity invaded his room, his bath prepared, the others long gone, he realised that he might know she was safe, but he didn't know she was *all right*. He didn't have physical proof of that. He hadn't properly even looked in her eyes, or

touched her—not that he should be touching her or gazing into her eyes—but that was about the time he had
been about to go back downstairs, and find her, and then
he'd heard her key in the lock, and now...

Here she is.

With me.

Lawrence took a few tentative steps forward, until
he was standing right behind her—not touching, but
close enough that he could smell her. *Feel* her. From
his higher vantage, he could see her chest rise and fall
with measured slowness, and then, still clutching the
bucket before her, she was leaning back against him.

Closing his eyes, he revelled in that moment. The
surrender. The breaching of a gulf. Her trust. The relinquishment of the weight on her shoulders to him. He felt
it all, seeping through him, and he took it, *gladly*, dropping his head so he could take a long inhale of her hair.

This is what I needed.

'Lawrence...'

He'd never been particularly talented at understanding people.

Emotionally. Oh, he could see anger, and deception,
and desire. He could recognise mischief and glee, and
sarcasm. In fact, he'd spent a long time studying people,
to be able to see what he could. He could deduce for
the most part a person's reasoning, the flow and pro-
gression of their thoughts and goals, if they followed
a logical order.

When they did not however, he often failed to see
what was coming. To understand, the path that person
had taken to arrive at such a decision, or conclusion. It
was in part that which made him so distrustful of the
human race as a whole, that, and, in his experience, that
the human race as a whole tended more often than not, to

cheat, deceive, or lie. Not always on a grand scale, more often than not, on a small scale—but still.

His lack of understanding of reasoning which defied logic, was in great part what had made his marriage to Milicent...fail. Not so much the distrust—it hadn't been quite so bad back then and he would never say Milicent had prompted him to distrust *all* women— because the fact was, he'd trusted Milicent. However, he had failed at seeing all the hints, the subtle requests, the unspoken needs. When she'd explained them, he'd understood, rationally, and tried to meet them. Still, it hadn't been enough. He'd accepted that, accepted that failure of what he for so long believed was his character.

Except that with Bobby...

It felt like he could understand her. She was the most infuriating, vexing creature he'd ever had to deal with. Yet, those emotions he struggled sometimes to understand when people concealed them, deep beneath politeness, civilisation, and manners, he saw them clearly with Bobby. He could hear them, in every word. Like now.

Now, he could hear the regret, the apology brewing in the simple utterance of his name.

And though he knew there was much to be said, he found that right this moment, he didn't want any of that to be said. Perhaps he was afraid it would all... explode again.

No.

It was... It was that he needed to be with her. Just breathe, and exist with her. No matter what they'd said to each other, which they would address in time, he needed her now...simply. The talking, the apologies, all felt like the prescribed thing. Merely being with her, that felt...truer. More natural, more...

Primordial.

'Tomorrow,' he told her.

Asked her; begged her.

She sank into him a little more with her next breath, and he smiled. Lifting his hands, he gently ran them down the length of her arms, until he held the damp rope of the bucket. She relinquished it to him, and transferring the weight to his right, he stepped around her, dropping a kiss at her temple as he did.

Finally opening his eyes, he blinked a few times, the dim room somehow as bright as white sands on a summer day, then went and set the bucket by the already full tub near the hearth.

And then he stood there, by the tub, staring out into the shadows, at Bobby, drinking her in. In the gloom, she still shone brightly. Her exhaustion, weariness, and frustration had diminished somehow, and he liked to think it was thanks to him, and his chest filled with pride at the thought. The tiredness that remained in the lines of her face, and her body, felt different now.

A weary sort of vulnerability. A reluctant openness; as if the armour she sported every second of every day, had been stripped.

As mine has been.

He realised that then. That he hadn't felt the weight of it on *his* shoulders for days now. The corners of his mouth tipped up in a smile, and that seemed to be what Bobby had been waiting for.

Because then she was moving towards him, into the proper glow of the firelight, ever so slowly, but with clear intention. Her coat dropped to the floor first, with a gentle *thump*. Then her waistcoat. Her boots, and stockings, which made her pause in her advance, as did the trousers and underthings. Lawrence swallowed hard, not bothering to hide his interest.

It hadn't been his intention to invite her in for...*that*, but that didn't mean he would pretend to hide his interest in her. First, he would give her a bath. Then, he would take one. The woman was exhausted. He would see where they went after that. As he'd said, he merely wished to exist with her.

Though Bobby did appear to be offering more than existence, the way she was moving again, not particularly seductively, but fully aware of what she was doing, slowly lifting that shirt over her head, and letting it drip like water from her hand. Unravelling the band of fabric covering her breasts without haste, and intense care, until a trail of it was behind her, and she was standing across the tub from him.

Lawrence held out his hand, and when she took it, he released the breath he hadn't realised he'd been holding for...years, perhaps. Strength, and warmth, filled him through her touch, and the relinquishment was there too again. The relinquishment of control, which she passed on to him.

A responsibility he would not carry lightly.

Guiding her into the tub, he only had one thing on his mind.

Make it better.

Chapter Ten

Presented with this same situation at any other time or place, Bobby would've been fleeing. Swiftly, and without ever looking back. There were different types of trust. Trusting a friend to tell you the truth even though you knew it would hurt. Trusting a horse not to throw you. Trusting a lover to...well, to not hurt you. There was trusting the baker not to poison your bread; trusting the doctor to give you the right cures.

And then, there was this. Trusting another person to...

Take care of you.

It had been a long time since Bobby had known such; *allowed* herself to do such a thing. Such a gesture, it engendered an intimacy, a bond, that was not easily shattered, and never forgotten. To her, it meant more than sexual intimacy. Sharing pleasure with someone was vastly different to...being vulnerable she supposed. She worked hard to keep the reins in all things, in every aspect of her life. The last people she'd truly let care for her had been Lady Rothwakes, and Julian. One could argue that the latter still did in some ways, giving her a livelihood, a roof over her head. Only, those bonds had all been created long ago. And she hadn't let anyone take care of her since then.

She'd never wanted to.

Never wanted to be tied to another, have her freedom diminished by another tie to yet another person.

And she didn't *consciously* want Lawrence to—consciously she wanted to run far, far away. Consciously, she knew it was dangerous, that creating this bond with him would be…trouble. But she was just so…*tired*.

Too tired to fight it. To reason it out and walk away.

All it took was for Lawrence to stand there, silently beckoning, and she answered. She wanted to fold herself into the sweet, welcoming heat of his very presence. There was so much to be said; she didn't deserve his kindness, his care, she knew that too. But he asked her to leave it be, *told* her it was tomorrow's problem, asking her to merely *be*—though in not so many words, but it was there, in his voice, in his touch—and she was powerless to refuse.

Too tired to fight it anymore.

Falling against him, feeling him at her back, strong, and steady, protective and yet… *Soft*… It stirred desires she'd not had. Ever. Or perhaps, that she had long buried.

This desire, so profound her bones ached with the intensity of it—to be taken care of.

She felt it again, as he guided her into the tub, the water blissfully warm, and the heady scent of lavender, rosemary, and clove, rose from it, enveloping her in a delicious cloud as she sank further into the water, her back coming to rest against the copper, and her eyes drifting shut for a moment as she felt everything within her…release.

A sigh escaped her, and Lawrence's hand slid into

the crook of her neck, gently massaging the muscles there, his thumb paying special attention to the place where her skull and neck met. Releasing another contented sigh, she felt herself sink even further into the water. It was the most luxuriant, lush, sensuous feeling she'd ever experienced.

The massage ended, and his deft fingers untied the knot pulling her hair back, before he took away the strand of leather. Her head followed his movement as his hand left her skin, her eyes opening as it did.

He was on his knees beside her, the rim of the tub just below his chest, and when he caught her looking, he smiled at her—that sweet, relaxed smile she'd never have thought him capable of. His eyes still held the flame of desire, but there was something even more tender along with it. His whole…being, emanated that softness that was so very much at odds with everything she'd thought she'd known about him. Before, and even since she'd, well, got to know him better than by mere reputation.

Bronzed skin glowed in the flickering of the fire, the dark mop of his hair, the sharp contours of his growing beard, glittered, highlights of gold shimmering with every breath, the only movement he seemed to make as he gazed right back at her. She'd called him stiff before, and from experience she knew he could move his body in a way which told her he wasn't so much so after all, but she'd not witnessed this… Immovable, relaxed state of his before. It was lulling, quieting, and reassuring, all at once. Reinforcing what she'd felt earlier.

Lawrence was a man you could lean on; in every sense of the word.

'Are you thirsty? Hungry?'

Bobby shook her head slightly, loath to stop…*looking* at him.

She'd had some bread and cheese from the kitchens when she'd taken the things for Arion's poultice; though she should've been hungrier from the day, the grimness, the disappointment of it, had spoiled her appetite.

'I was worried about you today,' Lawrence admitted quietly, sinking back on his heels, leaning his arms on the tub, and his chin into a little holder made by his hands.

His words, what they suggested, didn't scare her as much as they might've coming from…someone else.

And that was it, wasn't it? The crux of it all? Lawrence terrified her in a way, because things that might've scared her with other people, didn't so much with him. Had she been the same person she had been two mornings ago she would've fought succumbing to it tooth and nail. Now, she'd ceded control. Will. If only for a short time.

So she could rest.

Dark, burnt coffee–coloured eyes studied her for a long moment, tracking across her face, as if searching for something. She let herself, *forced* herself, to not shy away. Even as a blush bloomed on her cheeks, sweat pooling on her forehead.

Only from the heat of the water.

Then his sweet smile was widening, the lines at the corners of his eyes crinkling, as if he'd heard all her thoughts, seen them pass across her face, and realised she accepted his concern. His worry; not easily admitted, she knew.

Nodding, he lifted himself away again, reaching to the side for the soap. Turning her head away, she closed her eyes again as she leaned back, knowing if she was going to surrender to this, she couldn't quite watch. Doubts, questions, fears, they would overpower her.

Water moved against her chest and arms as he dipped the soap in the water, then long fingers trailed against her skin, from armpit to wrist, lifting her arm from the water before he ran the soap along it, ever so slowly, tortuously, but firmly enough she could feel it lathering, the bits of herbs cooked into it abrading her skin lightly.

Satisfied, he lowered her arm again, circling his hand around it this time, to wash it all away. The process was repeated on the other arm after she heard him shift, linen and cotton rustling, light fading as he moved above her. Then her legs, one by one, inch by inch. They received exceptional attention, deep, breath-stilting massages that turned her into a lump of oozing mush.

Moans, and breathy gasps escaped her, edging him on, begging him to do his worst. Desire rose as slowly as melting metal, pooling below her belly, tightening and heating her inner self, overwhelming in its certain, but leisurely rise. It, the heat, and the lassitude that every touch gave her, made her dizzy, transported her to a state almost beyond herself. Where there was no reason, no pain, no fear, merely delectable sensation.

A cry was strangled in her throat when he reached her feet and toes, the soreness of them not forgotten, but ignored, swallowed, until Lawrence's clever fingers untwisted every knot and ache within them forcefully. Tightness swelled in her chest, there, in the middle of her breastbone, as he worked on the strain where the ball of her foot met her arch. It felt as if years of her were in that infinitesimal place, and as he expelled them from her body, she felt she could breathe again, better than before. The tension in her chest released, tears along with it, which she prayed he wouldn't see before they disappeared into the water below.

She would never know—by the time she felt him at her side again, his breath fanning the skin above the waterline where it met her nipples, teasing them into thick, aching points—the tears had dried or fallen.

His tender ministrations continued along that exposed skin, taunting her even more, before they continued down her belly, then finally he returned to her breasts, no longer hiding the sensuality of his intent as he caressed and clutched her, pinching her nipples as he cleaned her, shards of electricity racing through her languorous body from her clenching core with every touch.

Arching, she pressed herself into his hands further.

'I won't rest until I see these lines erased,' he promised, his voice smooth, and decadent as the thickest chocolate.

'A necessary evil,' she told him, knowing he spoke of the lines her bindings left on her skin.

It was a sad fact there weren't many options for women to be comfortable whilst bouncing about on horseback for hours.

Even she, with her generous but not overly so, assets, suffered if she dared go without for too long. Most of the time, a tight waistcoat was enough—but not for rides such as she'd face on this race. She'd be damned if she ever chose a corset.

Lawrence hummed, and she drifted further into the land of soaked pleasure as he held true to his promise.

Then his hand drifted down, back down her belly, to her aching nest of curls. Her knees and legs fell further apart as she opened to him, and to his credit, he did make an attempt to wash her, to flit the soap untantalisingly along her innermost parts, but then the tip of his finger caught some of her slick secret wetness, and then the soap was abandoned, clunking against the bottom of the tub.

His finger returned, sliding down between her folds, from her sensitised nub, down to her body's opening. He slid inside with ease, first one finger, then another, his hand cupping her as his thumb pressed against that nub, swirling, flicking, massaging; the fingers inside her delving into her depths with a maddening, dizzying, exquisite diligence, as if he were learning every line and bump inside of her, committing them to memory.

Her body undulated with him, responding to every nudge, every press, every rub. Water sloshed against her skin, and the copper surrounding her as she panted, the climb to utmost pleasure sure and steady, but increasingly rapid. Her fists clenched in the water, and she felt his hand again, at the back of her neck, steadying her, guiding her, his thumb there smoothing the skin along the divot of flesh behind her ear.

Everything was hot, and slick, and her heart beat a tattoo in her chest, as she felt her skin blush, from toe to forehead. Lawrence's pace followed her climb, still tender, and dutiful in its profundity, but faster, and faster, until finally she shattered, clenching tightly around him as he continued to work himself in and out of her, pressing against that nub until it was almost unbearable. She came with a squeak, her whole body tensing and clenching as she flowed away from the seen world on a wave of pleasure unlike she'd ever known.

Easy, drugging, and yet immensely powerful.

When she returned, sweaty, and sated, her eyes floated open, to find Lawrence still by her side. His hands, not working her, but still against her, holding her safe.

He stole her breath, literally, when he leaned forward and kissed her, his tongue, and lips as driven as the rest of him, as compassionate as the rest of him. Not demanding, but not unsure.

Reassuring, and reviving.

Bobby let herself fall into that sensation, it wasn't really hard, when the rest of her was so…spent. Exhaustion, and the feeling of having released a lifetime of tension, left her pliable, and sleepy.

There was a soft kiss to end it all, and then she drifted away into nothingness.

Chapter Eleven

Despite the lack of sleep, Lawrence was awake at his habitual predawn hour. Though unusually, he lay there a moment, allowing himself to enjoy a lazy enjoyment of the soft, feathery bed, which was currently disappointingly empty. Had been, for a while, if the cool crispness of the spot where Bobby's body had been last night was anything to go by.

He understood her quiet departure. Last night… had been a lot. For the both of them. He might not be able to sense much, but he sensed that. Knew, how precious it was to have had what she'd given him—*trust, control*—for the time she had. And practically, he did know they were on a schedule, and eventually—*very soon*—he would have to rise himself, and get everything ready for the new day, just as Bobby likely already was, knowing her.

Which he felt he did—even as he knew he didn't.

Last night… He wasn't sure words existed to explain it.

Transformative. Easy. Hypnotic. Transcendentally, heart-stoppingly…

Magical.

Not a word he'd ever thought he would use. Other than to describe something belonging to that realm of a belief system he could never adhere to. Because he'd never have believed it could be real. Seeing Bobby come undone, feeling her beneath his own fingers, exploring every inch of her, taking care of her in every possible way... It had felt magical.

Picking her up, drying her, once she'd fallen soundly asleep in the tub, settling her in bed, then curling up beside her, and watching her sleep once he'd washed himself, that had been of the same transformative ilk. Sleeping with her nested in his arms, his body curled around hers...

He'd never had that before. Not that he wished to compare everything to Milicent—but she was the only woman he'd been with in what could qualify as a *relationship*. Not that he considered what he had with Bobby to be...*that*, but he couldn't qualify it as the experiences—limited as they'd been—with other women. Those had been...studies. Exploration. Expected rites of passage; or releases of transient pleasure.

It had all been...functional. He enjoyed sexual congress, sexual intimacy, but he'd never felt the burning need for more. Though he enjoyed the act itself, it had always been...something he could live without. He hadn't felt the passion of poets the world over; which had been part of the problem with Milicent. She'd wanted him to demonstrate that insatiable need for her; wanted all the soulful intimacy that came along with it, and which Lawrence hadn't been able to provide. Of which he'd thought himself incapable—one of those lacks in his character—but which now he began to doubt. Like so much more he'd thought part of himself, he supposed.

In any case, no, he'd never slept the night with a woman—not even his wife. He'd thought it all…normal, before. Finding pleasure, copulating to beget an heir, then padding off to sleep in his own bed. He liked sleeping alone. And though he couldn't say he liked being woken by flailing limbs or kicking legs—though he couldn't say he liked overheating because the woman beside him was a *goddamned furnace*—he could say that overall the experience had been…

Wonderful.

Full of wonder. Yes, that was it. An object of astonishment. For astonished was what he'd been, at how pleasant it felt to share a bed with Bobby. To feel her in his arms, to be… There, *for her.* It felt as giving her pleasure, watching her come apart under his touch, had. As before, but also, *more.* It felt…special. As if he'd discovered a new purpose to his being, a new facet to his character. A new function for himself. He could make Bobby feel good. He could make her feel safe. Make her lay down her armour, if only for a time. Those were good things, that filled him with pride, and accomplishment, as nothing else ever had.

Rolling onto his back, he linked his hands behind his head, and stared at the bleak beige ceiling above him, its tones muted in the dark grey of early morning.

These feelings, revelations, were all well and good, yet the more he discovered, admitted, revealed to himself, the more he felt… Lost. What did one do with such information? Did it prompt action? If so, what kind of action? Was merely acknowledging it all, enough? Taking care of Bobby now was one thing, but when this race ended…what possibilities existed then? She seemed to suggest there were none, and days ago he might've—*had*—agreed with her, but surely, something had changed now. Hadn't it? Did he mind that?

A light rap on his door tore him from the troublesome thoughts, and he pulled himself to sitting as Barnes shuffled in, a tray of food in his hands.

Lawrence was relieved then that Bobby had already made her escape.

'Good morning, my lord,' Barnes said, spotting that Lawrence was awake.

Strange.

It had never struck him before, the presence of servants. Being waited upon. Constantly. Being shepherded, aided through even the most intimate functions. He'd grown up with servants, but this morning, he felt the intrusion in a sense.

The past few days without Barnes attending to him, he'd survived. Very well, in fact. Not that there hadn't been times in the past when he'd had to make do without for some reason or other—such as his escapes into nature much like the recent days—but these past few days were different. He'd *fully* enjoyed the…independence in a way, of attending to himself. Depending on himself. Without knowing a servant was a shout away, in the house at the edge of the forest. Now, the man's duties seemed almost…

Unnecessary.

Extravagant.

'I trust you slept well, my lord,' Barnes said, laying the tray across Lawrence's lap.

'Yes, thank you,' he replied, frowning down at the delicious, welcome, but oddly troubling plate of food. 'Barnes,' he said when the man went to begin his duties, stopping him. The man had always been candid with him over the years, when Lawrence had asked. It had been one of the conditions of his employment actually, as Lawrence required at least *one* person in his life who he could trust to say what he meant. 'Do you find it odd, serving me?'

'My lord?'

'Witnessing what you do, every day,' he explained, raising his head to look the man in the eye. 'The intimacy of attending to me. When you do such as you do for me, for yourself, every day.'

Barnes quirked his head, his eyebrows drawing down into a frown.

'I can't say I've ever given it much thought,' he shrugged after a moment. 'It's what I was trained to do. It's part of... The privilege of your title I suppose. Like, would you ask a blacksmith if it were odd for him to wear a leather apron?'

'The apron serves a function.'

'And I don't?' Barnes chided.

Lawrence snorted, conceding the point.

'I suppose I wonder at your necessity, when I can perform what you do for me...for myself.'

'Are you displeased with my service?'

'No,' Lawrence said, waving his doubts away. 'I'm just...wondering at my own purpose I suppose,' he admitted quietly.

'To be lordly?' Barnes teased him, garnering a laugh. 'Ha. Ha.'

Smiling slyly, Barnes went off to do what he always did, though there was less to do as Lawrence was not about to go sit in the house or attend some society dinner.

As he ate his food, he did continue to ponder the question. *Questions.*

Of purpose, of necessity. Of ritual, and function; magic, and change.

No satisfactory answers came to him miraculously as his belly filled, but by the time it was, and he was dressed, ready for the day, he did spy a sight from his window that seemed to reassure him that no answers were needed, for now.

He could do as he'd told himself to before.

Just live.

'A sight, isn't she?' Rothwakes said, as Lawrence approached the fence where he was standing, watching Bobby warm Arion up—and likely checking his sore hind—in a mist-covered field the colour of twilight despite the rising sun. Lawrence had intended to find another spot, far away from his rival, before the man spoke, and though he wasn't sure he wanted to have a *friendly chat* with the little baron, he changed course and came to lead beside him.

'Indeed,' Lawrence agreed.

He wasn't quarrelsome for the sake of being quarrelsome, not on any day, so he had no choice but to agree with Rothwakes.

Though *a sight*, seemed a paltry description of what Bobby was. Even *an arresting vision* failed to quite capture the rapture she provoked like some ancient goddess, born from the mists, her steed a god in his own right. The way she moved with him, the way she communicated with him, silently…

It was incredible, and he was spellbound yet again.

'You are lucky to have her,' Lawrence said, breaking the silence, meaning it, in every way possible.

Perhaps it was evident in his tone, for the little baron turned slightly, raising a brow.

'She told you?'

'I guessed,' Lawrence corrected, and Rothwakes nodded, turning his eyes back to Bobby. 'I'll be the first to admit that had I not seen your horses in action before I knew who your trainer was… I might've—likely would have been—the first to disparage you.'

'You didn't need to know a woman ran my stables to disparage me,' Rothwakes pointed out with a smirk. Lawrence shrugged, conceding the point. Again, it was nothing but truth. 'It isn't out of… It isn't for myself I keep Bobby's involvement quiet,' he continued after a moment, with more solemnity. 'I do it for her. To protect her. It's the only way I know how. My father… My parents… They kept her involvement, her work, as quiet as could be. They never wanted her to lack…opportunities. And I… I want the same. She faces enough as it is.' Rothwakes glanced at him, as if asking for Lawrence's understanding. Lawrence nodded—he did understand—even though, he wondered… *Many things.* 'But anyone who sees her, like this… She's worked with horses people said were beyond help. She was born for this.'

'What's her secret? To taming them? Training them?' Lawrence asked.

He didn't actually think the man would respond—risk giving away the precious key to his own kingdom, troubled as it was, but then, Rothwakes was determined to surprise him it seemed today.

'Her secret is that she doesn't,' Rothwakes said, immeasurable pride and wonder in his voice that made what Lawrence suspected was jealousy bloom in his chest. 'Tame them, break them, even train them. She… befriends them. Asks them nicely to do things for her,' he laughed, shaking his head. 'Even as a child…she had this power… As if she speaks their language. Sounds mad, I know, but it is the truth as far as I know it.'

Lawrence nodded.

It did sound mad. But then again, he couldn't deny the bond he saw between rider and horse. He couldn't deny the way his own horse, a spirited beast who didn't like many people, responded to a few hushed words, and gentle touch.

And somehow, it didn't seem mad at all, knowing what little he did of Bobby.

It fit.

The two men stood there for a while together, both watching the spectacle before them, thoroughly engrossed. Finally, when twilight blue turned to pinkish purple, Rothwakes tapped the fence, pushed himself off, and hopped away.

Lawrence remained even after Bobby had disappeared from the field, heading back for the stables, though he knew very well he should be getting ready for the ride ahead himself.

Still, he didn't move, caught in a moment he wasn't ready to leave just yet.

Chapter Twelve

'Looking much better, my friend,' Bobby said, patting Arion's neck before swinging down, and tying him to a post at the side of the stables. He whinnied, and then bent down to get some water from the trough. Patting him again, she smiled wanly, and sighed, turning to look out at the road, and rolling hills beyond it.

All in all, it promised to be another good day for riding, with none of the rain which had foiled her yesterday on the horizon, and Arion was looking much better. With any luck, they could make good time today—the route was not a treacherous one far as she could tell, so as long as the mud and rivers weren't too bad, they'd be fine—though she wouldn't be able to push him too hard, and therefore make up much of the time deficit yesterday's disaster had created.

We will. Maybe not today, but yesterday was not the end for us.

This morning she'd woken early—so early she doubted it could truly be called morning—and come out here to check on him, get him ready for the day, massage his own tender hind, and…think. Though a solitary creature for the most part, Bobby had never really had cause to…spend as much time *thinking* as she did now. She went on instinct most of the time. And her life was not particularly trying, so there wasn't much to think on other than…making plans really.

The past few days had transformed her into a *ponderer* however, and she knew damn well and good what the cause of it was. *Who* was the cause of this…unsettling soul-searching, she supposed it could be deemed. She'd never really understood the people who spent hours thinking, and usually talking, of those they were…*interested* in. Never understood the urge to analyse it all, to wonder what it all meant. Her own affairs were short, and sweet, and happened with people who sought nothing more than her company for a brief time. This morning however, she understood it.

As confused and unsettled as she was, she felt as if she…understood it all.

Waking up curled into Lawrence's body had been… *Nice.*

More than that, but with him, it seemed all the best words were the simpler ones. Because it was simple, and easy with him. Last night, surrendering to him, had given her so much. Made her feel so much. But as nice as waking up next to him—*in his arms*—had been, it also had proved to be the catalyst for the return of her innate fear of…closeness, she supposed. She understood the others when they spoke of guarding their hearts. Because she could feel it now—as she had before—this *liking* that could so easily turn into more. Be turned into more by her mind, her own hopes, when truly, it wasn't. Couldn't ever be more.

Not solely because she didn't want it to be more— to risk caring for another, and losing her precious freedom—but also because her and Lawrence's lives, though tangled right this moment, weren't…as compatible as their bodies seemed to be. She might not know much, but she knew that much at least.

Still, do I hope for more? When I never hoped for it before?

Staring at that empty room last night…

No. Let be.

Nodding to herself, Bobby marched off to get her packs in the stables. She finished preparing Arion for their, not imminent, but approaching departure, then wagered she had enough time to perhaps speak with Julian for a moment—not that she truly needed to, but well, it would be nice and she was curious to know what he and Lawrence had been chatting about as they'd watched her, because she had seen the pair of them, and no she wouldn't think on how it had made her feel to show Lawrence what she could do, or to think perhaps he and Julian were becoming less hostile towards each other and how *that* made her feel—and perhaps she could get some hot breakfast too.

Nice hot eggs and ham…

Stomach growling, Bobby was so engrossed in her thoughts of a delicious breakfast, that she didn't notice the three locals heading towards her, smoking cheroot, until one of them addressed her as they passed—at least if *hey, girlie* constituted *addressing*. For the briefest second, she wondered if perhaps he was going to prove to be inordinately polite, and merely ask for the time, or who knew.

Stranger things…

The words which came out of his mouth next proved she had no such luck.

'Ye're that li'l girlie ridin' with the toffs 'cross the

country, ain't you?' he said, in that lecherous, mocking tone commonly used in such situations.

Considering he looked to be younger than she, and might've been handsome if not for his words, she took more umbrage than normal at the word *girlie.*

Or maybe that was the exhaustion and all the other emotions she'd been dealing with.

'That's me,' she sighed, her teeth clenching.

Through them, she did try to shoot him her best placating smile, and attempted to make the smart choice by turning away, only he *hailed* her yet again.

'Heard 'bout you and yer lot in the papers, never thought I'd see such a sight in me life.'

Squaring her shoulders, she took a deep breath, trying to tamp down her anger; trying to remain civilised as she turned.

Glaring at the idiot in front of her—a young local farm worker from the look of him—she raised a brow.

Don't, Bobby told herself, because she knew well and good what would happen if she *did.*

Storing away the information about *papers*—which was definitely something she would need to speak to Julian about, because since when had this gentleman's bet made the papers this far afield, really, it was never supposed to be…*so public*, at least beyond those of their acquaintance, those in the business of horses, London Society, even—she took deep breaths, reminding herself to…*not.*

Only, the other two laughed, and that irrepressible anger rose up higher inside her, and well, she *did.*

'How enthralling this encounter must then be for you,' she drawled. 'And you can read newspapers to boot. Your mother must be so proud.'

'Ye mockin' me, girlie?'

'So your limited cognitive abilities *do* allow you to understand sarcasm,' she said, exaggeratingly impressed. 'Congratulations.'

'Who do ye think ye are?' he growled, taking a step forward, and Bobby stood taller, meeting his gaze with no hesitation. 'Just cause ye're friends with some high-and-mightys? Ye ain't nothin' but an abomination not fit to lick me boots! Ain't right fer a woman to be as ye are, doin' what y'are!'

Don't.

Only she did, *again*. The red mist of rage clouded her judgement, her reason, everything, and her fist flung high and powerful, catching him in the nose, and he fell to the ground. She felt the other two close the tiny distance, and she whirled to face them.

'Suppose now you'll be saying it ain't right for a woman to fight idiots like you lot? Well, come on, then!'

'Feral bitch!' one of them shouted, lunging for her.

She got him too, but not before the other had grabbed her hair, and jerked her nearly off her feet. Stumbling back, she righted herself just in time to be punched by the one who'd called her a *feral bitch* as the other held her.

Vaguely, she heard shouts, and saw blurred figures pour out of the inn.

We have an audience it seems.

Not that she cared. Stars shone before her eyes, and she bit her tongue, but she'd been in worse scrapes before, and going by the seemingly distant cries of the onlookers, they would enjoy what came next. Shaking off the wave of blurred dizziness, she recovered just in time to prevent another blow by kicking the one before her in his most private area.

Whirling to the side, she launched the palm of her

hand upwards, catching the hair-grabber under the chin. He stumbled back, and she bounced a few feet away, to get her balance back before they came for her again, but just as they were all scrambling to their feet one figure stepped forth—not from the inn—but behind her.

Oh, fantastic.

Lawrence had just tied Beowulf up next to Arion—both mounts packed, and ready, and was making his way to the inn to meet with the others, when he spotted Bobby, with what he suspected were three locals. A rush of something resembling concern filled him at the sight of the probable farmhand speaking what looked far from *politely*, but though he quickened his step, he hadn't made it far enough before things…*devolved*.

He heard Bobby taunt the man, then something about things not being right for women, and then Bobby swung, knocking the man before her to the ground, and he had to admit, rushing over to help was momentarily forgotten as her strength awed him somewhat.

But then there was more taunting, and the words *feral bitch* sounded in the crisp morning air. More blows were being meted out, and his feet were moving fast beneath him as he closed the distance between himself and the fighters, even as others poured from inside the inn. Panic, and what he could not deny was *worry*, and disgust filled him as onlookers shouted encouragement, or insults.

Despite the burning urge to pound the men into the ground for daring to even *look* in Bobby's direction with ill intent, Lawrence knew as he ate up the space between himself and the fighters, that remaining level-headed would be the key to preventing things from getting worse than they already were. At the same time, he found a different anger in his heart; one for Bobby. For…punching first, he supposed. Starting a fight, *not* using her words.

Though she could obviously handle herself well enough, it was reckless, and foolish, to launch herself into a potentially life-threatening situation like this.

'That's enough,' Lawrence shouted as the three wastrels rose, making to attack Bobby again. The crowd froze—the tone he'd used which demonstrated both his position, and the threat it alone would carry in such a situation, enough to halt them in their…enjoyment of the spectacle. 'That's enough,' he repeated.

The men stopped, and turned to look at him, surprise and dismissal gleaming in their eyes.

'Ye mind yer own business,' one of them grumbled, apparently not too clever nor aware of what Lawrence could do without ever lifting a finger. 'She struck me, and the bitch needs remindin' of what she is. And what a man is.'

'What she is,' Lawrence drawled. 'Is the person who just knocked you all on your arses. And I don't think any of you could pretend to know what a man is, considering,' he spat.

'We wasn't finished,' one of the others objected.

'You are now,' he retorted, not quietly, but not shouting either, because truly how dim were these idiots? 'I suggest you leave, and should I see you skulking about again, I will be forced to educate you in what means a gentleman has to subdue others. I'll warn you, they aren't so simple, and easily cured, as mere blows.'

Crossing his arms, he raised a brow, and let his words sink in for a moment.

He daren't look at Bobby. Somehow, he had a feeling she wouldn't be taking his intervention well, but damn it if he would stand aside and watch this sort of grotesque spectacle.

Finally, the one with a cracked bloody nose seemed to get the message.

Spitting, he shrugged, gesturing to the other two.

'Ain't worth it anyways,' he sneered, stumbling away with his cohorts.

'What the Hell's happenin' here?' the innkeeper shouted, pushing through the crowd, finally it seemed, making an appearance.

Voices melded together, rushing to explain *fight, fight, fight*, and then Rothwakes and the solicitors were pushing through the crowd, even Barnes too, eyes wide as he surveyed the scene.

'Bobby? What the Hell is going on here?' Rothwakes demanded.

Lawrence took the opportunity to chance a glance at Bobby.

Wonderful.

There was no missing the indignant glare of anger in her eyes as she stood there, breathing hard, as she swiped a sleeve under her nose.

'This how ye fine people behave, then?' the innkeeper huffed loudly.

Another rush of voices—from the crowd, from Rothwakes, demanding to know what sort of establishment the man was running, but Lawrence's eyes didn't leave Bobby.

Hers finally met his, and if anything, the indignant anger seemed to multiply tenfold, as if she were angry at *him* for having intervened. She shook her head as he made to take a step forward, and bolted, heading around the stables.

'Bobby!' Rothwakes called, extirpating himself from

the crowd even as the innkeeper, finally dissuaded from making more of the situation—likely thanks to the solicitors—herded everyone inside.

Bobby kept running, and Lawrence closed the distance between Rothwakes and him.

'I'll find her,' he said, and Rothwakes looked at him, distrusting and appalled.

Lawrence looked meaningfully to the man's crutches as if that were the only reason to explain his volunteering on this mission, and though Lawrence could tell the man was not convinced in any way—he nodded nonetheless.

Inclining his head to the little baron, Lawrence returned to Beowulf, removed his medicinal box from his pack, then went off to find Bobby, knowing there was much to be said.

And I won't wait to confront it all this time.

'You should tend to those properly,' came Lawrence's voice, and Bobby sighed, clenching her teeth. She might've known he wouldn't just leave her be. If she'd thought she'd have more privacy in the stables, she'd have retreated there. Only then she risked Julian or someone else finding her, and confronting her. *No.* 'I brought my kit.'

'I'm fine,' she gritted out, plunging her hands into the frigid stream again, more for him to see, than for anything else. She'd already soaked them until they were blue, though she tried to convince herself that was merely because of the strange blue light that remained here as the rising sun still failed to reach this stream, and cleaned what blood she could feel from her face. 'Please, go away.'

'You need some salve, and some bandages,' Lawrence

said, and she could hear him, closer now, and also she could feel him, and she didn't like it, not one bit.

'I'm. Fine,' she repeated, slowly, loudly, deliberately, as she rose, shaking the excess water off, and wincing as her knuckles ached and burned. 'I don't need you, or anyone else. As you saw, I can take care of myself.'

'You call fighting like that taking care of yourself?' he demanded angrily, and by God, the man had some *damned nerve*.

'Yes, I bloody well do!' she shouted back, turning on him, adjusting her stance when she realised just how close he was, so she had to step back not to have to look up at him quite so much. 'I'm not some useless little weakling that can't defend herself! And lucky, that!'

'By God, Bobby, no one in their right mind would ever say that of you! But you weren't defending yourself—you started that fight because you stooped to their level! You could've just walked away!'

'I had that under control,' she hissed. 'I had *them*.'

'Well *excuse me for* taking umbrage with you fighting with three grown men!'

'I will not! And I suppose you wish for me to be grateful!'

'I wish you hadn't put yourself in such a position to begin with!'

'You think I *put* myself in that position?' she raged savagely. 'Oh, the privilege of you... I did not *put* myself into any position,' she seethed, stepping towards him, as if she wanted to strangle him. 'I was minding my own *damn* business when those lackwits began heckling me!'

'Do you deny provoking them? Do you deny striking first?'

'How *dare* you?' she seethed, lunging forward to

shove him, the anger, the hurt, his stupid judgement, all of it, welling up inside until she couldn't contain it anymore. He let her, stumbling gently back as if she'd not barely touched him. *Not nearly satisfying.* 'Would you call it provocation if I were a man? Would you begrudge a man who used his fists to defend his honour? To defend *himself*? No, I don't think so.'

Stomping past him, she sniffled, and wiped her nose on her sleeve.

Dammit, now I've another blood stain to get out.

'Yes, I would,' Lawrence said quietly, and somehow, that made her stop, and turn to him, and it made some of her ire melt away. 'I would say that to any man who behaved thus.'

'You have no idea,' she breathed. 'No idea, what it feels like, to be taunted, and tormented, and insulted, day, after day, after day, when all I wish, is to live in peace. Yet somehow, my mere existence, is so vile, so repulsive, that people feel the need to begrudge me it. Why? Because I don't dress nor behave as a woman *should*? You have no idea...' Sucking in a breath, she wondered why she was... Explaining all this. To *him*. 'You have no idea, you never could, of how it feels, to be...afraid. All the time. That someone will corner you, and either attack you, because they find you unnatural, or because they want to...*take*. I may live in safety most days, live under the protection of Julian's name, but by God, Lawrence. That doesn't mean I haven't had to deal with threats, and men coming after me for one reason or the other. For years,' she continued, all the poison, all the thoughts she'd expressed to no one, came pouring out, *why*, well, not because she wanted them too, that was for certain. 'I tried, to let it roll off me, like nothing. To take the high road, to be the civilised one.

To be the *polite* one, the smart one, who walks away, ferreting off to find safety from another. The one who laughs it off, and makes nice with the man blocking her way, because by standing up for myself, I create a challenge. Worse problems. But let me tell you, that doesn't work. *It shouldn't.* I shouldn't have to back down, and scurry away, because of what could happen to me— worse than merely taking it all. So I struck first. I met words with fists. They want *feral*, and *unnatural*, well, they can have it. But the truth is, sometimes, a fist to the face, it's all they understand. It's all that will make them stop, either insulting you, or coming after you. If not, they keep coming, more, and more, and there's only so much you can take, before it pierces through your skin, and cuts you. Or before something worse happens.'

'You're right, I could never understand what it means to face such situations,' Lawrence admitted quietly, and it caught her off guard, because there was an acknowledgement, a relinquishment in his eyes. 'To be alone, cornered. Though, I do know what it feels like,' he continued, tentatively. 'To want to hurt those who've hurt you. I do. But I'll never believe you can regain your honour by pummelling another man into the mud, or taking his life in a duel, or whatever other nonsense we come up with.'

'It's not about honour,' she protested.

He can't understand.

'Perhaps not entirely, I see that now. There is an inherent threat in any unwanted approach. And I hate that you ever had, or have to defend yourself against such behaviour,' he said earnestly. 'I was so… Angry when I saw them…touch you.' Raking his fingers through his hair, he blew out a breath, and Bobby wondered where exactly he was going with this. Because he seemed to understand it all one moment—and then not the next. 'But I heard you goad them, Bobby. I saw you swing first. Is every village numbskull who comes along calling you names a threat? Or do you, sometimes…look for a fight?'

Clenching her jaw, Bobby shook her head, and looked away.

She hated it—that feeling rising up within her, grabbing at all the rest, and turning it into pain, and hurt. Most of all, she hated the tightening of her throat, and the prick behind her eyes. Actually no—most of all, she hated *why* all that was happening.

Because he's right.

Thinking back, she realised just how many times she had thrown a punch, when the threat of more than words did not loom above. When she hadn't in fact, defended herself, but defended her supposed *honour*. Even today. She hadn't felt threatened today—she'd only felt anger, not the familiar panic born of true threat. Though she *was* right, she shouldn't *have to* be the better, smarter person, and walk away, she could've…

Not goaded them. Not swung first.

Only, she'd taken the vile words, the insults, the dismissals, all her life; at least until Lady Rothwakes had passed. After that, she hadn't had the strength to do so anymore. She hadn't wanted to. Not on top of all the rest. It had all…conflagrated somehow. One could only take so many bad experiences, so many *real* threats, before everything became a threat.

And, in a sense, as she said, if they wanted feral, they would get it. They would get the low-born ruffian; all vestiges of good breeding, and being a *lady*, flung far to the wayside because that wasn't who she could ever be. And she'd had no reason left to even pretend anymore. Everything she did, including her sexual escapades, were done in some manner to both tell the world to go hang it itself on their expectations of her, that she didn't care what they thought; but also to confirm they were right.

Because if they were right, perhaps then, finally, they would leave her in peace.

'The first time I discovered my wife was being unfaithful, I wanted to strangle the bastard,' Lawrence told her, cutting through her thoughts, cutting through much more, not that she'd admit it. She met his gaze, and saw the pain his confession was causing, but also, his conscious decision to eviscerate his soul before her, as much as she had before him. She recalled the hurt she'd caused, that she'd planned to apologise for, before this giant mess. 'Luckily, in order to do so, I had to travel up to London, so I had some time to truly ponder everything. I realised, hurting him, in any way, would do my own hurt no good. And what had he done in the end? It was my wife who'd betrayed our vows.'

'What did you do?' Bobby asked quietly, after a long moment's silence.

'I confronted her, and also, myself. We… It was a business arrangement for me, and only ever that, but I suppose the terms hadn't been properly agreed to beforehand,' he said, flatness, and a twinge of self-reproach tingeing his voice. Bobby felt her feet move, until she was standing a little closer. To better hear him. Not to be nearer to him, naturally. 'We agreed that after an initial period of fidelity—three years, during which we would resume attempts at children—she would be free, to seek what she wanted, and needed, elsewhere, discreetly, of course.'

'You don't have children,' she said quietly, and he shrugged.

'No, I don't.' Lawrence cleared his throat, and shot her a wan smile. 'My wife had a daughter. She's ten now; I ensured she had a good life, and was raised by a good family. A better man might've taken her in, but… I could not. I'm not quite sure who the father was; I don't think my wife did either if I'm honest. She broke our pact within a year, and when I found out, I swear I might've razed the city. But again, I knew, it wouldn't have helped. The thing is… Some days, I think I clung to the anger, the resentment, because it made me feel better to have all that rather than admit I didn't actually care. I was glad she left me. I was glad she showed me what a farce our arrangement was. I was angry about the dishonesty, but not about her actions on their own. And I think, I only ever wanted children because it was expected. Heirs, and all that. Not because I truly wanted to be a father, and that isn't right, bringing a child into that. I should know.'

Lawrence heaved in a deep breath, and ran a hand through his hair again, dislodging it this time, just like she liked.

No.

'I'm sorry,' he sighed. 'I shouldn't have just… Said all that,' he continued, waving his hands between them, and that's when Bobby noticed the box in one of them— presumably his kit for her wounds, which still smarted, but had been long forgotten. 'Don't quite know why I did. I didn't mean to make things…about me.'

'I'm glad you did,' she admitted. It was true—and Lawrence seemed to bring out all her truths, ugly, and painful though they may be. 'I am sorry about what I said to you before, about your wife. About you.' She didn't clarify why she'd done it, but Lawrence nodded, seemingly understanding; or at least, accepting to leave it all unsaid now. They had…moved past it. 'I wanted to tell you last night, but… Well, even this morning I suppose I was working up the courage.' Shrugging, she shot him a tiny smile, and received one back. 'I don't know how to function in the world sometimes,' she told him, biting her lip as she attempted to put it into words. 'Lord and Lady Rothwakes, they…tried to raise me,' she said, not quite willing to go entirely into *that* sad tale. The sorry tale of an orphan, taken in by good, upstanding people, who tried to give her all the best the world could offer, only to find the little orphan could never be what they'd hoped she could be. *Only in fairy tales do orphans become princesses.* 'I tried to live by what they taught me, the rules of the world they, and others, instilled in me. But then, when it came time to live in it… I don't know how to be it all at once. Myself. Who they raised me to be. All the while, living in this world that doesn't know me. Doesn't want to, for the most part. Only wants to…make me into something I don't want. I think I got so used to fighting all the time, being on guard… And truth is, if I give them all what they expect, it's easier.'

'Is it?' he asked, barely a whisper, licking his thumb, before sliding it under her nose, wiping some of the blood away.

Bobby shrugged.

She didn't actually have an answer right then.

She'd thought it was.

And maybe, it was—but that didn't make it the better choice for her.

The right choice.

'I'm not saying you can't fight for what's right, nor

defend yourself. I may not feel it every day, as others do, but I do know the world is a harsh, dangerous place. And perhaps this is me being selfish, because the truth is… I feel as if we've been fighting since we met. I don't think I want that anymore,' he said simply, and yet it was all far from simple. Truth was, she didn't really want to fight with him anymore either. Still, she saw that she'd done with him as she had with the rest. Attacked, raised up the portcullis, and then hidden behind walls of stone so as not to face the potential hurt he could cause. 'And perhaps, you could save your fight for when you truly need it. Or when it can make a true difference.'

'What do you fight for now, Lawrence?'

'The future. At least, I like to think so.' He smiled, and chucked her under the chin again. 'Would you let me clean you up now?'

'Yes. Won't be able to stand your harping if you don't,' she mumbled, grateful for the steering onto more solid ground.

Lawrence smiled, and tapped her nose gently, before nodding at a nearby rock where they could both sit.

And then, ever so carefully, tenderly, and sweetly, he cleaned her up, and put salve on her wounds, and bandaged her up, and they sat there a while in peaceful and comfortable silence, before it was time to get back onto the road.

Chapter Thirteen

A road, which they were sharing, for a time, at least; a fact both realised when they came upon each other at the confluence of two paths, some fifteen miles after having left the inn, and civilly bid each other *good luck* for the day. Lawrence was inordinately more pleased with the idea of sharing the road for a time with her than by rights he should've been.

After all, this was meant to be a race. A competition. So agreeing to ride together for a portion of it, made absolutely no sense whatsoever. No matter that their paths were the same, he should've ridden hard and fast in an attempt to lose her, or at least, cement the generous lead he had thanks to her delay the previous day. Except he used that very fact—that he already had about two and half hours' lead—to justify that really, what use was it *racing* her on this stretch, attempting to grow it, when in fact he'd planned for this portion to be made at a slower pace. Really, no use tiring Beowulf so early to add perhaps minutes to his lead.

No use at all.

Though he justified it all very well—his logic, as always, unshakably sound—he was also acutely aware of the fact that he had agreed to—*suggested*—sharing the road, because he wanted to. He wanted to spend time with Bobby. Just the two of them. When she couldn't distract him with promises of sensual passion, or rather, distract him with sensual passion, because he saw promises of it in her eyes nearly every time she looked at him.

He wanted time with her where she wouldn't be fighting him, or anyone else. Though, despite what her…nonrejection of his declaration that he didn't wish to fight her any longer, he didn't think she would ever give up fighting him at any given chance. Which, despite his words, he didn't truly mind. As long as…it was good fighting. Fair fighting, he supposed. Then, he wouldn't really mind fighting with her, always.

Not that they had always.

Regardless, the point was, he wanted this time with her. In the clear light of day. Alone. To…talk.

To just be together.

'I know your secret,' Lawrence said, once they'd ambled quietly for a while.

He saw Bobby perk up beside him, like a squirrel, and he let a satisfied grin spread on his lips, as he idly wondered what other secrets she might have.

Not many, I think.

The thought was an odd one, but he found it to be true; he *felt* it to be true. She hadn't perked up as if in fear that he'd discovered something ghastly in her past, or present, but rather merely as if he'd captured her attention. Capturing such a precious thing, he had to acknowledge, was rather wonderful.

One of the reasons he was decidedly glad to have time alone with her like this.

'To training horses,' he specified, and she quirked a brow.

'Is that so…'

'Indeed,' he said, with a touch of mock seriousness. 'Rothwakes and I made a truce this morning long enough for him to reveal it all. Come to think of it, perhaps it wasn't a truce at all, but rather a more civilised attempt at bettering me.'

Frowning, he pretended to mull on that for a moment.

In truth, he didn't believe it.

Rothwakes was as astounded by Bobby's powers as Lawrence was; perhaps it was the one thing they shared.

'So that's what you two were gossiping about this morning…' Bobby said, laughter in her voice. Lawrence made a moue of disgust at the idea he and Rothwakes were *gossips*, and then Bobby truly laughed. 'And what did Julian tell you exactly?'

'He said you don't train them. He said you…befriend them. Then ask them nicely to do things.'

The man's words had played on his mind every second since they'd been uttered.

Not that his answer had really given him much, hence this very choice of conversation. He felt as if there was more, to reveal, to discover. He was utterly fascinated by the spell, the power Bobby seemed to hold, not only over her own horse, but over any beast she met. He needed to understand it, to make sense of it, not as magic, but as technique. Not to lessen it, remove its power, but rather, so he could…

Replicate it perhaps.

Not steal, but borrow.

Learn from.

Learn about.

Understand it—and her.

Yes, that is what it boiled down to, he supposed.

An unchangeable urge to…understand *her*.

'Is there a question in there, Lawrence?' Bobby asked, apparently amused, and he shook his head, coming back to his surroundings.

'I suppose, quite a few are in there,' he admitted, glancing over at her, catching a glint of onyx even in the shade of her hat. 'I would ask if that were a true summation of your technique. I would ask if that precludes others from working with the horses when it isn't you asking the animal to do something. I would ask… How you do it all, I suppose.'

'So you haven't learnt my secret then, is what you're saying,' Bobby chided, and he laughed.

'Yes, well, I suppose not.'

'I wouldn't say I'm their friend, and ask them to do things,' Bobby said after a long moment. Lawrence had hoped she would read his silence for what it was, delicate prompting, an open ear when she was ready. 'I mean, some are my friends. But not all—same as every person you meet cannot always become your friend. As for the training proper, I suppose, I ask them to learn, and I promise I will learn too. It's…a conversation. I don't know, I've never really had to put it into words before—it's not like I have some great technique or secret. I just… Respect them.'

'As do I,' Lawrence pointed out, leaning forward slightly as they began up a hill. Trees shaded the left side of the path, and he was mindful of overhanging branches, dodging this way and that. 'And I speak to my horses as I've heard you speak to Arion. Still, I am not so proud as to not see the relationship I have with Beowulf, who I've known since his birth, isn't close to what I've seen between you, and some strange horse you've never met before.'

'You speak to your horses. But do you listen to them?'

'Of course, to the degree to which I can. When they tell me they're frightened, or hurt, as one would a child, I imagine,' he told her, as they levelled out on higher ground, the path narrowing slightly so their legs nearly touched as they rode side by side.

Here, though not so high, they could see shimmering seas of grass, wildflowers, and tufty tree tops for miles.

Exquisite.

'Then that is where we differ,' Bobby said softly. He glanced over at her, to find a little smile on her lips, one which seemed to say, *Oh, you simple man.* Not condescending, yet the smile of someone who had the wisdom of the ages. 'You see only what is plainly there. You don't search any deeper, open yourself to anything more. You respect horses, for what they can do for you. Perhaps even for their strength, grace, agility, and talents alone. But you see them as something lesser than man. Something other. Something to be tamed, *broken*, and trained.'

'They are,' he said blankly, trying to make sense of it, his rational, logical mind, agreeing with her summation of him, but not finding the fault in it. 'Something other, that is. They are…animals. Clever, wondrous creatures, but they do not have such things as we have. Reason, art, language—'

'And those are things which in your opinion make us superior? Their masters? Which give us the right to break their spirits?'

'No. Well, yes. I am not alone. It is the natural order. And I don't believe it is breaking their spirits…it is merely a turn of phrase.'

'You do not strike me as someone who chooses words casually,' Bobby pointed out, and he supposed, in that at least, she was entirely correct. 'As for the rest… You believe it is the natural order because we trained them, domesticated them? They had not the reason, the free will, to stop us, therefore they are lesser?'

'I feel you will condemn me for my answer,' he said, somewhat frustrated, yes. It felt like he'd stumbled into a philosophy debate at some university, when all he wanted to know was how the woman trained horses. 'So I shall simply say, man, and beast, are two very different, unequal things, yes.'

'To me, they are not. Different, yes, as all things are to each other. As each person is to another. But in my heart, I've never believed that we are any better than any other living thing. We inhabit this world together.'

'Do you believe all those living things, even that tree, there,' he said, pointing to a lone oak amidst a field of yarrow. 'Are your equal? You with your reason, your passions, your freedom, even.'

'Look into Beowulf's eyes, and tell me what you see. Do you not see freedom of spirit? Passions, emotions— perhaps different from our own, but present nonetheless? Should we ignore what we see in his eyes, all because men have written the laws of God, and Heaven? Because men for millennia have claimed there is a natural order? I mean no blasphemy, or offence, but when a preacher tells me we were merely created to have dominion over this earth, this gift from God, I'm afraid, I cannot help but disagree, and think, what a sad sort of place Heaven must be without all the world in it. What a freedomless existence it is, to merely rule over what has been given to us. I know in my heart, what I see, what I feel. We may not comprehend the way of other living things, but perhaps we simply haven't quite reached a point where we can. That doesn't mean there isn't intelligence, emotion, freedom, in them. Even in that tree there. It doesn't mean we are their masters—merely because a man wrote in a book that we are.'

Leaning back as they descended the hill on the other side, Lawrence let Bobby's words, her beliefs, truly penetrate his mind; permeate into his heart, and soul.

The rational part of him scoffed, and rebelled at her thoughts. They went against everything he'd been taught his life through—everything great scientists and holy men—yes—declared the truth of things. But the other part of him wondered, if this was truly the key to her success with horses, then perhaps it had merit after all. Men for centuries had believed notions to be true—only for another to come along and prove them wrong.

Still, one—*many, but one original*—question remained unanswered.

'So… When others ride, or purchase the horses you have trained, I don't dismiss your words,' he added, shooting her a meaningful glance. 'But training is the best word I know for now—do you tell them all this? How do the horses respond when interacting with another rider?'

'That is a rather strong point of contention between Julian and I,' Bobby admitted wryly. 'I've never shared my thoughts with anyone before,' she said, a little quieter, and Lawrence couldn't help but grin, the privilege warming his heart. 'I do work a while with our riders, for the races, to gauge them, and their fit with particular horses. When it comes to sales… I try to get to know those who purchase them, those who will be taking care of them, but it isn't always easy. There has only been one instance where I've asked Julian not to sell to a particular person, and it cost him a lot. A good relationship, and some good money. But the horse he wished to have, and I... We both felt the man had no kindness or respect in him.'

'So there have been no issues with those who have purchased, or ridden? No reluctance or difficulty leading the horses?' Bobby shook her head, and he nodded pensively. 'Do you believe me to have kindness, and respect, in me?'

He was asking for a specific reason—which was categorically not that he wished to know she didn't think as ill of him as she had upon first meeting. Even despite all that had passed between them, he couldn't help but doubt her good opinion of him.

But this wasn't about that—this was merely in the interest of...*science.*

'I do,' Bobby admitted quietly, her gaze steadily affixed before her, *purposefully.*

'Then, if I wished to ride, or work with Arion, he would obey me?' Bobby's eyes shot to his, a panicked look on her face. 'I don't mean to buy him, or take him from you,' he reassured her, and she relaxed. He began to believe she told the truth of horses understanding more than he typically gave them credit for when Arion let loose a disapproving snort. A twinge of guilt pierced him then—knowing that if he did win, technically, Arion *would* become his. Though he decided then and there, come what may, if it was in his power, he would ensure the two were never separated. *The very least I can do.* 'I'm only curious. Did Julian have the same relationship with him, as you do?'

'Arion would do as you wished. As he did for Julian. But neither of you could ever have the same relationship with him as I do. Just as I could never have the same relationship with Beowulf as you do.'

'Arion is special to you, isn't he?'

Bobby shot him a look which held a measure of guilt, and reluctance, but Lawrence didn't release her, compelling her silently to answer.

This wasn't about her skills any more, this was most definitely about *her*, and he wouldn't lose this chance.

Or I'll regret it.

Bobby sighed, knowing Lawrence wouldn't let this go. She wasn't entirely sure why it bothered her so much, his question, his probing, in this matter. It wasn't that it was personal—somehow, they'd already ventured far into the dangerous depths of *personal*. Between what they'd shared after her fight this morning; and all they had before then even. But before, perhaps it had felt, less *intentional*. Less, pointed, as his question was now.

Even though a voice in the back of her mind whispered that his fingers, his exploration of her body last night had been *very pointed* and *personal*. Except that even then, as with all else which had passed before, it felt as if circumstances had pushed them into the murky waters of *personal*. The journey they were on, the increasing exhaustion, all of it, bonded them together as they faced the same trials.

However here, and now, circumstances weren't conspiring to loosen lips.

Lawrence was doing it all on his own.

Probing into all that made her who she was.

The questions about her…*methods*, could be dismissed as arising from professional interest, even though her answers were far from conventional she knew, in their *milieu* at least. Even though her answers revealed a part of her she typically preferred to hide under a coarse, unapproachable exterior.

She'd answered him, honestly, openly, because she

knew that whether or not he agreed with her, he would listen, without judgement. For all she'd heard about Lawrence before she met him, that he was a lord with a turned-up nose, that he was arrogant, and prideful, and judgemental, ambitious, jaded, and harsh, well, perhaps the rest was true to an extent, she'd seen traces of it all—save for the judgement part. If there was anyone guilty of being judgemental, unfortunately, she had to admit, it had been her.

And it had felt good to put her thoughts into words, to share them with another. Julian never asked, he merely appreciated the results—most of the time, when it didn't cost him anything. Everyone else seemed to merely accept her talent, with no interest in it otherwise. If it could be called a talent.

Asking about Arion, however…

It hit…

Too close to my heart.

To my own past; to myself.

Glancing over at Lawrence, somewhat covertly, she found him still looking at her, waiting, quietly asking, for her answer.

And though she couldn't tell him *all* of it, the polite thing to do was to answer.

Since she didn't want to be impolite, she figured she could give the simple answer—without any sad, sorry context.

'I found him,' she said finally, breaking the compelling spell of Lawrence's expectant gaze. He had this way of looking at her… Head slightly tilted downwards, eyes, not wide, but *wide open*, as if he wanted to…see all he possibly could. Of her. 'A new born foal, abandoned outside the market in Kinnerston. Probably wanted to make sure his mother sold or something. I hate that market,' she muttered angrily.

Kinnerston was one of those small, little-known places, that prided itself on exclusivity; in buyers, sellers, and horses.

So it was no surprise that no one would own up to having a tainted mare—nor a mixed lineage foal like Arion, unless his blood was *purposefully* mixed and chosen. Considering how she'd found him it was obvious he hadn't been an intentional creation.

Man playing God.

And in Kinnerston—in the horse trade—there were many of those. Like any other place which prided itself as *untainted*, *special*, people participating in Kinnerston did their worst to ensure profits—one way or the other. Not that she'd seen anything, or she would've publicly decried it, but there were rumours enough. Julian insisted on going—and she went reluctantly, at least until she found Arion. After that, she'd refused to return; Julian followed suit a year later.

Which she had been immensely glad of.

'I wish I could say I was surprised,' Lawrence said, some of her own disgust in his voice. 'But that place is a den of vipers. Haven't been there for years.'

'I made Julian take him home with us,' she continued, shaking her head to rid herself of thoughts of that terrible place. The notion that Lawrence didn't go there made her feel a little better—as if she wasn't alone in feeling what she did. 'And I took care of him. Nursed him back to health. Everyone said it was a waste of time, that he would never amount to anything worthwhile.'

Bobby cast her mind back to those days, those years, she'd barely spent a waking hour away from him.

Not always her choice—once he'd begun properly

walking, he'd been determined to follow her everywhere—fences, doors, and locks be damned. Everyone had been as perplexed about his talents for escape
as they had been about her own, once upon a time. But
just as they had with her, eventually, they stopped trying to keep Arion where they wanted him, and let him
go where he wished; let him go and find Bobby.

Even most nights she'd spent with him, sleeping in
his stall until about a year ago.

No one really understood it—but then again, they
didn't have to.

'He's your favourite, isn't he?' Lawrence asked, gentle amusement in his voice.

'It's not nice to play favourites.'

'If you saved him, it would be natural for there to be
a stronger bond than with others.'

'He isn't the only one we've saved over the years,'
Bobby pointed out, and Lawrence raised a brow in question. 'There have been others, and people know to come
to us. Some we've kept, others have gone off to various new lives.'

'But Arion is special.'

'Yes,' she admitted. 'We…understand each other in
a way I've never felt before.'

'This race… It's also about showing the world what
he's worth, isn't it? That no matter what they said, his
life was worth saving.'

'Despicable isn't it, that one should have to find
worth to justify saving a life?' Lawrence nodded grimly,
and Bobby continued. 'But it is how this all started,
isn't it?' Bobby shrugged. 'You challenging the notion
that a horse like him could win against your pureblood
stallion. If Arion wins… Perhaps people will rethink to
some degree, this whole business. It's less about find-

ing worth in the act of saving his life, but rather, about challenging the need to in the first place I suppose. It's about challenging all the edicts which make up this business—arbitrary as they are.'

'If you don't agree with racing, why are you doing this? Why work in the business at all?'

'I don't agree with using animals for sport,' Bobby argued. 'I don't agree with the way many are treated, in a quest to seek fame, and fortune. I don't agree with breeding, as it is, not in this world at least. I think it hubris, and barbaric. If Arion can change people's minds with this race, I like to think he'd not consider it hypocritical to participate. As for me working in a business with faults, well. For one, all industries have faults. Refusing to participate, rather than working towards change…that is not my preference, in this case.'

'Well,' Lawrence said after a long moment. 'Whatever the outcome, I will say you've changed my mind about *him*. He's made it much further, much faster, than I ever thought he could, even with what I imagine is a measure of draught in him.'

Snicking his tail, and blowing out a long breath as he shook his head, Arion seemed to say, *I'll accept the compliment even if you were foolish to doubt me*.

'He says so have you, even with the measure of stuffy viscount in you,' Bobby said wryly, waggling her brows.

Taking off with a laugh, she heard Lawrence mumbling something about *getting her*, *little vixen*, and she laughed harder.

After all, she wouldn't mind it so much if he did get her.

Chapter Fourteen

'I'll walk you out,' Julian said after she'd made her appearance before the solicitors, handing them her route for the following day, before she could even think to escape. He sounded *cheery, politely unaffected*, but Bobby knew better. *That* was in fact his *polite for show* tone—the one he used to excuse himself from company before he revealed how he was *really* feeling.

It was a talent Bobby found fascinating—that she didn't envy because she didn't have much, but her candour and lack of restraint, were two things she *did* pride herself on having—when it wasn't her on the receiving end of whatever came next.

As they strode out of the inn—so like the others if a little smaller, more intimate, and seemingly older; she would swear it should've been demolished in the middle ages—Bobby pushed away her apprehension, reminding herself that actually, she had a thing or two to say to Julian. No matter how nice her day had been—fight notwithstanding—full of...*niceness*. She wouldn't let the *niceness* distract her.

Best remember that, always.

Instinctively, she led Julian away from the inn and

its somewhat busy yard to a semidiscreet spot nestled by the hedgerow, beneath a mighty oak, cloaking them in more shadows than necessary for whatever this conversation was to be.

Crossing her arms, she faced him, and waited, as he adjusted himself on his crutches, wincing slightly as his foot knocked against a rather large stone encased in the dirt. Concern automatically flooded her heart, and despite the dimness of their chosen spot, it wasn't hard to see this whole expedition was beginning to wear him thin. Never mind the stakes of it all.

But nothing whatsoever should distract you from your purpose.

Not niceness—not concern.

'Care to explain what the Hell that was this morning, Bobby?' he said harshly, with no preamble, and instead of giving into the feeling of *smallness*, Bobby leaned into the feeling of…*annoyance*. 'Did we not have—oh, perhaps a thousand talks about you controlling your temper? Do you have any idea what kind of mess you might've created had I not been able to smooth everything over?'

'I'm sorry you had to clean up my mess again, Julian, but—'

'No *but*! And this isn't about me having to clean up after you, this is about you jeopardising everything we've worked so hard for!'

'It was just a little brawl,' she countered.

She didn't want, or need, another speech about her fighting.

And somehow, Julian's attempt was more irksome than Lawrence's had been—because she didn't feel like… Julian cared to know the *why* as Lawrence had. It was the same reason she'd been so candid with Lawrence, and couldn't—hadn't before—to Julian. Despite all they'd shared, a life, friendship, parents...

Some days it felt like he didn't understand her and didn't care to.

'I don't care if it was a bloody arm wrestle or a battle the size of Waterloo,' Julian growled. 'I care that your behaviour reflects on all of us. On me, on the stables, on everything we're trying to achieve!'

'If I were a man—'

'Don't start with that again, Bobby, damn it,' he exclaimed. 'I'd upbraid you all the same, Hell, I'd upbraid myself! If we lose this, all we'll have left is our reputation! And this isn't what we want to be known for!'

'And how would we be known for it?' Bobby asked, mustering as much calm as she could. Not detracting the conversation, but rather, turning it so it wasn't just Julian telling her how she was doing everything all wrong again, and her either explaining herself, or taking it silently. So it became about what *she* needed to know. Wanted to confront *him* about. 'I've had my share of brawls, and I don't think any of those men would be off to spread the word among Society—among our business associates.'

'That's not the point—'

'Why are we in the papers, Julian? And more importantly, why didn't you tell me about it?'

Julian at least had the decency to look somewhat caught off guard, if not a tad sheepish.

Sighing, he shook his head, angrily swatting a fly away, tottering slightly on his crutches.

'I had to do something to be useful,' he said begrudgingly. 'Something to benefit us, no matter the outcome of the race. I couldn't just...sit in carriages, and stand by, waiting for you. It's a great story—already I've had hundreds of requests to attend the London event, and apparently people are talking about coming to watch parts of the race... It's good for us.'

'I understand that, Julian.' And she did. Having the Rothwakes name in the papers, as he said, regardless of the outcome, it would bring their enterprise interest. *Not that it will be of much good if we lose the estate...* 'It still doesn't explain why you wouldn't tell me.'

'You had enough on your mind.'

'I've known you since we were children, Julian. Don't you dare think you can lie to me.'

Sheepishness morphed into guilt, and her stomach tumbled downwards, feeling like it had been filled with lead.

Casting her mind back to this morning, Bobby realised *why* Julian hadn't told her. She wouldn't admit it, but tears stung her eyes.

Judas.

'I wonder what makes a gentleman's bet such a great story,' she said hollowly.

'It's not like that—'

'How could you use me like this, and not have the decency to ask, or even tell me?'

Julian reached for her, but she stepped back, out of his reach, her heart aching with betrayal.

He may not have ever understood her, but they were friends, and he didn't need to fully understand her to know what this would do to her.

'I didn't use you. Bobby,' he said, but the weakness of his conviction was apparent in his tone. 'But I won't deny that when they heard a woman was racing four hundred miles against someone like Hayes, well, it captured their attention. As it should—what you're doing is incredible, people cannot wait to meet you—'

'Is it incredible? I shall have to tell Hayes you believe him incredible too, for he is doing the same as I am,' she spat, and Julian clenched his jaw. 'You *used* me, Julian. You dangled me in front of those journalists like some curiosity at a menagerie. For years, we've kept my involvement in the stables quiet, for the good of our reputation. And now, because it serves you, you flaunt me about? Let me guess, should I chance to look at these papers, I'll read all about how a woman is *racing*, yet I won't see a single trace of all else I do, have done, and plan to.'

'The time isn't right, and you know it,' Julian shot back angrily. 'I intended to tell everyone in London. The kind of people we need, *you* need, will be there, and with all this press, they will be falling over themselves to speak to you. Don't you see how perfect it is? They'll be so awed by you they won't be able to wait before they agree to work with you.'

'I don't want to *awe*!' she shouted, taking a breath before calming herself. 'Justify it however you like, Julian. Truth is, you know what you did was wrong, and cheap, and disloyal. Make yourself useful tomorrow by spending some time thinking about that, and staying well clear of me until we have to appear in London together.'

Bobby strode off without another word, swallowing the hurt, and anger, and feelings of uncleanliness until they filled her stomach almost as well as a meal.

And then she swung onto Arion, and went to find her actual dinner, hoping that Lawrence had made something good for once—she had won today by a meagre five minutes—ignoring the fact that it wasn't the dinner she was craving in the least.

It was only his company, his comfort.

* * *

Lawrence was immensely proud of his creation—though he was beginning to wonder if he would be alone in enjoying it. Considering Bobby had beat him today—by five minutes, but still—she was sure taking her time. He'd had the time to take care of Beowulf, himself, and make this damn salt beef stew, and yes—his potatoes were already beginning to soften.

He wasn't entirely sure why he'd used up some of his stored victuals to make it, he could have very well caught a rabbit, and roasted it—Bobby would've been more than happy with that as long as he didn't subject it to the same treatment as she had those fish the other night. He liked that about her, that she asked for nothing, wished for nothing grand, as far as he knew. In any case, the best explanation he could come up with was that he'd wanted to do something…special for her. To mark the…thawing between them he supposed. To show her that last night's care hadn't been…an isolated incident.

That he cared for her in some measure.

A greater measure than I have many others.

He was still somewhat unsure about what to do about that in the future. Letting her go to live her own life if she won—or taking her livelihood from her, and letting her go live her own life if she lost… Both possibilities were becoming increasingly…distasteful.

The sound of hooves drew his attention, and he looked up to find Bobby and Arion bounding towards him along the bank of the little lake he'd found for their encampment. He smiled widely—something he'd noticed he seemed to be doing a bit more regularly recently—and felt himself relax more than he'd been, which was a feat, considering he'd thought himself to be quite at ease already.

Odd.

Odder still was how his heart skipped a beat, even as he quirked his head inquisitively, when Bobby slid off Arion, and strode straight over to him. He blinked as she came to stand beside him, and then in a flash she was leaning over, one knee on the log he was sitting on, and she took his face in her hands, staring down at him with barely leashed need. When he said nor did nothing to stop her, she sighed, as if he'd just given her the greatest gift in the universe, and that made his heart skip another beat—which really couldn't be healthy—but it calmed itself when she kissed him.

As ardently, and messily, as their first attempts, but with an underlying desperation and search that felled him. He gave her all he could, all it was she sought from him—whatever it was, he found he didn't care. She could have it all if that would make her better.

Finally, she released him, with a tender, sweet kiss, and a contented sigh.

'I made stew.'

A faint smile swept away some of the dark cloud he noticed around her.

'Thank you.'

Lawrence knew it wasn't merely a thank-you for supper, but a thank-you for so much more.

He wondered at this ability he had, to read so much into what she said, what she did, but as she untangled herself from him, and began taking care of Arion, he realised Bobby wore her emotions on her sleeve. Whatever she felt, she seemed to feel it so strongly, it couldn't be concealed. Or rather, she felt no need to conceal it, from him at least. Though he suspected it was more of a general thing, than something specific to him. Not that he minded. In fact, with her, he knew where he stood—whether or not it was good—and he found her emotional candour, well, he supposed he could call it, refreshing, and…

Endearing.

'Dare I ask what happened after I left?' he said once Arion was unsaddled, gently stirring his stew.

'Julian being a tactless, unthinking ass,' she muttered darkly.

'Far from unusual in my—I'll grant you—limited experience.'

Lawrence knew he had his faults—but he never really denied them.

In his experience—not that, as he'd said, it was extensive, because what reason did he have to associate much with Rothwakes—the little baron was rather full of himself, and swanned about expecting the world to grant him any whim because of his good looks, title, and success with horses. Not to the same degree as others, but to a degree which was noticeable, and insufferable.

The man seemed to be constantly self-involved, and for Lawrence to say that, meant something.

'What did he do this time?'

'Did you know our little race has made the papers?' Bobby asked as a response, heaving a sigh before she began brushing Arion.

Ah.

'I didn't,' he admitted. It was rather odd, that was the sort of thing Barnes might've made him aware of, Matthews even. Perhaps they didn't know either. But then how… 'How did you find out?'

'The men this morning… They said something about papers. I had it in my mind to ask Julian about it, and I did, and… Apparently, I'm the story.'

'He didn't,' Lawrence said, though he knew the answer already.

Unthinking ass indeed.

'He had a lot to say about the *why*, but not much to say about the *why he didn't tell me*.'

'I'm sorry, Bobby.'

She paused her brushing efforts, and looked over to him, a frown appearing—one of doubt, not displeasure.

'It's both heartwarming, and profoundly sad that I don't need to explain why I'm upset to you, yet that I did to Julian, and I've known him all my life.'

Lawrence opened his mouth to say something—*anything*—but found there wasn't much to say.

She was right. It was strange. Both heartening, and heartbreaking.

Bobby turned back to Arion, finished settling him in, then disappeared for a short while to bathe and change. He noticed that she'd settled Arion closer to Beowulf than ever before—not that either horse minded, quite the contrary.

Finally, she sat down beside him, and he spooned stew into bowls for them both.

'What is… That is to say… What are you to each other?' Lawrence finally managed to get out.

It wasn't merely his own curiosity that drove him— she'd assured him there was no promise or romantic aspect to her relationship with Rothwakes—but also that need to understand her better. She had mentioned something about Lord and Lady Rothwakes raising her, and he'd forced himself not to think too hard on that, as he didn't wish to pry, and she obviously wasn't ready to share that part of her tale yet, still, it meant there was a closeness between Bobby and the Rothwakes family which went beyond…the norm. Like it or not, Roth-wakes was part of Bobby's life.

He felt her stiffen slightly, then relent.

'We're friends. He's my employer,' she said flatly. Then, drawing in a deep breath, she stirred her stew for a moment, then continued. 'I don't… I don't want to talk about how it all came to be, but the fact is we… grew up together. He was…*is*, my oldest friend. We… tried to have something else, but it wasn't meant to be. We didn't function well that way.'

Well then.

That was…a lot of information.

Lawrence digested it all, as they ate his stew—which he had to admit he was quite pleased with in the end. He understood her reluctance to delve even now further into her own personal history, from the first he'd felt it was…a tender subject.

And though it might inform their discussion, he felt as if he had enough material to go on to reach a solid enough conclusion regarding their relationship.

'It's just…' Bobby shrugged.

'What?'

'I feel like the longer we know each other, the less he knows me,' she frowned, studying what was left of his stew as though it contained the answer to all the questions she'd ever asked. 'I'm not making much sense.'

'You are, actually,' Lawrence said, and he felt her turn to study him as she had her stew. 'I don't want to make this conversation about me. Again.'

And he didn't.

He'd initiated this, because he wanted to understand her. Hear what she had to say, even if he had nothing at all to contribute.

He just wanted to listen.

'Is it a real conversation if we aren't both sharing our experiences?'

Hm.

Lawrence hadn't ever really thought of it that way.

And not that he could refuse her—not when she looked at him like that, all doe-eyed and pleadingly— but he thought maybe, she wished to know him a little better too.

For once, he wasn't afraid she might find him wanting in some aspect or other. If she did, she would be sure to tell him, and that was…all he could ever ask for. This morning, when he'd abruptly, and unintentionally, shared what he had about Milicent, she'd accepted it, and listened, and understood *why* he was speaking of it all; as well as what it cost him.

So given another chance, to learn, and tell more, well, he found that apparently, he wanted *her* to know him a little better.

Whatever the outcome.

'I told you briefly of my wife this morning,' he said finally, ceding to her request. This morning he hadn't meant to say all he had either, but just as he did now, he felt it…*relevant.* 'I mentioned that the terms of what I'd thought to be a business arrangement weren't agreed to beforehand.' Bobby nodded, and he forged on. 'It was true. We barely knew each other, save for having met at a handful of events prior to the engagement. It was all done very properly, but as I later found out, Milicent… She wished for more. She thought that once we were married, I would…become more demonstrative, I think. When I failed to, she sought, as I've mentioned, consolation elsewhere. I found out, terms were renegotiated, and I thought she understood then, who I was. What I had it in me to offer her. But as days passed, she continued to begrudge me my lack of…love, and passion, really, to put it frankly.' Lawrence drew in a breath, looking out over the fire to the lake so still it seemed a mirror in the dusk. 'I never felt what I should for my wife, and that is my failing. I accept that now. But it took me a long time to understand that demanding it, expecting it, not trying to understand me or communicate her needs in a manner I could comprehend… Not giving us time to get to know each other…to find some manner of love… Well, I will merely say that I was not alone in failing at married life.'

Bobby nodded, and followed suit in staring out at the lake.

'We used to have these great conversations, Julian and I,' she said quietly. 'Hours we'd spend, well into the night, just *talking*. About our dreams, telling each other silly stories, moaning about tutors…whatever it was, it was *easy*. And then…his parents died, and he became master of Rothwakes, and I know we had to grow up in some measure, that he had responsibilities I can't even fathom. But it seems as if these past years, he doesn't care to talk to me, not really. He just trudges forth, and only if I truly take umbrage, or stand before him, and say *stop*, will he even take notice of anything else around him. I suppose… I suppose I miss him. This whole race… I feel as if we aren't in it together anymore. I want my friend back,' she breathed, and Lawrence reached over to lay his hand on hers.

'Rothwakes may be a selfish cad on the best of days,' he said, and Bobby laughed, the sound yet again music to his ears. He thought he'd never tire of it. 'But I doubt even he would fail to see what a loss your friendship would be. Give it some time, and tell him what you told me. If nothing else, you'll have an answer as to what he wants for the future.'

'You're very good at advice, you know that?'

It was Lawrence's turn to laugh.

In all his life, he'd never been accused of such a thing. If it related to business, a professional, or moral choice, perhaps. However, when it came to matters of people, and *the heart* as the saying went, well, not so much.

Bobby, however, was not laughing.

'I mean it, Lawrence,' she pressed. 'All you've done it seems is pull me back from whatever edge I court. You make sense of what I cannot.'

'And you make me lose what sense I have,' he said quietly, his heart full again with her words.

Perhaps…perhaps he could…*be there* for another, despite what he'd believed.

Been told, so very often.

Perhaps, his failings were not failings, but mere… incompatibility with others. With the language others spoke.

And because there was nothing else to say, not right that second at least, he put whatever he wished her to know in the kiss which followed.

As she did, and together they had a rather long, rather beautiful, silent conversation, before they fell asleep entwined again, the croaks of the frogs a strange, but enchanting lullaby.

Chapter Fifteen

Bobby wasn't sure what she expected their arrival in London to be, other than perhaps, she didn't expect very much at all. The final portion before London, into Guildford, had been as quiet, and uneventful, as the majority of the others. If anyone had seen or heard anything about the race, or the riders, there was no sign of it.

Not that Bobby tarried long after arriving, and learning that she was in charge of dinner that night—Lawrence having beaten her by five minutes and left her another silly map demanding she come provide sustenance. Julian kept his distance, and silent, which Bobby was immensely grateful for. He did have much to think on, and so did she. She wasn't making up any of the gap between her and Lawrence, and though all was not lost, she knew it could be soon if she didn't…

Pick up the pace.

Ride better.

Ride faster.

She'd thought she had been, but then apparently, it wasn't enough.

There is still time.

And after London, the portions were shorter—which meant more speed on longer distances. So, she wasn't worried. She wasn't feeling wonderful, and pleased with herself, but she was determined, and that was enough. And being with Lawrence…it helped. Rather than distract, it calmed, and settled her in a way she couldn't explain. Sitting with him last night, sharing a meal, sharing their blankets and much more—though there hadn't been quite so revelatory a conversation as before—felt *ideal*. She tried not to think too hard on it all, simply enjoyed it, knowing that once they reached London, things would change. It would be…the beginning of the end.

Only…three more days.

Three more days to win this, and show them what we're worth.

In fact, more than the race itself, it was the event that evening that consumed her thoughts as she rode into the city. Between nerves for the coming evening, and a need to be very mindful as she navigated the busy roads, Bobby didn't really have much time to think on how their London arrival might've been different from the others. No matter that they were finishing in Hyde Park, to her, it was just another stop on the road before she could head to Julian's townhouse and get ready for the night ahead.

Only, it turned out to be much more than merely *another stop on the road*.

At first, she didn't really grant much importance to the crowds on the public road as she entered the park. It was always busy, particularly when England was graced with such sunny, breezy weather as today. But then, it was *exceptionally* busy. And a great clamour rose when she and Arion trotted forward, shouts of *'That's her!'* and *'Bobby!'* reaching her ears.

Stunned, her heart beating a mile a minute, Arion's nervousness adding to her own, Bobby properly looked at the crowd around her, and noticed the purposeful gap they'd left as they lined the road—for *her*. There were hundreds of them. From all walks of life; families, dandies, groups of young women, elderly, and children. Some waved flags, others handkerchiefs, others knots of ribbons with…

The Rothwakes colours.

The Hayes colours.

All of them smiled, and cheered, no matter their newfound allegiance, looking absolutely thrilled to be here for this. Beyond stunned, Bobby simply rode on, a confused smile on her own lips, as her eyes tried to take it all in, and she waved occasionally, awkwardly, her nerves somehow fading slightly to be replaced with… *pride.*

What do you know…

'They're here for us, Arion,' she whispered to him, leaning forward, patting his neck to keep him calm. 'Will you look at that…'

As always, he seemed to understand her, she might've sworn he trotted with his head that little bit higher, an added spring to his step.

On they rode, towards the statue of Achilles, encouragements still loud in her ears.

'We believe in you, Bobby!'

'Tally-ho!'

'Ye've got this!'

The crowd was, if at all possible, bigger at the arrival point—though perhaps that was merely how they were packed around the statue, and men waiting beneath it.

Another great cry rose up as she arrived, and slid off Arion, careful to keep him close as the crowd seemed to surge a bit closer, tightening the ranks around them.

Swallowing hard, she stepped towards the solicitors, Julian—who was unfortunately looking rather satisfied with himself—and Lawrence.

Damn, he's won again.

Disappointment prickled at her as she forced her smile to remain, and watched the solicitors mark the time. Hands tapped her shoulder, cheering her, trying to shake her hand, and she breathed deeply, trying to find an escape.

Lawrence must've seen her oncoming distress, for in a flash he was there before her.

'Let's give the lady some room, what do you say?' he grinned, gesturing for the crowd to settle.

Mercifully, they listened, giving her and Arion space to move, breathe, and think.

Not much—it was all so overwhelming—but enough.

'Well raced, Miss Kingsley,' Lawrence said loudly, offering out his hand. She took it, and he placed his other over them, leaning down slightly. She knew it was for their audience's benefit, but the name chafed nonetheless. 'Are you all right?'

'I'm fine,' she breathed.

'Quite a surprise.'

'You can say that again.'

Lawrence nodded, and whistled, somehow being heard above the clamour, and in an instant, Barnes was bringing Beowulf to him, making a clear path through the throngs.

'Follow me,' he winked, once he held the reins in his hand.

Jumping onto Beowulf in a most dashing and entertaining manner—Bobby was not alone in her admiration, the crowd whistled and laughed—Lawrence addressed them all once again.

'Miss Kingsley and I have much to do before we celebrate our progress to this great city later this evening,' he announced, in a booming voice that made his position and power all too clear. Sometimes, Bobby forgot who he was, but in moments like this, it was impossible. She wasn't entirely sure how she felt about it, but luckily, she didn't have any time to ponder it. 'Thank you all for coming, and we hope to see you all when we set off tomorrow morning!'

Another loud cheer, and another wink.

Bobby mounted Arion—adding a little flair because *why not*? The crowd certainly appreciated it, and well, there was nothing wrong with that. Lawrence turned Beowulf, and as Bobby was about to follow his lead, she felt a little tug on her trousers' leg. Looking down, she found a young girl of about five or six, holding up a posy of violets for her.

Touched, speechless, she leaned down to take the posy.

'Thank you.'

'Welcome, miss,' the girl said politely, and Bobby's eyes met those of the girl's mother, standing behind her—a working woman if she were to guess. 'One day, I'll ride a horse too.'

'How about right now?' Bobby asked, more so the mother than the child. The woman's eyes got big, and she looked a bit wary, which Bobby could understand. She wasn't even sure why she was doing this, there were lots of other children—why was this one special? Still, she knew it was what was…right. 'She can ride with me out of the park, we'll meet you on the road.'

The woman glanced down at her hopeful daughter, then nodded, and Bobby opened her arms to receive the child.

'Comfortable?' she asked when the child was settled securely on her lap.

The young girl nodded, and Bobby looked up to find Lawrence watching, and waiting, an amused smile on his lips, his head quirked so that his eyebrows almost seemed a diagonal slash.

Bobby shot him a look which said: *Well, what?*

With a shrug, he turned, and waved to the crowd again, before making his way through it, and across the way so they could exit the park, luckily no one really following them.

'What's your name?' Bobby asked the young girl who was sitting very calmly, fascinated by everything, especially Arion's mane.

'Maureen.'

'So how do you like riding, Maureen?'

'Very much! We saw ponies once, and I got to ride one at the fair.'

'That explains it,' she said seriously. 'You're a natural.'

Maureen turned to beam at her, and Bobby couldn't help it, she felt her heart and spirits lift at that.

No matter all the rest. Out of it, had come this. A little girl's smile.

Worth it, I think.

It took only a few minutes to get to the road, and Bobby spotted Maureen's mother in the bustle there, less daunting than the one they'd left behind thankfully. She wished she could do more, promise something, *anything*, but with her own future in jeopardy—her home and livelihood in jeopardy—she wasn't sure what she could. Hell, at the end of all this, she could lose Arion; something else she hadn't really let herself think on, the pain, too sharp. The fear of failure, the fear of what lay in her future hadn't felt as tangible, as bitter, for a while.

Not until that moment.

'Thank you so much, Miss Kingsley,' the woman said as though minding her elocution, as Bobby handed Maureen back down with a smile.

'My pleasure,' she smiled. 'Sorry it couldn't be longer, Maureen. Thank you for the posy.'

'Thank you!' Maureen piped up.

'Come by my townhouse in September,' Lawrence said to the woman, startling everyone as he bent down to hand her a card, and what Bobby thought was a coin. 'I'll take the young lady for a ride around the park, if she likes.'

Everyone stared at him for a moment, various expressions of surprise on all their faces. Wariness too—the woman was right to wonder what precisely this man's motives were.

'He's bit of a stuffy lord,' Bobby told her casually, fixing Lawrence with her gaze. She saw him fighting not to smile, and she grinned wide. 'But he is honourable.'

'Thank you, my lord,' the woman nodded, taking the card, and Lawrence seemed to grow taller, and prouder.

Whether she would ever use it, well that remained to be seen.

'Good day to you both,' the woman said.

'Bye, Miss Kingsley! Bye, Your Lordship!' Maureen chirped, waving as they turned their horses to head into Mayfair.

The pair of them waved back until the little girl and her mother disappeared.

'That was very kind and thoughtful of you, Lawrence,' Bobby said once they'd made it across the road, heading in the general direction of Berkeley Square—his and Julian's townhouses wedged in the streets before it. He shrugged, as if it meant nothing at all to him—the gesture, her words—but somehow, she knew better. 'Thank you for getting us out of there. I admit I wasn't quite prepared for…all that.'

'Neither was I,' he admitted. 'And you're welcome. I was glad to help. Besides, we both need all the time we have to get these gentlemen settled, and dress up like peacocks for this evening. And nap. I feel I might need a very long nap.'

Bobby laughed—somehow Lawrence napping to prepare for an event was…incongruous.

She herself wouldn't say no to a nap generally, but she was a bit overexcited to consider it properly.

'This is where I leave you, Bobby,' he said, pulling her back to the moment as they stopped. 'Until tonight, at least.'

'Until later, Lawrence.'

With a smile, and touch to the brim of his hat, he turned away, heading south one street.

Bobby watched him go, pondering for a short moment, the beauty in the unexpected.

Chapter Sixteen

Well, now, that is a lot of people, Bobby thought as she and Julian moved away from their hosts, into the ballroom, which hosted yes, a space for dancing, there, by the floor-to-ceiling French windows, but had been also filled with small tables and chairs, a feast of delicacies on long tables along the walls, and so many candles the light nearly blinded her.

Bobby had expected *lavish*—after all this was Cheston House, London residence of the Marquess and Marchioness of—but she hadn't quite expected… so many people. So…*much*, really.

When they'd all decided on having this event, the words *party* and *dinner* and *business* had been thrown around generously. It was to be a chance for Julian and Lawrence both to meet with investors, celebrate burying old rivalries, and generally meeting and greeting. In Society, anything was a good excuse for a party.

They had all agreed—after some heated debates—on having it here, as the marquess was an acquaintance of Lawrence's, and no one else could come up with a suitably impressive space to entertain. Despite the grandiose venue, with its crystal chandeliers, polished mirrors and floorboards, gilt and gold and art—which Bobby knew went with such houses—she hadn't expected a *business dinner party* to be anything as overwhelming as this.

And especially not as busy.

Julian had said more were clamouring to procure invites, and she suspected even after their conversation the other day that the original low numbers would grow, but…

Surely this is too many.

Taking deep breaths as they advanced further into the room, Julian greeting people as they went—her smiling and nodding and curtseying as she should, but neither required to, nor yet up to, being any more participative—Bobby tried very hard not to let it all overwhelm her. Sure, there were hundreds of dark evening suits, and feathers, and wide, bustling silk skirts, and shiny diamonds, rubies, and emeralds. Sure, there was a cacophony of music, laughter, chatter, and yes, the scents, natural and manufactured, combined to make a rather nauseating blend. Yet none of this was new to Bobby. This wasn't her first *party*, not even in Society as grand as this, a mix of titans of industry, bankers, financiers, lords, ladies, and from the disdainful looks of some, journalists too.

In fact, underneath the initial surprise, she could still feel the excitement she'd felt all day—Hell, since she'd first learned that *she* would be attending as a rider. She knew as well as anyone what this could mean for her future—meeting all these people. Particularly if Julian remained true to his word, and introduced her as more than a rider or a groom. She'd even been excited about dressing for such an evening. It had been a long time since she'd worn a fine gown, and fine jewellery, and done her hair, and danced, and had this manner of fun.

Despite all the aspects of being a *proper lady* she rebelled against to some extent—even before she'd completely eschewed most of them—she had enjoyed some of it. Though she hadn't been *properly* introduced into Society—the purpose of such things clear even then, along with Bobby's rejection of such purposes, most of all *marriage*—Lord and Lady Rothwakes had made sure Bobby was *introduced* into society. That, as their *ward* as she was introduced, then, she was made part of their social lives. That no matter her leanings towards other occupations—she remained part of another world too. That she saw more than what she *wanted*; that she experienced all they could offer her.

Though Bobby viewed those times with a measure of pain, and bittersweet regret—the Rothwakes always emphasising the need for her to keep her *unusual occupations* quiet, further proof that she would never be a *true* lady, truly part of their world, truly accepted in all she was—most of the time, that hurt, even in memory, was tamped down by the pure joy, the comfort she'd felt, from her special times with Lady Rothwakes.

Every social event was an excuse for them to spend time together, in private. Lady Rothwakes brushing and fixing her hair rather than a maid. Lady Rothwakes helping her choose the best garments for the day, or night. Lady Rothwakes…being with her. As a mother. Not choosing the ruby earrings because they were best suited for whatever social event—but rather because she thought they suited Bobby best. Those moments, they were so full of love… Well, Bobby could only really cherish them.

When Bobby had found the fabric for the dress she

wore tonight—a rich pink silk that flowed like water—she'd felt *excited* about it. It had felt as though Lady Rothwakes had been there, in the shop with her, guiding her to it. Silly, for someone so staunchly unbelieving, but then, it was how it had felt. And then, Mrs Murray in the village had done it up for her, adding a trim of hand-embroidered ivy...

Bobby felt beautiful. It had been a long time since a dress had felt like her—since she'd had occasion to wear one, and since she'd allowed herself to feel, well, vain, she supposed—but this one was simple—gorgeous, in her opinion, but simple—with its simple lines, lack of ruffles and ruching, save for some around the top of the bodice and sleeves to add shape. It fell off her shoulders, and though she knew it wasn't ladylike to show the marks of the sun on her skin—and it was true the vee around her neck looked a bit odd compared to the paleness of her shoulders—well, she liked it.

Besides, the delicate diamond and sapphire set Lady Rothwakes had gifted her for her sixteenth birthday did a perfect job of offsetting the dermal markings of her daily occupation. They also made her feel...confident. Despite the bittersweet feelings they brought to her heart, there was no denying she stood a little taller, a little straighter, with Lady Rothwakes' jewels on her.

The reminder of who she represented now—what name she represented—and of this afternoon's surprising, but heartening arrival in London, settled her unease somewhat, and she felt ready to truly invest in this evening, and in herself. Glancing around the room as Julian asked some Manchester man about hunting, Bobby idly wondered where Lawrence was.

It wasn't that she was...searching for him, *per se*. It wasn't that she was excited to see him, or even that she

particularly wanted him to see her. Wishing for a man
to see you when you felt beautiful, particularly a man
who'd already shown his appreciation of you when you
looked as far from a *lady* as you could, was absolutely
foolish. She hadn't worn this dress for him, she'd worn
it for herself, because she liked it, but still, if she was
being completely honest, well, maybe she did want him
to see her...

In another light.

Absolute balderdash, she chided herself, shaking her
head, and following Julian when she felt him move on.

'Mr Marshall is up ahead, and that is Mr Spellman
with him,' Julian said, stopping them for a moment, as
he grabbed two glasses of champagne off a passing tray,
handing her one, and sipping his own before passing it
to her as well as he couldn't exactly walk with crutches
and hold a glass at the same time.

They were the first words he'd spoken to her all
evening, since she'd met him in the townhouse's hall,
and he'd muttered something about '*looking well*', and
'*best be going then*'. It hurt her—no denying that—
that he hadn't yet made any attempt to apologise. Perhaps he was waiting for a better time, still, it felt as if
a distance had come between them, when really, he
should've been...

There for me.

'Very successful in shipping. And that is the Ver-
nons with them,' he added, his eyes gleaming as he surveyed the trio made up of an older, portly gentleman, a
tall woman in her mid-thirties, and a young miss who
seemed to have inherited half of everything from her
parents. 'Americans,' Julian told her. 'Shipbuilding.
Very interested in investing over here.'

They wandered over to the group, who stopped their chattering when they caught sight of her and Julian.

All looked her up and down with undisguised interest, though somehow the stares of the greying shipping men seemed altogether less…

Just less.

Introductions were made quickly, and Bobby offered the group a smile as she sipped her champagne.

'Well then, Miss Kingsley,' the man called Marshall said genially. 'How is it you got yourself involved with all this, then? I admit, the papers did not quite say.'

Bobby opened her mouth to answer, but Julian beat her to it.

'Miss Kingsley has been part of the family for years, my parents' ward. As it happens, she's the brilliant mind behind the success of my stables.'

Julian offered her a meaningful glance, and she smiled.

He kept his promise.

'How very interesting,' Marshall nodded. 'How did you become involved with horses then?'

'I suppose I just fell into it in a way,' she told him, shrugging a little, though she knew that was certainly not something she should be doing. 'I was very lucky to be given the opportunity to develop my skills at Roth-wakes, and help His Lordship build a reputation worthy of the name.'

'And what a name it is,' Mr Vernon agreed. 'Heard all about it on the other side of the Atlantic.'

'That is very heartening to hear, sir,' Bobby blushed. 'We do our best.'

'So you train all the horses?' Miss Vernon asked eagerly.

Another couple—who were introduced as the Far-
thingtons, joined the group.

'I do,' Bobby told them all, though she held Miss
Vernon's gaze. 'I have help, of course, but I suppose
you could say I steer the ship.'

Messrs Spellman and Marshall apparently appreciated her nautical reference, laughing, and raising their
glasses.

'Miss Kingsley does more than merely steer the
ship,' Julian corrected. 'She handles every detail, and
it will be a loss indeed when she leaves us to pursue
another path.'

'When is the wedding, then?' Mrs Farthington asked,
and everyone stared at her for a moment.

Everyone was confused—except for Bobby—who
merely blinked, forcing herself to smile through the
expected but unwelcome reminder.

Nothing ever changes.

'Wedding? Are you getting married? Did I miss
something?' Spellman asked, frowning.

'I am not,' Bobby said gracefully, but with a coldness
that could not be mistaken. 'I plan to leave Rothwakes
and start my own farm,' she announced, with as much
cheer and joviality as she could muster.

'My apologies, Miss Kingsley,' Mrs Farthington said,
looking at least a little abashed. 'How dreadfully silly
of me to assume. Very original of you to start your own
farm, what a capital idea,' she ground out, though no
one could ever believe the woman thought it *capital*.

'You can truly steer the ship then,' Mrs Vernon offered, and it didn't matter whether she was trying to be
altogether more jolly, and encouraging about it all, keeping the conversation going like anyone with true manners would. It chafed. It all just, *chafed*. Like sandpaper

on already raw skin. 'Though I wonder why anyone would wish to have to endure all that business which goes along with new enterprises when you obviously have a good position, in a good house.'

'The chance to build something of my own,' Bobby said, not harshly, but not kindly either. 'Mr Vernon, you started your own enterprise I would wager—what prompted you to do so?'

Her smile, her tone, it was all polite.

No one failed to detect the underlying sting of it however.

At least it amuses Messrs Spellman and Marshall, she thought vaguely, catching the gentleman snorting into their drinks out of the corner of her eye.

'The chance to build something of my own,' Mr Vernon agreed, raising his glass, and tipping his head. 'A legacy, for the future.'

'Then we are alike in that,' she said graciously.

The conversation moved on for a short while, Marshall and Mr Vernon both promising to call on her when her own operation was up and running. A success, Bobby supposed it should be called.

Julian said nothing about her behaviour, and she did nothing of the sort again as the evening wore on, more conversations—all following the same track of that first one—filling each interminable minute, until Bobby couldn't stand it anymore. Until she thought she might scream, right there, in the middle of the packed ballroom, toss the untouched plate of food in her hands across it, and tell them all where to go with their opinions.

Luckily, before she could follow through on that desire, the man she'd searched for all evening, but never found, appeared right before her, looking sinfully exceptional in his expertly tailored black evening dress, blacker for the contrast with the pristine starched white shirt and cravat, and beige brocade waistcoat.

'Want to get out of here?'

'God, yes.'

Lawrence swept away her plate, before sweeping her away from that place altogether.

My knight in shining evening dress.

Lawrence wasn't entirely sure of the how or why behind it, but apparently, this race had made him more approachable. More likeable. People he'd known for years, and who he knew barely put up with him and his *gruff aloofness*, greeted him cheerfully; and from what he could tell, it seemed, *genuine*. Others fell over themselves in an effort to get to know him, just speak with him really, as if all of a sudden, he was interesting. If it had only been journalists, he supposed he might've understood, but these were young people of Society, hungry pillars of trade and industry.

Thinking about it, which he did, as he experienced this change when he finally began making the rounds in Cheston House's ballroom—having spent a good amount of time catching up with the marquess and marchioness, the former having been one of the few school chums he'd ever had, and if not a *good friend*, then someone he hadn't quite managed to alienate in all the years he'd known him—the only reasonable and logical explanation he could come up with was that somehow, racing four hundred miles across country made him adventurous, and therefore interesting. At the very least, less *stiff*. He might not believe that all followed, but it was all he could reasonably come up with.

It was a rather stark contrast to the majority of events

such as this he attended, and a stark contrast to the way he'd seen his evening going. In his mind, it had all been rather simple; uneventful, and uncomplicated. He would spend some time with Cheston, wander around the party, find some other people to chat to—he knew several of his investors, in both his racing and railway endeavours would be present—perhaps have a glass or two of champagne, and some food, and then he would quietly escape and retire.

He did add *Dance with Bobby* and *Generally spend time with Bobby flirting and having fun* to his list when he first saw her enter the room. It was impossible to miss her, not only because of the excited chatter bouncing off the walls when she arrived with Rothwakes, but because in a room full of opulence, show, and frippery, she was breathtakingly, and refreshingly simple. He'd not really given a thought to what she might wear this evening—he'd only thought about spending more time with her—but if he had, somehow, he would've got it wrong. Because never could he have imagined so glorious a sight as she made.

Oh, he'd thought her beautiful and captivating before. It wasn't the dress, the jewels, or the neatly curled hair which made her so. Only, they did reveal another side of her, like the various facets of a gemstone. A side of her that glowed. Brighter than any of the flawless crystal in this place. He'd seen a glimpse of this light before—particularly that morning she'd been riding Arion in the mists—but something about her was different tonight. Brighter. Less...*contained*.

Lawrence longed to go right over there to her, to whisk her away, and ask her why precisely she was glowing, and could he please have some of whatever it was that made her do so, but when he made to move

the first time, she was already deep in conversation
with who he knew to be important guests, and potential investors, and he was not about to intrude. Evenings
such as this were vital to him—he could only imagine
what they might mean to her, looking to go off and
start a new venture on her own. Hadn't she said Rothwakes would reveal the truth of her talents tonight? He
wouldn't...intrude. She deserved all this room could
give to her, and more. It wasn't his place to stand beside
her, detract from all that. Even if the thought of standing beside her, helping her, singing her praises, well,
that would be rather nice, he wagered.

But it is not my place.

However, he did keep an eye on her—rather his eyes
kept finding her no matter where he was. And as the
evening wore on, as he solicited more business, reassured old, and fielded questions from various papers
about his thoughts on Bobby—*a tremendous horse-
woman, a worthy competitor, no I don't wish to comment on the strong likelihood of my win as the race is
not yet ended*—he found he didn't like what his eyes
were seeing a little more every time they spotted her.

Her light is fading.

It wouldn't do. It made him...angry, yes that was
the word. It made him surly, and angry, and he didn't
understand why no one else could see it. The tighter
smiles. The sadness in her eyes. The hunching of her
shoulders. Bobby wore every emotion on her—that's
what he loved about her—and even though she was obviously trying to play along, and be polite, or whatever
it was they were all required to do in instances such
as this, he could see it. Therefore everyone else—particularly Rothwakes—had to be completely dull not to
notice. Not to see the cracks, the pain, the discomfort.

He watched her closely, not wanting to intrude, or
attract attention. Finally, she slipped away, and stood
alone for a moment staring at the tables laden with food.
He watched as she unenthusiastically set some things
on a plate for herself, then stared at it forlornly.

Before he'd even reached her, asked her what was
going on, he knew what he had to do; what she needed.

To be outside. Away from here. So she can breathe.

And so, once he was finally standing before her, he
said the words he hoped would be the first step to lifting her spirits.

'Want to get out of here?'

The gratitude and relief in her eyes made him feel
a giant.

'God, yes.'

Bobby passed her plate to a passing waiter, and he
tucked her hand into the crook of his arm, before sweeping her out of the ballroom, and out of Cheston House
altogether, stopping only to direct one of the footmen
to put their things in his carriage, and send it to wait
by the park corner.

And then, he took Bobby to the nearest bit of the
natural world he could.

Chapter Seventeen

'Ready to talk about it yet?' Lawrence asked softly, breaking the tense, but comfortable, and enveloping silence between them. The night itself was far from quiet, creatures of the night—animal and human—abundant, even nestled here, as they were in Hyde Park, buffeted from the outside world by its natural offerings.

Somehow, Lawrence had known she needed this, a reminder of the pure world she loved, where she could escape the urban pit of remorseless vipers who only ever sought *more*, *more*, *more*. Somehow, she hadn't seen him, but he'd seen her, and *known*. It was…priceless. As all the moments they seemed to share were. *Even the bad ones*, she thought ruefully.

They weren't alone here—Bobby could hear the sounds of midnight revellers, lovers, and troublemakers alike—except that it felt as if they were. As if they were on the road again, and things were simpler.

Moving her feet about in the water, which felt refreshing and reviving—even though some part of her doubted it was as clean and fresh as a country stream—Bobby pondered his question.

Was she ready to talk?

Or, more aptly, was she ready to open herself more to him? To speak of things she never had to anyone, not even Lady Rothwakes, unable to find the language and will to reveal it all.

Was she ready to admit Lawrence *meant* something to her, already understood her in a way no one else ever had, and would not only listen, but hear, and accept, whatever she told him?

Was she ready to ask him without asking, for more advice?

I am not ready to not answer.

Only, how to even begin explaining it all?

'I was actually looking forward to the party,' she admitted quietly, thinking that was perhaps a good place to begin. *The sadness of disappointment.* 'Looking forward to... Making connections I suppose,' she sighed. 'Coming out into the world as someone...worthwhile, with a good plan for the future. Coming out on my own merits, not merely as an extension of Julian. And still, the only merits anyone seems to ever see are that I'm odd, or unusual. In a pitiable way. What a waste, that someone so well educated, pretty enough, and with connections, prefers to muck about with horses, rather than a husband and brace of children,' Bobby said, in a tone mocking those who had uttered such sentiments over the years. 'What a waste. One woman blatantly assumed I was to be married—and that was just the start of what I heard all evening. Some as open as she was, others more subtle in their unending judgement.'

'Casting off the judgement of others is not an easy feat, I grant you that.'

'Particularly not when they hold the keys to your future. Had I your position, not even your wealth, merely your title, and your sex, I would be accepted as eccentric. Fanciful, perhaps. But I would still be accepted. It was foolish of me to think I could change their minds, that people would think differently of me after I won. They won't—and though they might someday deign to buy a horse from me, they won't ever trust me enough with their patronage. Even I know the kind of place I seek to build will not survive long if I don't have custom from those with wealth, and power.'

'You haven't won yet,' Lawrence remarked, and Bobby turned to see a challenging smile on his lips which relaxed her immediately. 'Whether or not you do,' he added, with more seriousness. 'What you will have achieved will speak for itself. I know all the reasons why you, and Rothwakes, have kept your involvement in his business quiet, I do. People will always find something to criticise or judge. Some may never, granted, give you what you seek. Not all. At the end of this, what you've done will speak for you, just as it will speak for me. I mean, I've seen the change in them all in my regard already. I'm adventurous apparently,' he grinned, answering her silent query. 'And no matter what, *I* will speak for you.'

'I don't want any favours from you,' Bobby muttered, turning away from him again, her fingers toying with a rock before she tossed it into the dark, metallic water before them.

'It would not be a favour, Bobby,' he sighed, exasperated. 'It would be the truth. Not that I believe you will truly need it. Already your name is on everyone's lips. Whether you like it or not, fame is its own weapon, its own asset.'

'My name is on everyone's lips for the wrong reasons,' she countered.

'Some people's, perhaps. Regardless, it is on their lips, and that is all you need.'

'It's the very last thing I need. The very last thing I want,' she shrugged. She'd thought, for a moment, that he could understand. But it always came back to the same thing. 'They want me to be something I'm not, and when I turn out not to be, they hate me for it. They don't merely rethink their stance, they turn away. This dress, for example. I love it,' she admitted, lifting the skirt up a little, as if to show him again, the delicacy, the water-like beauty of the sumptuous fabric. 'I was excited to wear it. I am more comfortable in my every-day clothes, granted, they are part of who I am, but I do like a good dress, too. But the second people see me in one, they have expectations. It's always been like that. I can't be Bobby anymore. I have to be Miss Kingsley. A proper woman. A *lady*. That's why I stopped wearing them, altogether. They gave people the wrong idea.'

'I understand the weight of expectations, believe me,' Lawrence said, chucking her under the chin so she'd look at him. 'Everyone in this world does, to some degree, I think. And as much as we like to deny it, we all know very well that though clothes may not *make* the man, they do often tell us about him. You'll never change that. But I look at you, in that dress, that is worth being excited about, and all I see is the Bobby I know. A different side of you, yes, but it's only you I see. Were Rothwakes here, loath as I am to give him any credit, I think he would agree.'

Bobby smiled weakly, and Lawrence shrugged.

It felt good, to know that, to know that he did see her, for all she was, but it didn't change the fact that not everyone did.

Not everyone who mattered had.

And it didn't change that no matter how much she wanted to tell the world to go hang itself, and be *herself* always, life didn't work that way.

To succeed, to have a good life, she'd been taught she must abide by certain rules. She'd cast off the rules to a degree, because she'd had the freedom to, but in this next chapter of her life, to succeed, she couldn't.

Could she?

'Why do you hate Miss Kingsley so much?' Lawrence asked, putting a screeching halt to her private deliberations, as if he'd seen what they were before she even could, cutting straight to the heart of it.

Glancing over, she tried to find some trace of mockery, or judgement, but as ever, it seemed there was none.

Not since that first day in Julian's office, had she seen any sort of judgement—and even then, he had seemed more affronted by the suggestion he shouldn't race someone of his class, than disapproval of her.

'Miss Kingsley is all Lady Rothwakes dreamed I could be,' she confessed, her voice merely breath, though seemingly as loud as a brutal cry. 'All I failed to be, even for her.'

Grimacing, she turned away from Lawrence's empathetic gaze, refusing to show the weakness of tears gathering in her own eyes.

Clearing her throat, she continued, knowing it was time to share her sad, sorry tale.

Of the orphan who could never be a princess; even if she wanted to.

Lawrence watched Bobby, as he always seemed to now, even though there were times when all she was seemed too much to bear, and he forced himself to look away lest he forget… Everything. Looking at her—

watching the not-so-subtle shifts of her emotions across her face, the thoughts in her eyes, simply taking in what he now had no choice but to admit to himself was her untethered beauty—it was hypnotic. As in it emptied his mind, filled his body, his soul, with something more, and paused the ticking of time; the movement of the Earth, even.

Now, the hypnotic trance held pain, pain for her, for all the anger, the doubts, the disappointment and fear she'd felt trying to fit herself into a world that couldn't even begin to compare with her wonder.

He wasn't sure what to say—only sure that she needed to express it all—to *him*.

And now, he saw the decision she made, to answer the question he'd posed so lightly at the beginning of the voyage.

The question of her beginnings; her link to the Rothwakes family.

'I'm told my father was a blacksmith,' she began, her eyes on the liquid-like waves of her skirts. 'My mother... Tended a small patch of land, made preserves and jellies and such to help when times were leaner. Good people by all accounts, God-fearing and such.'

Bobby inhaled a deep breath before continuing, though Lawrence knew how this chapter ended.

Perhaps he'd always known, though perhaps he'd hoped for something different than a sad beginning—perhaps a stroke of fortune, a chance meeting.

Anything but death.

'I don't remember much from that time,' she said, stronger now. 'Flashes of feeling sometimes in my dreams. Don't have anything of theirs, except for a box of little trinkets I suppose my father made for my mother, iron tulips and things like that.'

Bobby shrugged, as if that weren't important, and yet, Lawrence knew it was.

Both what little she had—and all that she didn't. For all that he had perhaps lacked, mementos of family had never been part of that. Particularly portraits. Not perfect renditions, but enough to jog his memories.

Memories which were, in themselves, a blessing too. 'I remember being cold,' she frowned, nearly whispering now. He wanted to reach out, hold her hand or something, but then, he felt like she needed to finish before he could. Baring herself like this, was enough for right this moment. 'So very cold. I feel it sometimes, icy cold flesh beneath my fingertips,' she continued, looking down at her hands, as if she could now. 'And then nothing else. When I was older, Lord Rothwakes told me he'd heard me crying, when he rode past one day. It was so quiet, he nearly missed it—would've, had his horse not baulked at moving on actually. He found my parents, dead, presumably of a fever that I'd either not caught, or survived somehow. He brought me back to Rothwakes, and was going to have me sent off to the parish, but Her Ladyship wouldn't have it. She believed God had sent her a daughter,' Bobby smiled meekly, looking back at him, imploring him to understand, and oh, how he did. He nodded, and she took a breath before continuing. 'Though I was never lied to about my heritage, I was raised as their own. Or at least, they tried to. I had a room, beautiful clothes, the best education, but in the end, all I kept was the education. From my first nights there, I'm told I would scamper out of the house—how, no one knew—and make my way to the stables, to sleep with the horses. For years, they tried to stop it, until finally, they gave up, and made me a nice proper room in the stables. Lord Rothwakes gave me a position in the stables when I was fourteen, though he asked I continue my education as a lady too. I think they hoped, eventually, that I would…decide to want something other than my work. I know Her Ladyship was sad, disappointed that I couldn't be the daughter she wanted. One worthy of her. I tried,' Bobby breathed vehemently. 'So hard. I *wanted* to be Miss Kingsley for her, make her proud… Especially after His Lordship died. But it made me so miserable…she told me I shouldn't bother anymore. Not long after that, she fell ill. She was ill for a long time. And then, she was gone. She said…she always used to tell Julian and I that we'd never disappointed her, and never could, even when we got into trouble. And she said she loved me, and I believe that, but it doesn't change the fact that I couldn't be the daughter she wished for so.'

Shrugging, Bobby turned to the Serpentine, and Lawrence pondered her words, her story, for a long moment.

He hadn't known Lady Rothwakes well—after all their families had been feuding for years, hence why he'd likely never heard of Bobby—but he heard enough to not doubt she was a kind, gentle, and understanding woman.

'Would I be wrong to say, that isn't quite how she put it?' he asked, and Bobby shot her eyes to his, narrowing them inquisitively. 'I didn't know Her Ladyship, but I know what she wasn't. And I think, the truth was in your own words. You were miserable. Perhaps, she didn't wish to see you miserable any more. Perhaps she recognised that forcing you to be who *she* wanted, rather than who you were, was not the kind of mother she wished to be. I think, in the end, those words she uttered to Rothwakes, and you, stood fast. She was not disappointed. And never could be.'

Bobby's eyes widened, as if she'd never imagined that possibility before, and then, he saw her mind turning back to whatever time it had been, when Lady Rothwakes had told her to cease pretending for her sake.

'She said it was wrong of her,' Bobby whispered. 'To force me down a path I was never meant for. I always thought she meant that the daughter of a blacksmith could never be the daughter of a lady, but now... I wonder.'

'I don't think you have to wonder, Bobby,' Lawrence said gently, resisting the urge to touch her no more. He tucked a loose strand behind her ear, and she turned to him, the tears she'd tried to hide away earlier, tumbling out onto her cheeks. 'You knew her, knew her heart. But nothing you've said to me, of how she was... Telling you she loved you, that is enough to know she merely wished for you to be yourself. That was who she loved. The woman with spirit, and fight, and who sees the world in a way no one else ever could. A woman not bound by convention, but capable of forging whatever path she chose to. There is no one like you, Bobby. However, I do think perhaps you've spent too long in your little corner of the world. There are so many incredible people out here, people who have defied society's dictates of who they should be, how they should live, even how they should dress. Scientists, artists, adventurers... I don't pretend to know what it took, what it cost, for them to do that, but perhaps, there are people in this world ready to accept, to champion, you. If only you open your heart to the possibilities.'

Another round of tears tumbled from her eyes, and he shuffled closer to gently swipe them away with his thumbs, before extracting a handkerchief from his pocket and offering it out to her.

She blew her nose, in the most unfashionable, unladylike way possible, and he grinned, somehow charmed by it.

It was that gesture, that moment, that brought a jolt of understanding to him, and he stared at her in awe, as she fixed herself back up.

He trusted Bobby.

Categorically, implicitly; more than he'd ever trusted anyone in his life.

Because despite her fears, her doubts, she was never anything but herself with him. It wasn't merely her emotions she wore on her sleeve, it was *all* of her. She said what she meant, even if she didn't quite mean all she said at certain times. There was honesty in every breath, every gesture, every word. Despite what she might think, as long as he'd known her, all he'd seen her do was present herself to the world, daring them to see her as she was.

Just, Bobby.

He huffed a laugh to himself, and Bobby turned back to him, a question in her eyes, though she did not offer his handkerchief back, tucking it away somewhere.

'I was just thinking... That dress should have an opportunity to enjoy the evening, *properly,*' he said, meaning it, but also not saying what he truly meant to. It was neither the time, nor the place, and in reality, it didn't change anything at all, so there was no point mentioning it. 'Would you be offended if I was ever so presumptuous and invited you to my home?' he asked, and she laughed, the sound convincing him he'd made the right choice. 'I am sure I can rustle up some food if you are hungry, and well, perhaps I can bribe one of the servants to play a tune on the fiddle or something. Actually, come to think of it,' he added excitedly, scrambling to his feet. 'Barnes, my—well, you know him—he is rather accomplished at the piano.'

Waggling his eyebrows, he offered out his hands, and Bobby took them, carefully rising from the slippery bank.

'I wouldn't want to put them out,' she said tentatively. 'They'll be waiting for you to return to go to bed.'

'I do intend to ask them, you know. I'm not a completely ignorant arse.'

Bobby laughed again, and bending down, he picked up their shoes, before offering out his arm.

'Debatable,' she mused, lacing her arm through his. 'Besides, you are their lord. Do you truly think they will refuse you?'

'Barnes will,' he assured her. 'He is the very Devil. Only, ever so clever with starch.'

'Ah, so he is to blame for your starchiness.'

'I shall be sure to tell him you said that.'

Bobby shoved him slightly, though she kept her arm in his, and when they had recovered from the sidestepping, she remained closer by his side than she had been.

Lawrence smiled, as they fell into a pleasant silence walking through the park, back to where his carriage waited.

It wasn't until they arrived back at his townhouse, and his butler raised an eyebrow in rather exceptional surprise, that he realised they'd never put their shoes back on.

Chapter Eighteen

'Lawrence, wait,' Bobby said, reaching out to stop him even as he made to go find Barnes once his butler had seen to taking their things, and gone to ask for a tray of food and drink to be prepared. As touched as she was by what he wanted to do for her, it wasn't what she truly wanted, nor needed right now. There was actually only one thing she needed, other than food. 'I… That is… Would you mind if we remained just the two of us?'

He raised a brow, studying her carefully, as if ensuring this wasn't some attempt to be unobtrusive, then relaxed, and smiled.

The butler chose that moment to reappear, and Lawrence turned to him.

'Keats, please instruct the rest of the house that they are free to retire. We will require nothing further this evening.'

A bow, and the butler went off to do as instructed.

Taking her hand in his, Lawrence led her upstairs to the drawing room, where a roaring fire, and generously laden tray of food awaited them already. Bread, cheese, cold meats, chutneys, fruit…

Bobby's stomach growled when she spotted the feast, and Lawrence laughed.

'That answers my next question then,' he mused, leading her to the small coffee table the food was set on.

He glanced at the settee beside it, and the chairs, then back at her, and, decision made, grabbed pillows from the surrounding furniture, setting them on the floor.

'Will you be all right with that skirt of yours?' he asked.

'I managed well enough in the park, didn't I?'

'Good point. Wine? Gin? Whisky? Brandy?'

'Wine, please.'

After helping her to a nest of pillows on the floor, which proved to be tricky only in that the crinoline made it difficult to get close to the table, he strode off to the corner, and returned with two glasses of a rich red vintage.

Depositing them, he then sat himself to the side of her, and Bobby was once again struck by the naturalness of the picture they made. A viscount and what could pass as a lady, sitting by the fire on the floor of an exquisite—though tame and far from ornate—drawing room in Mayfair. It fit, in a way she couldn't quite explain, nor comprehend, only in that she never would've really thought about imagining the Lawrence she'd thought would race her in such a fashion. But then, she was reminded he hadn't been that Lawrence, not since that first night.

They feasted in companionable silence, alternating sending each other soft smiles and staring into the hypnotic flames before them. Caught in a strange, comforting haze, Bobby distractedly noted that her mind was… at peace. Oh, she had doubts, and fears, and questions, and so much more, but sitting there, she felt settled in a way she hadn't in a long time. Or perhaps, ever.

There were no expectations, there was nothing *to do*, merely to live, breathe, eat, and be. It was a most exceptional feeling, she decided. When they were both sated, Lawrence helped her back to her feet, then dragged the table across the poor Persian rug beneath it, then tucked it beside an armchair.

She frowned quizzically, but Lawrence ignored her, too invested in searching for...

Something.

Only his form was visible as he moved about the room, opening drawers, studying bookcases, nooks, and shelves.

'Aha,' he said triumphantly, coming back to her, cradling something before him. 'I thought I'd kept this in here.'

He strode over to the mantel before she could glimpse what he held, and fiddled with whatever it was for a moment, before he finally stepped back.

There was a tiny tinkling sound, a tune which Bobby didn't recognise but which sounded rather like...

A waltz.

'I did promise you a dance,' Lawrence shrugged, almost embarrassed, as if the small gesture wouldn't be enough, doubt darkening his eyes. 'It was Mother's.'

Unable to speak for fear of revealing just how much the gesture touched her, Bobby smiled, opening her arms so that he could move into position.

With a sigh of relief, he did, and it didn't matter that the music box was barely audible over the sounds of their swishing clothes, or the crackling of the wood. It didn't matter that they only had a small portion of floor, or that they could only dance a condensed version of the typically grand waltz. Being in his arms, swaying more than sweeping across the floor, his heat, and strength, and steadiness holding her fast, Bobby felt more cherished, than she ever had before.

As the music waned, their form slipped, until they were merely embracing and swaying, her head tucked against his chest. One of his hands rose from where it rested gently on her lower back, and he stroked the nest of slowly fading curls atop her head ever so tenderly. Taking a deep inhale of him—*more warm chocolate, less Beowulf today*—Bobby squeezed him tightly, before leaning her head back so she could look him in the eye.

It was odd, looking up at him thus, the fine features of his face sharper; the patches of varying coloured hair and thickness in his growing beard, somehow reminding her of his *realness*.

She realised then, that these past days had, in some way, felt a dream. *He* had felt a dream. By seeming to know her, understand her so well, so quickly, despite their differences. A kindly sprite appearing to a weary traveller. He'd felt like someone come from the pages of a storybook—because no one as exceptional as he could possibly exist.

But he is real. And he is here, with me.

'Thank you,' she breathed.

For everything.

A slow nod, and he bent down, curling into himself, his body leaving hers somewhat so he could accommodate their difference in size. He kissed her, slowly, torturously slow at first, until she swiped his tongue with her own as he went to trace the seam of her lips, and then, there was that profound, soul-searching, desperate quality to it.

Bobby gave him just enough of a push to start him moving backwards, somewhat confident she knew where she was leading him, their lips and tongues still tangling, until he met the settee with the back of his legs and half fell, half sat, making to drag her down with him, but she resisted, managing to stay on her feet. Surprisingly, had she been wearing her normal clothes, it wouldn't have been so easy a feat.

Crinoline and petticoats are good for something.

Breaking the kiss, despite the protesting moan Lawrence emitted, Bobby straightened, and he must've seen something in her eyes—perhaps the request he let her do her worst—because then he quirked his head, and settled back down, waiting, his eyes glittering with need, and anticipation.

She stood there for a moment, just, taking him in, because in his evening dress, his hair dishevelled from her fingers, lips glistening and swollen from their kiss, the firelight dancing across his skin and casting him in that irresistible warm glow... Well it felt an image she needed to commit to memory.

Just in case.

Once she had, praying silently the image *would* remain with her, always, not be lost as so much was to time, she reached behind her, untucking the bunch of strings from inside the bodice, then unknotting it—in what she hoped was at least a *slightly* seductive manner, despite the contorting necessary to the task.

If Lawrence's licking of lips, and clenching hands into the settee's upholstery were anything to go by, it was.

She continued, until she had loosened the bodice enough to remove it. Then she set to work on the skirts, and crinoline, until she stood before him dressed only in her corset and underclothes.

This will be much easier now.

Coming to stand before him again, she nudged his legs apart so she could stand between them, noticing the rapid rise and fall of his chest. The hunger on his face was hard to miss, but he was letting her do what she would, and that relinquishment of power and control made her heady. Or perhaps that was just Lawrence.

Bending over—so close his breath fanned on her cheek though she did not let their skin touch—she slid her hands under his coat, over his shoulders, so she could slip it off him. He moved only so she could take it away, lifting his back and nudging her neck with his nose, his own sharp inhale of her skin tickling, and heating her all at once. After folding, and setting his coat on the chair with her own garments, she returned to him, and continued her work.

Temptingly, teasingly, stroking every inch of yet to be uncovered skin, she relieved him of his waistcoat, cravat, and shirt. Kneeling, she made quicker work of his shoes and socks, then rid him of his trousers and under things. She took a moment once she had to admire her work, and the striking figure she'd revealed. It wasn't as if she hadn't seen him in all his naked glory—for it was glory, something to be revered and celebrated—but this was different. Him sitting there, all luminescent skin and sinew and muscle, a god of old, on a settee, in his house…it was profoundly more intimate. The intrusion of the world—the furniture, the house—made it all more of a…conscious choice. To be with him thus.

Once she'd drunk her fill, she knelt before him once again, her hands running up his thighs, cupping his hips, and beckoning him forward a little. He followed her command, sliding lower, closer, his eyes hooded as he watched her, sucking in breath, after breath, after breath, through his nose. His hands rose to the back of the settee, giving him more of a relaxed air—or at least it might've had his knuckles not been white as he clutched the carved wood.

His head lolled back, and he inhaled sharply when she finally put him out of his exquisite torture, taking him in hand, and guiding him to her mouth. His thighs tightened where her forearms rested on them, and he fought the instinct to thrust. Letting one hand travel up his chest, fingers dancing through the light dusting of curls, over the ridges and valleys of ribs, and stomach, she tightened her hold on his steel, warm, and silky in her palm, then began to love his baser self.

Closing her eyes as she sucked, and kissed, and nipped, and laved, exploring this part of him as she had the rest of him, running her tongue along his veins, catching the wetness which escaped him—salt, and musk, and yet the most delicious ambrosia—she slowly edged him closer to ecstasy. She listened to every moan, every growl; felt every muscle strain, and followed the directions his body gave her, repeating that little twist of her hand, or that swipe of her tongue around the engorged head of him. His hips rose and moved with her despite his attempts at control, not that she minded. She was cautious of how deeply she took him, but otherwise, let him explore her mouth with this flesh.

His pants grew harsher, shallower, and she ran her fingers over his nipple.

'Bobby…' he ground out. 'Bobby…'

She knew the warning he gave—and she was grateful, but she didn't relent.

Only kept on as she had, until he released himself inside her mouth, and she drank all he had to give. Still, she did not release him until his pulsing shaft was empty, and he was melting into the settee, loose-limbed and sated. Then, she released him, kissing him once more on the tip, before rising, and settling herself across his thighs.

With as much speed as he could muster, he embraced her, his arms holding her tightly to him as she nestled into the crook of his neck, peppering tiny kisses on the scruff there. And when he'd recovered a little more, his hand moved to its favourite spot at the back of her neck, and he guided her to him, kissing her with a bruising possessiveness she'd not quite felt before.

Breaking it after what might've been minutes, or hours, he held her face close to his, his other hand coming to cradle her cheek, his thumb tracing the line beneath her eye.

'You have the power of the gods in you, Bobby Kingsley,' he said, awe in his voice that made her heart skip a beat. Or maybe it was the use of *both* her names— together. Reconciled, for perhaps the first time. 'The power to reshape worlds.'

She frowned, unsure of his meaning—other than it was *good*, but before she could ask anything, he kissed her again, a man possessed.

A man on a mission.

If anyone had ever asked him whether a woman pleasuring him with her mouth would make him feel as though he was experiencing some manner of faith-restoring religious ecstasy, Lawrence would've laughed in their face. Likely for hours. Only he'd never been pleasured that way before by Bobby. And somehow, it did feel as what he imagined a faith-restoring religious experience would.

It wasn't that she was *very* good at what she did, it was…the intimacy. The care, the devotion behind every lick, every stroke, every touch. She consumed him, in every possible meaning of the word, and he realised that first time he'd lain with her, he hadn't been wrong. Being with her, sharing pleasure with her, it was beyond anything he'd ever felt before. And it went beyond compatibility or attraction—or at least that which was physical. Especially tonight.

He couldn't explain it, and he didn't want to. He didn't want to know the *why*, the meaning of it all, and that was a first for him. He didn't want to understand it, cheapen it all with words, and logic. He just wanted to feel. *That* was what he meant when he'd said she had the power to reshape worlds. Because she had reshaped *his*. Not just tonight, but every minute they'd spent together, as if she were breaking down the stone walls of his fortress, and carrying them off to build something new. Something better.

He liked it.

It seemed a very poor, simple word, but that's all his brain could conjure up.

He was too lost in Bobby to think much at all. He kissed her with every ounce of passion he'd never known he could possess, thanking her for all she'd ever given him, and giving what little made him, to her. Clumsily, his damned hands shaking again, he searched, then thankfully found, the strings of her corset. He untied them, though he was entirely sure they would be profoundly knotted when she found them tomorrow.

Impatient, possessed, by this feral, and primal need to possess her—as she possessed him, drove him to do her bidding, to be hers, for as long as she would let him—he tore what remained of her clothes off her, and then settled her back on his lap. The thought struck him, that he should be taking her to bed, enjoying the downy comforts of it, but at the same time, this felt more…them. As if they could love each other like this, any time, any place.

Kissing her again, for he couldn't breathe if he didn't, he cradled her buttocks with one arm, holding her close, as his other hand sought out her breasts, and *yes, those delectable nipples*. He caressed them for a moment, then, unable to resist any longer, he lowered his head, and suckled, teased, nipped, until *she* was gasping, arching and offering more of herself. His hand on her hip tightened, and he felt her buttocks clenching, as her legs hugged him tightly.

He feasted on her flesh, her glorious skin, everywhere he could find for a long time, the scents of their coupling rising between them, filling the air with a powerful, lustful potency that set him on edge. Finally, he was ready to rise to the occasion again, and he brought her closer, releasing the breast he'd been paying very close attention to for a moment, so he could guide himself into her.

When he did, the breath which escaped them both was, he thought, the breath of life. The first, supposedly given to man. The beginning of all things. Bobby tore the next from him, before leaning back, her hands on his knees, her whole self offered out to him. He took all she gave, reverently, aware of the preciousness of her. It wasn't lust that drove him—not entirely. With her rising and falling as she did, rolling her hips in tandem with his thrusts, the slick heat of her caressing, cradling, and worshipping all at once, it certainly felt more than a mindless quest for pleasure.

It was a rite. Of passage, of prayer. An act of true devotion, true worship.

He didn't have time to find the meaning, the words he truly sought, seemingly on the tip of his tongue, but ever unreachable, because it was all just too overwhelming. She clenched around him, nails digging into his legs as her voice echoed against the walls of the drawing room. He felt as if he was tearing his own flesh when he removed himself from her—but he had promised, and he would never betray her trust—releasing onto her belly and breasts with a groaning cry of his own.

She collapsed against him, sweat and seed mingling and tying them together once again, and he held her tightly to him, wondering how in the Hell he was ever going to do without her when the end came.

Chapter Nineteen

The enclave they'd created in the drawing room, was, in Bobby's opinion, perfect, and complete with everything they could ask for—food, drink, fire, pleasure—and Bobby thought it felt almost a world in itself, a place where she could happily end her days, though she would miss Arion, among other things.

However, once they'd finally untangled themselves from each other, Lawrence had made a good point, in that the drawing room lacked other *necessities*. And before she could even say a word, offer to leave though that was the last thing she wished to do, Lawrence had slung her onto his back, and somehow contrived to gather all their things into a pack made out of her crinoline. Meanwhile, she was charged with transporting the pack of victuals he made out of a napkin, and a decanter of claret.

Once they were ready, he brought her upstairs to his bedchamber, and after adding fuel to the fire, they cleaned each other—which took longer than it might've on their own, because of all the stolen kisses and touches—took care of their personal needs, then snuggled into the impressively large bed dominating

the room, packed with downy pillows and blankets.
Famished again, they feasted on their makeshift picnic,
and once sated, merely lay there, together, as they were
now, Bobby nestled in the crook of his arm, staring at
the dancing shadows on the ceiling.

Unwilling as she was to acknowledge it, she couldn't
deny that something had profoundly changed between
them. Between their earlier conversation, coming here,
the way he'd...taken her in the drawing room. Things
had felt different with Lawrence from the beginning—
the ease and the simplicity had terrified her—but now,
it felt as if there was something greater behind it all.
Something that transcended pleasure, and for which
she had no words. How did you know which word to
use if you didn't know what the word was meant to explain and define?

A conundrum, if she'd ever encountered one.

A fearsome mystery if she'd ever encountered one.

'I know we should be attempting to get some rest,'
Lawrence said softly, breaking the silence, but not truly
breaking, as his voice seemed to blend in with the summer night itself. 'Considering we have an early start in
the morning. However, I feel a long sleep tonight simply isn't in the cards.'

So she wasn't alone in feeling as if every nerve in
her body was still vibrating, and alive, and all the world
was there, *right there*, for them to grasp and enjoy with
all their might.

Or perhaps not the world, merely life itself.

'Tonight was a party,' Bobby pointed out. 'In my
experience it is most unseemly to end the revelry too
early...'

Lawrence chuckled, and she turned into him, and
grinned against his chest.

'I will defer to you, then, as my experience in most recent years has been more limited, I am sure.'

'Did you just say I was right?' Bobby asked, propping herself up so she could look at him, making her very best *excited surprised* face. Raising a brow, he shook his head. 'You did. That is certainly what it sounded like.'

'I said nothing of the sort.'

Bobby shrugged, settling back into her cosy spot and he laughed.

'Agree to disagree,' she muttered. 'Why don't you go to parties much?' she asked after a long moment.

She thought he might not answer—she had a feeling already of what that answer might be, and should be sorry for picking at what could possibly be old wounds—but at the same time, she had shared so much, and he had too, only…

I am greedy. I want more.

I want it all.

'In my, sadly not limited experience, they are merely a necessary evil.' Bobby's fingers ran lightly down his side, as she waited for him to continue. 'It was always made clear to me that parties were merely a means to an end. A way to make, or foster connections. Even at school…it was all about meeting the right people. Then, it was about finding a wife. Cultivating business relationships. Add to that the fact I am easily overwhelmed when there are masses of people, and the result is a rather grim endurance of parties, as opposed to any sense of enjoyment. There's always this…pressure, to say, and do the right thing, to further your gains. So many things to think about at once, on a large scale… It's maddening.'

'I can understand that. With the exception of this evening, I admit I haven't had much stake at such events

before. And even when I was younger, once all the revelry had started, I had a tendency to escape the stuffy
ballrooms and abscond with the help to more interesting
locales. Other than that, most parties have been jolly old
things, where the only purpose was to amuse ourselves.
In that, I see now that I have been lucky.'

'My lack of enthusiasm for such social gatherings
was one of the things Milicent reproached me the most,'
he admitted hesitatingly.

'It doesn't bother me that you speak of her,' Bobby
reassured him. 'She was part of your life, Lawrence.'

Unbidden, however, a flash of jealousy coursed
through her, for another woman, long-dead, whom Lawrence had already confessed he hadn't loved, nor held
particularly dear.

Merely because the other woman *had* been a part of
his life, good or ill. In the end, Bobby would perhaps
be able to lay claim to being a footnote; not a chapter
as his late wife had been.

Though it didn't change the fact she *did* want Lawrence to share.

'You're the first person I've ever really spoken to
about her,' he confessed, and her heart clenched a little
for him then. 'My parents made their disappointment in
my ability to fulfil my duty clear, and their even greater
disappointment when I refused to take another wife
after she passed, inescapable. Then, they too passed,
and it is true what they say about me. I am rather too
much of a misanthrope for my own good.'

'I won't disagree with you on the latter point,' Bobby
teased, and he pinched her bottom lightly. 'Ow,' she
said, swatting him away lightly. 'You're making my
point for me, you know.' She felt him shrug, and gave
it a moment before she continued. 'What was she like?'

'Very beautiful, I won't deny that. Gregarious…she had this air about her, always laughing, and eager, and… It was attractive, I'll not deny that either. She was witty, and…all a viscountess should be.' Lawrence inhaled deeply, and Bobby focused on him, his needs, rather than the own pang of her heart at the mention of what a viscountess *should* be.

Because I neither care nor wish to be that.

Like love itself—it would require…too much relinquishment of self. Too much loss of freedom. Not that she'd thought about it.

Certainly not.

'I thought our differences would be good. Useful—making up for lacks in each other. I was wrong. She needed others to feel alive, I think. She needed parties, and attention, and lavishness. I…couldn't give all that. I tried—gave her the keys of the kingdom so to speak—and when she begged me to be with her, always, I did try. It apparently was never in the way she wished, though whenever I asked her how I should be, she said it meant nothing if I didn't *know*. I cared for her, she was my wife, and everything I was taught demanded I feel that at least, but… As I said, to me, it was a business arrangement. Attractive, enticing as she was, I didn't feel the passion she craved so dearly. The other side of her… I couldn't love her lacks, as one should. Her childishness, impishness, her manipulative demonstrations of affections… They ensured I could never love her. And for all her claims, I don't think she loved me.'

Silence engulfed the room, only it was, as it ever seemed to be with Bobby, a comfortable, freeing silence. Not one full of regret, anger, or guilt. Merely, contemplative. He would say he wasn't sure why he had just told her all about Milicent, except that he was sure. It came back to the same thing, reflected what she herself had said. His wife, had been his wife. Part of his life, for better, or worse.

And no, he hadn't spoken to anyone about it—after all they were his private affairs, his private failings. Yet he didn't fail to see now how it might've helped, to speak of it all to someone. To have someone he could speak of it all *to*.

A friend. Family. Someone…who cared for him.

Which, despite what he would say should anyone ask, he knew Bobby did. As he did for her. *Friends* seemed a poor choice of word, but only in that it didn't quite encapsulate *all* they were. Otherwise, it was a good word.

To him, at least.

'Why didn't you remarry?' she asked finally, tearing him from his etymological musings. 'Having gained that experience, wouldn't it have been easier to find someone who would agree to your terms? Create the partnership you sought? You said before…well, that is… I understand you don't wish to be a father, but as you've pointed out, it is considered a duty for someone like you. You've built…a legacy. Is that…enough for you? Does the knowledge it won't remain in your bloodline bother you at all?'

'No,' he said, with no uncertainty. 'I do have an heir—my cousin. A very hardworking, enterprising young chap I admit I don't know well, but that I know well enough. He will be a good Viscount Hayes when the time comes. As for remarriage…' Lawrence trailed off for a moment, putting his private thoughts into words, as he'd never before. 'Truth is, I married because it was expected, my duty, and the key to building a legacy. After Milicent died, and I was without a *direct* heir, I realised then that I had never truly wanted a child, and that there were other ways to create a legacy. To fulfil my duty to those under my care, and to the country. And if I am being *entirely* honest, I was scared. I've never truly trusted people, as a general rule, but after Milicent, wondering if the next person would decide to renege on the deal after it was sealed… I didn't feel I could do that. And I didn't want to sour things with my own distrust either.'

'If your parents had known, perhaps they might not have begrudged you your choice as fervently.'

'Perhaps… They were not cruel, or unkind, or un- feeling,' he said. 'I feel as if you should know that—that proper dues should be given. In fact, I admired them. Together, they were a most worthy team, and they did much to restore the prestige of the title, success of the estates, even build for the future, for me, and my leg- acy. They cared for each other, and they cared for me, I know that. Even if I heard things…felt things. That made me understand a child was their duty, never a choice. I think they wanted the best for me, and knew what a good marriage could be, only I didn't have it in me, and we didn't have the manner of relationship which allowed…frank talk, shall we say.'

'I think Lord and Lady Rothwakes loved each other,' she said thoughtfully, not dismissing his words, his thoughts, and feelings, but *sharing* as she was so often with him. 'His Lordship would look at her sometimes… One of the only things that's ever made me believe love isn't merely a fairy tale. Like the way couples would touch each other sometimes in the village. Or do things to ease the other's way. And they loved us too, Julian and I. I am lucky again in that respect, and I am glad that whatever your relationship lacked with your parents, that you felt cared for. Appreciated.'

'Did you ever wish to marry? To have children?' Lawrence asked, determined to ignore the little voice whispering that it wasn't merely the question of an objective party with no skin in the game.

He hadn't lied, there were reasons to his refusal to marry again.

And thinking of *marriage* and *Bobby* in relation to himself...that way lay madness, and danger. Because really, they'd known each less than a full week—discounting that first meeting at Rothwakes.

Thinking of marriage to *her* was then...frivolity, and nonsense, and besides, he hadn't even heard the woman's answer yet.

'The thought crossed my mind, it would've been hard for it not to with Lady Rothwakes,' she sighed. 'Not in a bad way, she never pushed for it, but she, and Lord Rothwakes both, did say that were that something I wanted, they could facilitate the search for a good husband. I tried to picture it,' she told him, her fingers idly tracing the spaces between his ribs, which was utterly distracting. 'However... Every time I did, I couldn't quite reconcile what my life was, how I liked it, what I did, what I *do*, and married life. That picture, void of what I loved...it didn't feel right. As for children... I've never felt that desire, strong, and unrelenting for some of my own. Perhaps for the same reasons—I enjoy my freedom, my independence too much. Though, I admit, I should like to fall in love someday,' she whispered. 'It seems to be a most extraordinary thing.'

'From all I've heard tell of it, it does,' he agreed.

Because it did.

He wasn't entirely certain he would recognise it for

what it was, considering how long he'd gone without knowing it—*romantic love* at least—but he did agree that it seemed to be a rather grand adventure.

Though he'd never considered himself the adventurous type, after this whole experience, he thought perhaps he should rethink that.

'I have a confession to make, Lawrence,' Bobby said seriously, so seriously his heart jolted.

With fear?

Hope?

All of the above?

Before he could figure out precisely what had prompted the jolt—and what he wished her words to be, she continued.

'I'm not used to speaking of my feelings. I *don't* speak of my feelings. But I've never been scared of them before. Until you. I'm not saying…*that*,' she specified, as if her admitting she had contrived to fall in love with him was the most terrible prospect in the history of the world. He should've thought it to be—after all, this…relationship didn't even truly have a name, though perhaps *affair* worked rather well—but he didn't. 'Much to my own regret, I do like you, though; care about you. But when I'm with you… It feels too easy. Too normal. Too comfortable. Too *right*,' she said, and hadn't he rather thought the same? 'And nothing in this world is all of those things. So, it terrifies me—because how does that end? How terrible will the other side of all this be?'

Lawrence sucked in a breath, her words hitting him deeply.

Her trust, her vulnerability, her courage in voicing such things, eviscerating him in a manner he'd not thought possible.

Truth be told, he'd thought about the end, of course

he had. As a faraway, distant, simple thing. The marker at the end of a book. The lines at the edge of a map. He'd never thought about, *considered*, the other side. The end as a tangible thing he would have to face, and endure, and live with. He'd refused to recognise its inherent ugliness, and terror.

Now that he'd been forced to, he realised that he couldn't fight it. Realising he cared for Bobby, wished to have the privilege of caring for her, didn't change the facts. What seemed a lifetime ago, he'd contemplated what realising his care for her meant. If it meant a change in the way forward. Now, however, as various possibilities flitted through his mind—working with her regardless of who won this bet, even offering her a long-term lovers' arrangement—he realised fighting the natural end of what they had now, would be denying the reality of what they had. Their situation, their differences, their diverging future paths. The fact that at no point had Bobby expressed a desire for things *not* to end, expressing in no uncertain terms that her freedom, her independence, were paramount to who she was.

Though, he could damn well make the end easier than Bobby promised it would be.

'I don't know,' he answered her. *Truth. It can be painful, but it certainly paves a smoother road.* 'I have no idea how terrible the other side of all this will be. Be sure, however, that you will not face it alone. We shall both be confronted with its ugliness.'

A nod, her silky raven hair, now completely devoid of curls, sliding across his chest.

He didn't really dare say any more, or even look at her.

Instead, he rolled her over, and showed her that he too, cared, and liked her, really, rather a lot in fact.

Chapter Twenty

Last night had certainly given Bobby a lot to think on. Which considering how full her mind had already been with *thoughts*, was quite an extraordinary feat. Some part of her considered chastising herself for saying all she had. Speaking of *feelings* and *liking* and all the rest was, as she'd told Lawrence, not in her habit. And she didn't want him to think she was asking for anything— at least anything more than what they already had.

Something had shifted between them last night though she couldn't put a name to it. Heavens knew she'd tried this morning as she'd shuffled out of his home and back to Julian's before the lamplighters had even come to do their duties. Wandering the deserted streets, the dark purple of the morning eerie and dreamlike, her dress under her arms, a borrowed coat of Lawrence's over her undergarments…she'd felt freer, happier, *lighter* than she had in a long, long time. As if her heart had wings, or floated like one of those great balloons inside of her chest, lifting her up. Not even having to scratch at the servant's entrance to be as discreet as possible when she returned to Julian's had dimmed her mood. Though she had been careful to be changed, and out well before she could chance to meet him.

It wasn't that she was avoiding him—after all Arion did need to warm up before the day's ride, and she needed to get everything ready for the day ahead—it was just... She didn't want to have to explain herself. She didn't want to have to explain her behaviour to Julian—who she was quite certain would have something to say about her precipitous departure the night before—and she certainly did not want to have to explain to him what was happening between Lawrence and her... Because...

Because it was none of his business.

Right.

It wasn't as if she was breaking rules or anything. It wasn't as if she was ashamed, only she was a bit... protective. Or private. Yes, she was merely being private. Discreet.

It's my business, not his.

A sound caught Bobby's attention, and she looked up to find Lawrence and Beowulf striding into the stables. Hell, how had she forgotten where she was? She'd been like this all day, ever since she'd left his bed—not reluctantly, only it was ever so comfortable, and he looked so inviting, lying there on his belly, naked to the waist, and that was all there was to the pang she'd felt in her heart when she'd snuck away from him—barely paying more attention to the ride than she needed to, to be safe and ensure they made good time.

Grunting and nodding when the solicitors marked her time and took her plan for the following day. The most conscious she'd been was when she'd decided to wait a few minutes here, in the dry warmth of the stables before setting out to find a spot for the night ahead—and no, she hadn't been waiting for Lawrence. Merely giving herself and Arion a moment more before heading into the misty spray that relentlessly fell from the sky.

And which made Lawrence look, rather than worse for wear—as she was sure it did her—utterly…

Breathtaking.

He literally stole her breath, and she could do nothing but stare as he came and tucked Beowulf next to Arion, planting himself before her. They both just stood there, wedged between the horses, and smiled like dim-witted fools at each other.

Clearing her throat, Bobby stepped into him even closer, teasingly taking out his pocket watch, and glancing at it.

'Twenty minutes,' Bobby managed to say in a voice that didn't betray her breathlessness. She whistled—that was a rather large margin. *So he's not too much of a distraction after all…* The thought warmed her. She could have it all—for now at least. 'And on one of the shortest runs… Tsk-tsk.'

'What would Madam care for for dinner this evening?' he asked, mischief glinting in his eyes as she slid his watch back into the pocket of his waistcoat.

The glint matched the sheen of sparkling specks all over him, giving him the luminescent quality of a fairy king or something.

'Surprise me?'

'If you promise to return that coat you stole from my closet…'

'I would do no such thing. How dare you call me a thief, sir?'

'So Barnes was wrong in reporting it missing? And

you traipsed across Mayfair in your undergarments then? What a sight that must've been...'

The grin that appeared on his lips was more than dangerous.

He leaned down, and Bobby tilted her head towards him, ready for—

'Bobby,' came Julian's voice, harsh, and somewhat reprimanding.

Like a bucket of ice water, it sent chills down her spine, covering her in gooseflesh.

She knew that tone well, it was the same as his father's, the one old Lord Rothwakes had used when she trampled mud on the rugs, or pushed boys into streams for being horrible. Lawrence stiffened, not moving away so much as putting space between them, albeit unnoticeably.

Bobby found she didn't like it, not one bit.

'A word with you. That is, if you wouldn't mind, Hayes.'

Lawrence's eyes met hers, and she saw the question in them.

Though she appreciated the silent offer, she nodded, telling him to go.

That she would be all right.

At least, she hoped so.

Whatever Julian was going to come up with, she had a feeling she wouldn't like it.

Probably why you avoided him all day...

'I'll be by the old castle road,' Lawrence whispered before he moved away.

Steeling herself, she watched Lawrence take Beowulf and leave, then Julian come to stand in the stallion's place, not missing the look of utter unguarded enmity they shot each other.

Idiots.

Not that she didn't understand it, the history between them, between the families, Hell, not so long ago she would've shot Lawrence such a glare.

Only I've since got to know him.

'Should I be worried about you, Bobby?' Julian asked after a moment.

'No,' she told him flatly.

Mostly truthfully.

'Let me rephrase,' he said, and there it was again, that *tone*. 'I am worried about you.'

'Don't see why,' she shrugged, moving to check the packs on Arion, though she'd already done that, focusing on the items within, the heat of her horse, anything rather than the feelings in her breast. Combativeness, defensiveness, and a smidgen of, not quite shame, but something close to it. Not that she had anything to be ashamed of, she reminded herself. *Quite right.* 'If I keep up my times tomorrow, we'll make it to the final portion with no clear winner. You know as well as I do that Arion and I can take that with our eyes closed.'

'You've done me proud on this race, Bobby,' he admitted, and she glanced over to find him leaning, arms crossed, against the tying post. 'Not that I ever doubted your abilities. It's not the race I'm worried about. It's you.'

Sniffing, Bobby shrugged again, moving to Arion's front, giving him a nice scritch on his forehead, before facing Julian, arms crossed, the dampness of her clothes, the chill they held, somehow helping her to feel grounded, to tamp down what she instinctively felt was coming.

Not that she wouldn't make it any easier for Julian.

Not that I want to hear any of it.

'You disappeared last night,' Julian said seriously.

'And I don't need to ask to know where you were. I'm not entirely stupid.'

'It's none of your business.'

'It is, actually,' he bit back. 'For better or for worse, you are my friend, and my family, Bobby. All I have left.' Swallowing hard, she felt her eyes drop against her will. True, she'd always felt that way, but they didn't speak of such things, say them out loud, and with his recent distance, it had been easier to forget the bonds tying them together. The loyalty, the love. 'Last night, there I was, trying to vaunt your merits, connect you with people who can help you, and you just *ran* off! All for what? *Him*? Did you ever think perhaps he wanted you out of there?'

'I left because *I* needed to,' she ground out fiercely. She wished she could explain it all to him, as she had to Lawrence, but despite the closeness and intimacy she and Julian had shared all these years, she didn't feel he could understand. At least, not as he was now. *In his stubborn, judgemental mood.* 'I appreciate what you tried to do for me, I do,' she continued, tamping down her aggression. 'Last night proved a little more than I could handle, that's all. Lawrence had nothing to do with my departure other than aiding me.'

'You don't know him, Bobby—'

'And you do?'

'I know he's ambitious,' Julian pointed out, straightening as quickly as he could with his crutches. 'I know he's an arrogant ass who'll stop at nothing to get what he wants. I know he's a bitter, jaded widower, and I know that he's a man who values his name, his reputation, above all else, and has a very clear idea for his future. And I know there is no way you could ever factor into that, no matter what he may have promised you in the dark of the night. He doesn't have it in him to commit to you. Even if he did, he wouldn't, because you're not the viscountess a man like he needs to achieve what he wants. You're not even the mistress a man like he needs. I'm sorry, but it's the truth.'

'You think I don't know that?' Bobby said quietly, proud of herself for not letting any of the hurt swelling in her breast now be heard, or seen. There was... too much to consider right this moment. Not only about Julian's summation of Lawrence—but about his words altogether, the cut they were. 'What do you think, Julian? That I'm fawning over him, waiting for him to propose marriage or some such nonsense?' As if she didn't know she was not made of such stuff as viscountesses—or even *proper* mistresses—were. All the hurt from before—from trying so hard to be Miss Kingsley, and failing—resurged, though she fought to keep Lawrence's words from the previous night in her mind. *She loved me. I was never meant to be a lady. I was never meant to be a lady...* 'I won't deny we've been spending time together, you and I have never hidden such things from each other,' she continued, pushing it all in her mind so she could...get rid of Julian. Once upon a time, it had been the two of them, against the world. The two of them, able to speak and share, now it seemed, a gulf separated them. 'But you should know, I carry no illusions, no desires for more. I've barely known the man a week! When the race ends—however it ends—we shall all go on to live our own lives, and that shall be the end of it.'

Perhaps Julian did sense some of the wound within her, for his expression softened, and he stepped—*hopped*—forward.

'What I said... You know I don't mean it against you.

I just don't want to see you get hurt,' he breathed, almost pleadingly. 'I love you, Bobby.'

'I know. And I love you.'

She nodded reassuringly, and he studied her for a moment before doing the same.

'Mama would've loved this,' he muttered, and the mention of Lady Rothwakes made Bobby's heart clench. 'She probably would've had my hide for not thinking of letting you run it to begin with, but she would've been so proud. Father too.'

Bobby heard the tightening of his voice, and she looked away, damned tears pricking her eyes again.

She heard him take a breath, felt his hesitation, before finally, she heard him leave.

Inhaling deeply, Bobby closed her eyes for a moment, forcing her body to relax. She hadn't even realised how tight every muscle had been, not until she breathed, and released her arms, every inch of her pulsing and stiff.

Arion nudged her shoulder, and she turned to him, running her fingers along the lines of his face, and smiled.

'It's all a bit of a mess, isn't it?' He huffed, sending strands of her hair flying about her, and she laughed. 'Yes, I do know I made the mess myself, thank you very much.'

Arion huffed again, and she nodded, her fingers still gently caressing him.

She did know she'd made a bit of a mess; just like she knew all the rest.

That Her Ladyship and Lord Rothwakes would've been proud. That Julian is; that he loves me. That he's trying to protect me. That when this race ends—we'll all move on with our own lives. That whatever is between Lawrence and I is not meant to last.

And that was all how it was meant to be. She'd meant what she said to Julian—she'd never had any illusions as to…anything more with Lawrence. How could she when it wasn't something she'd ever wanted for herself?

Commitment. Something lasting.

And yet, somehow, the stark reminder Julian had given her, it chafed. Not solely because he'd pointed out her unsuitability for anything more than a temporary mistress, but because…

I hadn't quite got around to envisaging the ending of this.

Yes, that was it. Despite talks of endings the night before, truth was, she'd been so wrapped up in the pleasure, the fun of it all—been so wrapped up in the moment—that she hadn't pictured the end of it as she normally always did. These past days had seemed to go on for ever—this whole race seemed to go on for ever—but in a *good* way. Something within her had merely…got swept away.

But now it is nearly over.

And you cannot lose sight of the prize.

Quite right.

'Quite right,' she told Arion, kissing his nose before untying him, and leading him outside. 'I'm going to fix this my friend,' she promised him, before mounting up, refusing to acknowledge the rather horrid feeling in her heart.

Because it had no value, no merit.

Told her nothing.

Only that endings were sad, and unpleasant things.

Nothing more.

All the while he built up makeshift shelters, for Bobby and himself, and for Beowulf and Arion—which didn't require much considering he'd found a rather nicely protected spot in a copse of old oaks—as he shot and prepared the four pigeons, then cooked them, Lawrence had a rather unpleasant feeling in his gut. Some might call it premonition—he merely assumed it was a wariness of what he believed to be the logical reason behind Rothwakes' desire to speak to Bobby.

Me. Us.

In a way, it was the man's right to confront it, and he had to admit he thought a little better of Rothwakes for him having chosen to speak to Bobby. Not come to him, to threaten him, or demand he wed his...friend or whatever she was to him. Demand that he leave Bobby alone. It was the woman's choice, and his, what they did or didn't do. They were adults.

Even if he did suppose Rothwakes was allowed to offer his thoughts, and counsel, as a friend. To Bobby. Certainly not a friend to Lawrence.

Shaking the unpleasantness of that possibility off him, Lawrence returned to his pigeons, reassuring himself that there was no reason to worry so about anything. Or everything. Bobby seemed to encompass both of those.

And speak of the she-devil...

The grin on his lips died almost as quickly as it arose, and it felt as if it had never been there at all. Lawrence tried to reassure himself again, that really, until the woman said anything, he couldn't know what was on the horizon, what she felt. Only, she seemed...*distant*. More so, if it were possible, than that first day.

Oh, outwardly, she did as had become her habit, took care of Arion—even settling him next to Beowulf—took care of herself, and sat down beside him, warming her pale little fingers by the fire for a moment. To the untrained observer, all was the same about her as it always was.

Except that Lawrence was a trained observer of Bobby now. Bobby, who could never truly hide what she felt or thought, no matter how hard she tried. She wasn't built for it.

Like those hunched-over shoulders, and that tight, clicking jaw. The darkness in her normally luminescent depths. The patently determined way she pretended all was well.

Only I know better now.

'These look delicious,' she said casually, but there was categorically nothing casual about the way she said it. It was forced. As if everything within her was tight, and being pulled in a multitude of directions. 'Thank you, Lawrence.'

Even the way she says my name.

It does not feel the same.

He studied her as he plated a pigeon and passed it to her.

An outside observer might have also thought she looked him in the eye when he did, but they would've been wrong again. She'd looked in the general direction of his eyes for a split second, offered a whispery excuse of a smile, but she'd not *met* his gaze.

She never backs down...

'What did he say to you?' he asked hollowly.

No point in trying to dissimulate his fear, his pain.

Never with her.

'Nothing I didn't know,' she told him flatly, picking at her food, but barely ingesting any of it.

'Like what?'

'That beyond Monday, there will be nothing left to tie us together.'

True.

They'd discussed the ending of this last night, so of course that was true, and they weren't blind to it, but still, the statement somehow bothered him. Immensely. Beyond reason.

And what precisely should I do about it?

'We both knew that when we began…whatever this is,' he said slowly, voicing his thoughts, unsure of what else to do at this point. 'We discussed it last night, even. And though it is an unpleasant prospect, I admit I'm confused as to why you sound so resentful of that fact.'

He'd thought…

Well, he'd thought she would have no reason to be resentful of it.

That clearly defined limits, a clearly defined temporary relationship, that those were things she wanted.

'I'm not resentful,' Bobby snapped, and he raised an eyebrow. Sighing, she set down her plate, and remained silent for a long while, her face contorting into little grimaces as every thought flitted across her face—but he couldn't decipher them. 'Why would I be, when as you say, we discussed this, and nothing beyond the end of this race? I know where we stand, Lawrence,' she said coldly, and he wasn't entirely sure why that hurt so much. 'I think I just forgot…our deadline was nearly here. There's only one section left before the final race, and I… I'm too far behind still,' she said flatly, and that didn't sound right either. It sounded like the truth, but not *the whole* truth. 'If I don't thrash you thoroughly tomorrow, Lawrence… It'll all be over for Julian. For me, for everyone at Rothwakes. And I can't…'

That last part—that sounded true.

Heartfelt, and heartbreaking.

He'd be lying if he said they weren't distractions for

each other, that their companionship didn't—*hadn't already*—clouded his judgement and softened his resolve. He'd already made the decision to rethink the railway plans—not that he'd told her, how could he, when he'd made the decision only this morning, when he woke alone, in a bed still warm, and full of her scent?

How was that only this morning? It felt… So far, so different from where they were now, figuratively and literally. This morning, he couldn't wait until this very moment, when they'd have time together again. He'd not liked waking alone—without *her*—though he understood very well why she'd left. It had felt so different, so wonderful, like that morning at the pub, only last night she'd been in *his* bed—*his* home. It felt all of those things she'd said she felt with him.

Comfortable.

Easy.

Right.

Now, he wished he was back there, in London, and that this…

Hadn't come to pass.

But now that it had… Well. He would behave as he was. A gentleman.

He wouldn't ask her for more than she cared to offer, and he certainly wouldn't ask her to choose where her loyalties lay.

She already has.

'I understand,' he finally managed to say, softer, with less strength than he might've wished, but oh, well. Relief flooded her eyes, but also a pain he felt strike his own heart.

This is for the best. No use fighting. It was good while it lasted.

'Will you stay tonight?' he found himself asking—

asking not begging—though it would've been easy to confuse the two in this instance. 'We don't have to… It's just I've already built the shelters, and Arion is settled…'

Lawrence smiled wanly, and Bobby nodded.

They returned to their food, eating it, but without much enthusiasm, merely because they knew they should.

A long road ahead…

When they had finished, and settled in for the night, Bobby slithered under his blanket, and nestled in the crook of his arm. He cherished that moment, more than he might've otherwise, for he knew it would be the last time he was afforded such a privilege.

One of the most awesome of my life.

Chapter Twenty-One

Part of the allure of this race, had been the adventure of riding across England. Not only proving herself, and Arion, to the world, but also, the sheer wonder of riding from one side of the great isle, to the other. To see and experience things, she might never have otherwise. Oh, she saw glorious countryside everyday with her work, but it was different from being alone in it. Experiencing it properly.

Sadly, not the rolling hills, not the thick forests, not the mediaeval castles, flats full to burst of crops, nor the lush and noisy marshes of Kent were truly experienced that day. They were seen, noted, but not properly enjoyed, and Bobby wasn't oblivious to the fact that it wasn't just due to the pace she needed to maintain to properly make up her time.

Thinking back, had she really enjoyed any of the race? Experienced it? *Lived* it? She had in the moments with Lawrence, and she'd had good days of riding, but she'd let herself get so caught up in him, and *thinking*, and all that for what? Good memories of night-time trysts, and no answers. This race was meant to be the ride of a lifetime. The beginning of something extraordinary. Instead, it only felt like a grand old disappointment. Full of…heartbreak.

She knew it had been more than that, but the pain in her heart, the sadness she bore like a shroud today, even as she ran herself and Arion ragged… It clouded all the rest. Made it difficult to swallow.

She knew ending it with Lawrence had been right. For the final portion of this, she needed all her energy, all her strength, focused on the race. On what mattered. On the man who *would* be by her side when it all ended. On her family. On all those depending on her to secure their futures, *their* homes, *their* livelihoods.

Knowing it was right didn't help ease any of the bitterness of it. She'd known—told him—the other side would be terrible, and oh, how it was. She'd never felt this way before. Restless and listless and like she could scream for millennia and as if her chest was just too tight to breathe properly. She felt angry, and sad, and annoyed at herself, and…

Heartbroken.

It had been about the time she'd passed Canterbury that she'd had to accept that word. A word she'd never thought she'd use, save for perhaps if Julian passed before her. It was something she'd felt when the Rothwakes had died. A chilling, gut-wrenching, eviscerating pain born from loss. And no, Lawrence wasn't dead. What they'd had was. And so, the grief for that was different, but it was a sort of grief too.

Slowing to a trot as houses and church towers cropped up on the distant horizon, signalling their destination was nearing, Bobby inhaled deeply of the salty air, turning to watch the gulls cry and soar over fields of wheat and corn.

Why am I grieving something that never was?

The gulls, the sun, not even the breeze whistling through it all, seemed to have the answer. But Bobby knew the answer was essential. If she could only find *one answer* after all this…it had to be this one.

You're not. You're grieving what might've been.
What you wished there could be.

Her hands tightened reflexively on the reins as she sucked in a shaky breath, the pain not dull and aching, but sharp and stabbing now. Her eyes pricked with tears, and she forced herself to see through them. Arion tossed his head, and she came to, loosening her grip.

Dammit.

Not so clever after all, was she?

All this time… All this time, telling herself she didn't want *more*, that she didn't want commitment, a future… It had all been true. For so long. She hadn't lied when she'd said she imagined marriage, and children, and found that picture wanting, for all it lacked of what she wanted, and loved. She hadn't lied about fearing tethering herself to another, what she might lose and feel if she did. She hadn't lied about knowing where she stood, and what she could or couldn't be.

Except there lay the rub. Somehow, her feelings for Lawrence had…whispered to her. Made her desire, so deeply, and yet so unknowingly, *something* with him. Past tomorrow, past this race. Though she knew she was not made to be a viscountess as Lawrence would require, something inside her *wanted* to be. Because then…

We could have a happy ending.
Like those girls in fairy stories.

She'd never been one to believe in those, to grant them much credence as other women did sometimes. Because…they were just stories.

And it didn't matter that from the very first, she knew where she stood with Lawrence—what she could, and couldn't ever be—somehow, her idiotic, treacherous little heart had given birth to some equally nonsensical hope that it could be different. That she wouldn't have to live her life…alone. That she could live it *with him*. Commitment, sacrifice, those didn't sound so very loathsome when said in relation to him. Because it felt as if he would never…ask too much of her. Lawrence wouldn't ask for Bobby to be anything but herself, though Society might ask for the new Lady Hayes to be what she could never force herself to be, lest she die from the inside out.

The tears she'd held at bay flowed freely now, and she sniffed, wiping her nose on her sleeve. The gaping loneliness she'd ignored so long would not be ignored. As if there were truly a giant hole in her, aching to be filled. She'd never really felt lonely; after all she had the horses, she had Julian, she had friends down at the village. Only none of them, none of them filled an empty room at night. None of them gave her the kind of love she'd secretly craved all her life. Oh, they gave her love, and affection. And for a long time that had been enough, covered up the hole and made it less. Lawrence had somehow made it reappear, with a vengeance.

I wasn't lonely till I met him. Or maybe I was, because…

Because she wanted… To be in love. With someone. To share that romantic love, to build a future together. To trust, to have fun. To have picnics in drawing rooms, and speak of nothing and everything all at once, and burn fish, and make up stories, and fight with, and…

It wasn't only love I wanted. Not any love. There was

no hole in me until he came along. I wanted Lawrence.
I wanted to love, and be loved by him.

She didn't complete that thought with the rest of the logical conclusion. That was quite enough for one day. Instead, she tightened her thighs, and spurred Arion onwards.

Because none of it mattered now.

The answer changed nothing in the end.

It's all over.

'It's bursting in here,' Bobby commented once she finally managed to make it to the table where Matthews, Watkins, and Julian waited. Not just in here, but in the yard too, and on the road, leading here and into the village. The pats on her shoulder, great cries when she'd arrived, and encouragements shouted in her ear as she pushed through the throngs—of villagers, urbanites, and gentry—gave her a pretty good idea of why that was, yet she still couldn't quite bring herself to believe it. London was one thing…

This is something wholly different.

'Are they honestly all here for us?' she asked.

Matthews looked his usual stern self, Watkins beside himself, and Julian…

Looked relieved she was speaking in his general direction but not as self-satisfied as he might've otherwise been. And there was a glint of concern in his eyes as they swept over her, making her wonder if she still bore traces of her…emotional outburst.

Just ignore it.

'They are indeed,' Watkins squeaked, eyeing the room—though not much could be seen beyond a mass of bodies. 'Isn't it most exhilarating?'

'Best of luck tomorrow!' someone cheered, patting her as they passed her in search of more ale.

Dazedly, Bobby smiled and nodded, though she needed to get out of here, and fast.

This whole packed place was making her feel... dizzy.

Just breathe. This is good.

'Most exhilarating,' she said, smiling vaguely at Watkins.

'You've made good time today, Miss Kingsley,' Matthews noted. 'Depending on His Lordship's arrival, we may yet be tied for tomorrow.'

Nodding, Bobby ignored the knots in her stomach.

They had made excellent time—but as to whether her little incident in Dorset would officially cost them the race... As Matthews said, only His Lordship's arrival would tell.

I need to win the day by at least an hour...

'Regardless of the outcome, Bobby,' Julian said gently, grabbing her attention back. 'This,' he continued, gesturing to the room, 'proves the success of our endeavour. One way or the other. I know you'll give them a proper show tomorrow. I've already heard people fighting over where to watch from. You and Arion have many admirers.'

Bobby nodded again, the lump in her throat preventing her from speaking.

It was all just so much...

Heartbreak, hope, determination, excitement even, all mingling within her.

'If it isn't contrary to the rules, gentlemen,' she said, addressing the solicitors. 'I should like to remain here a while to see where His Lordship and I stand. I'll remain outside, and not sneak any victuals, not that I need any.'

'As you wish,' Matthews agreed begrudgingly. 'I see no reason to refuse.'

Watkins nodded as well, and Julian smiled at her.

A genuine smile, that of her friend, and she didn't have it in her to refuse him one back.

Knocking a fist on the table, she slowly made her way back out—nodding and smiling and muttering thanks to the well-wishers in what she felt to be a satisfactory manner—to Arion, who she'd left near a fence at the back of the inn, having no other choice as all the other horses and carriages were tied and packed into every available space.

Arion seemed generally unfazed by all the excitement when she checked on him—though he did have a rather quiet, secluded spot all to himself—and much as she wanted to go hide away with him somewhere else entirely, she needed to know whether they still had a chance at winning this thing.

Winning the future I always wanted—the only one I can ever have.

Not losing all I already have. All I have left.

Rather than stand there waiting, Bobby wandered around, unable to sit still. She kept to the boundaries of the inn, away from people best she could, though their support did lift her spirits somewhat. She'd just finished wearing down a neat path along a stream, when a familiar squeal caught her ear.

No. Arion.

Her stomach twisted and churned, as panic rose in her chest.

Something was wrong. Something was very wrong.

Running, scrambling, tripping and sliding, Bobby made her way back to where she'd left him, cursing herself for leaving him in the first place.

Two men were with him—rather well-dressed gentlemen—but their intentions were far from polite. They'd backed Arion against the fence, and something shiny glinted in one of the men's hands. She had no idea what they wanted—beyond hurting Arion—and she didn't care. Her blood ran cold as she raced up to them, even as white-hot rage clouded her mind and vision.

Arion bucked and reared, thankfully keeping the vermin at bay, and they were so intent on watching him, that they didn't see her coming.

Bobby launched herself at the closest man to her, the one with the shiny blade, throwing him to the ground before he could even register what was happening. Rolling them both over so she could straddle him, she punched him, and took hold of the blade, tossing it over the fence before someone got truly hurt.

Not that she didn't want to gut these bastards.

'Get her off me!' the man beneath her screamed, raising his hands to protect his face.

'You swine!' she screamed, aiming for other body parts, satisfying grunts escaping the man as she did. 'You gutless cretins! I'll—'

An arm banded around her neck before she could react.

So stupid.

She'd known there was another one, but she'd just been so focused on hurting...

The arm dragged her off the man on the ground, and back a few steps, until her elbow collided with his diaphragm. His hold lessened somewhat, enough to stop the movement, and she stomped on his foot hard as she could, swirling when he released her to throw her fist across his nose. It provided a satisfying crunch before the man bent over, but before she could finish her work, the maggot she'd left behind grabbed her wrist, twisting her arm around before she could stop him.

Clenching her teeth, she held steady against the pain, preparing to get herself out of this, once she had her footing—except her moment never came. The maggot was too quick. He shoved her face down into the earth, and a scream tore from her throat as she heard a sickening pop, and felt the worst pain she ever had before. It felt like tearing flesh—worse than a broken bone; worse than the likely broken bones in her wrist—and she was sure that feeling wasn't so far from the truth of the matter.

Tears sprang into the grass as she tried to clear her head, tried to find a way to get up, and fight, but there was a knee on her back now, and that pain… She thought she'd be ill, and faint all at once.

There was a shout from somewhere seemingly far away, and then seconds, hours perhaps later, the weight lifted from her back. She cried in relief then, not able to conceal any of it. She tried to move, but found she couldn't quite yet.

Arion squealed and shouted, and nickered, and she just wanted to go to him…

There were sounds of a scuffle, and then the unlikeliest face came into view.

It was the last thing she saw before she let the pain overtake her—take her to a place where there was no pain at all.

Barnes. My saviour.

Chapter Twenty-Two

While it took Bobby most of the forty-mile ride to determine the truth of her feelings, it took Lawrence only fifteen. He was making his way through a patchy, youthful, and rather sweltering forest, where no wind seemed to reach him, when he stiffened atop Beowulf, the full extent of his own short-sightedness hitting him like some divine bolt of lightning.

Ever since Bobby and he had woken, the chasm between them, dark, dismal, and nauseating, ever since they'd started off on the road, he'd repeated to himself that it was *all for the best*. That the ending, terrible as it was, was as inevitable as a sunrise. A fact they'd both known, and accepted.

So he'd repeated that it was *all for the best*, *hoping* the truth of it would sink in eventually, like a habit one acquired that became part of one's nature, until he made the mistake of adding *because* to the end of it.

All for the best because…

Because nothing.

Yes, they were a distraction for each other—take him getting hit by a low-hanging branch because he was pondering all this—and yes, it was likely best to put some distance between them until the race was over. That didn't mean an *ending* was for the best.

This whole time...

This whole time he'd been convinced, as she had been, that an ending was on the cards for them. Because he and Rothwakes were...rivals he supposed. Because she disagreed with him. Because they wanted different things from life. Because she valued her freedom and independence so much. Because neither wanted something more.

Only that was a load of bollocks.

He would endure Rothwakes for her. She might disagree with him, and he her sometimes, but they talked—*fought*—about it, and expressed themselves. They didn't want such different things from life. Just the chance to build something lasting of their own. And he, for one, wanted something more. He wanted to wake with her by his side, and to share adventures, and to watch her work with horses, and to...share a life with her. So, the only thing keeping them apart, keeping them from having more, was this conviction that was completely foundless.

Well, for him at least.

And he thought, for her, perhaps. She'd told him she cared for him, and liked him, and it had made her sad to part, he knew that, deep down. He'd seen what it cost her. He couldn't be entirely certain of her *thoughts* on the matter, but when one spoke of hurtful, terrible endings...when one was as distraught as she'd been last night when breaking it off... Well, it suggested perhaps she wasn't so keen on an ending after all. It suggested she hated it as much as he did. Perhaps, she too also felt this dizzying, blinding, glorious rush of unspeakable light as he did in his chest.

Is this love?

It certainly felt like what people had written, sung, about. Overwhelming, and fragile, and breathtaking, all at once. He couldn't be certain, having never experienced it before, but actually, well maybe he could.

He'd been right before. Love couldn't be forced. It *happened*—or didn't, as he'd thought might be the case for him—when it happened. It was a choice in some ways, but also, it wasn't. How unreasonable that argument was. Oh, how little he cared.

He loved Bobby Kingsley. The way she smelled, the way she moved.

The way she challenged him, and showed him all of who she was.

'I love her,' he laughed. 'I love her!' he shouted to the trees and the grasses and the birds.

Beowulf neighed, alarmed, but also Lawrence thought, agreeing.

Of all the wonders he'd expected to find on this road…love was certainly not one of them.

And I won't lose it.

Short-sightedness, a refusal to accept what he'd already felt blossoming in his heart, because it was irrational, and improbable—particularly given the short time frame of their acquaintance—had nearly cost him everything. But he could salvage this. He knew he could. He just needed…

He just needed to speak to Bobby.

Perhaps her own reluctance would fade away, if he lay his heart bare to her. If he offered her a future. She'd said she'd not envisaged marriage because of the life it would cost her, but he would never ask for her to cast away her dreams. He'd help her realise them.

If she didn't want marriage—which he found didn't

bother him so much if it was a love match, and not a business arrangement—well, he found he didn't mind that either. They could be whatever they wished. Society be bloody well damned. And as for her freedom, her independence, he would never ask her to relinquish them. Together…together they could build whatever they wanted.

Right.

This was a good plan. If she rejected him after that…well, at least he would know. The potential hurt of that…paled in comparison to the potential of losing her merely because he didn't speak up. If she truly didn't want him, fine, but if she did…it was worth looking a love-struck fool.

Emboldened by his discovery, eager to get to her—because he wouldn't wait until after the race to confess all this—he made rather exceptional time, right up until he encountered a flooded river it took him a while to safely cross without risking going too far off route. Still, no matter if it cost him the day, he was altogether too excited to let a little delay mar his mood. In the end, he didn't really care about the race. He'd have abandoned it right there and then, given Bobby all she wanted if he thought she'd be pleased and not flog him until kingdom come.

Lawrence was smiling like the love-struck fool he really couldn't deny he was as he and Beowulf bounded into the…rather packed inn yard. When people milling around shouted *congratulations*, and *huzzahs*, he understood they were all here for the race.

I'll be damned…

Unfortunately, his rather high spirits meant he had to give it to Rothwakes for making such a spectacle— even if using Bobby had been misguided. The man had made the best of a situation that could cost him everything, and Lawrence wouldn't deny that.

Leading Beowulf to the side of the inn, inclining his head and waving to onlookers, it took a moment for Lawrence to fully realise who precisely was calling him, and why it didn't sound excited, but rather panicked.

Frowning, he searched for the source, and spotted a familiar blur rushing towards him best he could with—

'Oh, God, no,' he breathed, releasing Beowulf's reins and rushing towards Barnes. 'No, no, no…'

Fear pierced his chest, bile rising as he approached, and saw the full extent of the harm done to her.

Bobby hung limply in Barnes' arms, one of her own hanging awkwardly away from her, cuts and bruises on her face and knuckles.

No, no, no…

'What happened?' he demanded as he met Barnes, his fingers hovering over Bobby, not wanting to cause more harm, but wishing nothing more than to touch her. 'What the Hell happened?'

Why?

He couldn't lose her. Not like this. Not before…

'I just came upon them—two of them against her,' Barnes wheezed. 'Trussed them up back there,' he said, gesturing behind him, and Lawrence's jaw clenched as he saw two men tied to a fence, both looking worse for wear. Lucky Barnes, and Bobby, had got to them before he could… 'She needs a doctor, I was just getting her inside—.'

'I'll take her, and get the others,' Lawrence said in a tone that brooked no argument. 'You stay with them. If they wake, you find out what the Hell happened. And take care of Arion, and Beowulf.'

Barnes nodded, and it took a moment to transfer Bobby between them, Lawrence wary of the loosely hanging arm.

He felt marginally better once he had her in his arms, and he even dared kiss her forehead as he turned to rush her inside. She was warm, thank God. Pale, and in terrible shape, but warm.

'You can't leave me, Bobby,' he told her gently. 'Not yet. We're not finished yet.'

Chaos met him after that.

People screamed and he shouted at them all to '*Get out of the bloody way!*' And then he was shouting some more, ordering everyone to *move now*, so he could find Rothwakes and the others. He did—his entrance enough to gather their attention—and Rothwakes paled when he spotted Bobby, anger flashing in his eyes as he met Lawrence's.

The crowd gasped around them, murmuring, and an eerie silence filling the packed inn.

'Hayes—'

'The men who did this are out back, with my valet,' he said before the man could accuse him of anything. If he did, Lawrence might very well take his anger out on him. 'She needs a doctor.'

'Bring her to my room,' Rothwakes said, clenching his teeth hard. 'Watkins will show you the way,' he continued, shoving his hand in his pocket, then passing his key to the overly eager solicitor, whose eyes were in danger of popping out of his head. Lawrence didn't waste a second, he followed the little man through the crowd, parting like the red sea for him, then upstairs. 'Who will fetch the doctor—assuming you have one in this forsaken place?' Lawrence heard Rothwakes shout to the crowd as he did.

And then he was away from it all, in the little baron's room, and he lay Bobby down on the bed, wishing there was more he could do.

More than just lay a blanket over her, and take her hand, and sit there, and wait.

He knew he should go out there, sort out everything with the men who had attacked her—something telling him instinctively this was *nothing* like the fight Bobby had started—but he couldn't will himself to move.

'Please, Bobby,' he whispered, stroking her hair, kissing her cheeks lightly. 'Please, come back to me.'

How long it was he remained there, pleading with her, and any mighty powers that may exist and still hold him in their grace, he would never know.

All he knew, was by the time Rothwakes and the doctor kicked him out of the room, and he went to find Barnes, Bobby hadn't stirred. She hadn't come back to him.

He didn't know what he would do if she never did— but he refused to think on it.

Already, his heart felt as if it might never beat again.

Chapter Twenty-Three

'I told you once, I won't bloody well say it again,' Bobby growled, snatching the bottle from the infuriating man who looked far too young to be a proper physician. Not that she was judging, only right this second, she was; or rather she was searching for any reason, no matter how unreasonable, to discard his words and orders. 'I won't take your damned laudanum, you've already done your worst, now off with you before I show you just how capable I still am!'

To punctuate her statement, she launched the vial across the room, until it shattered satisfyingly against the stone of the hearth.

Knowing what was best for his own safety, the doctor scampered off, and she made sure to glower at Julian who'd been hovering in the room this whole time, to ensure he didn't try something sneaky, before finally, she collapsed back into the soft nest of pillows with a groan.

Christ, that bloody hurts.

She let her eyes close, clenching her teeth against the hot, fiery pain radiating from her shoulder to the tips of her fingers. Better than it had been before, since the doctor had put her arm back into place, but overpowering nonetheless.

Dislocated.

Likely muscle tear.

Broken wrist.

All as she'd expected.

She heard Julian lumber across the room and settle in the chair by her bedside. A wave of love for him filled her; for being here now, for having held her hand, and her gaze, as the doctor had done his work. For having wiped the sweat off her brow, and for...

Everything else.

She was grateful to Barnes too, and would have to find him at some point, to thank him for saving her. There was no doubt it all could've been worse—terror still filled her heart at the thought of what might've happened.

To her, and—

'How is Arion?' she asked, her eyes flying open. 'They didn't hurt him, did they?'

Julian shook his head, and she relaxed again.

Thank you, Heavens above. Thank you, Barnes.

'He's fine. Nervous, and anxious, but settled, and being watched by Hayes' valet,' Julian reassured her. 'Bobby... I'm sorry.'

'This isn't your fault, Julian,' she argued, wincing as she sat up a little straighter.

'I should have known this could happen,' he insisted. 'Those men... They were some of many who bet on the outcome of this race. Apparently, they couldn't risk you winning, for they'd be ruined. If I hadn't gone to the papers, fed this frenzy...'

Bobby reached out with her good hand—the left— luckily on the side Julian was, and placed it on his.

Sighing he closed his eyes and shook his head.

'It's not your fault, Julian,' she repeated, firmer, and

he met her gaze with regret and concern in his eyes. 'You were trying to capitalise on this. I still don't agree with how you did… But you couldn't know. And it isn't on you. It's on those greedy bastards,' she spat.

He nodded, but remained unconvinced.

'Are you hungry?' he asked, still blaming himself, but intent on putting on a normal face, for her. 'Or would you like some mint tea? Are you still nauseous?'

'I wouldn't say no to some willow bark,' she smiling weakly.

Her head was pounding—though it was rather distracting from the rest.

'I'll fetch that for you,' he said, almost too eagerly. 'Well, I'll have it fetched, not like I can carry it myself. I need to find Hayes anyway. Likely pacing the corridor still, with the other vultures.'

Her heart skipped a beat at the mention of Lawrence, but then her mind registered Julian's words—and his resigned expression.

'When did Lawrence arrive?' she asked, and she knew Julian thought she asked for another reason—until he saw her face.

'Bobby, no,' he ordered, shaking his head. 'Don't even think about it—'

'Think about it? Why in the Hell do you think I refused the laudanum, Julian?' she cried. 'When did Lawrence arrive?'

Julian fumed in silence for a long while, until finally, he spoke the words she had hoped for—going against all he wished to, she knew.

'A little over an hour after you.'

Relief flooded her, and she let her head fall back, tears gathering in her eyes.

It isn't over.

I haven't lost. The race, at least.

'Bobby, please, for the love of all things Holy, for the love you hold for me, and that you held for mother and father, I beg you, don't do this.'

She met his gaze again, and he winced, tears in his own eyes—though for very different reasons.

'I'll forfeit regardless,' he told her, though he already knew better than to think that an option. 'I will tell them right now—'

'I will never forgive you if you do,' she said simply. Julian's eyes closed, tears tumbling down his cheeks—opposites in their origin from her own. 'If you take this away from me, I swear to God, Julian, the bonds between us will be shattered for ever.'

'Bobby, you were lucky tonight,' Julian hissed. 'Those men might've killed you. But you are here, now, and you will live. Don't risk that all for some stupid race. For Rothwakes. The estate means nothing if you are not part of this world, or if you suffer some other injury. Mama, Father, they would tell you the same. Hell, the servants and people working on the estate would tell you the same. It isn't worth it, please.'

'I don't care if I have to walk the last two bloody miles of this race myself,' she growled. 'I will finish it. For you, for Rothwakes, for your—*our*—parents. But most importantly, for myself. I'm not asking you to understand, and I'm not asking you to agree. I'm just asking that you not stand in my way.'

Pleading eyes met hers again, before he bit back whatever choice words he had to say, and left as much in a huff as he could, slamming the door as he did.

Bobby sank back into the pillows, taking a deep breath. To ease the pain in her body, and the clenching of her heart.

Was she being foolish?

Risking her life…for what?

Was this another case of fighting the wrong battle? Being so profoundly stubborn she couldn't see another way to the future?

No.

In her heart, she knew she'd meant what she said to Julian.

This was for her now. It had been, perhaps since the beginning. So many doubts, her whole life, had plagued her. Now…now she could prove to herself what she was truly capable of.

And if she didn't…she would regret it her life through.

I need to finish it.

Chapter Twenty-Four

The slamming of the door behind which lay the most important thing in the world jolted Lawrence from the worried stupor he'd let himself fall into as he paced the corridor, waiting for news, Watkins' and Matthews' eyes following his progress. The doctor had been and gone, but not tarried long after muttering something about *dislocation*, *broken wrist,* and *otherwise unharmed.*

The relief Lawrence had felt at those few words was unmatched by anything he'd ever felt before. Relief felt a cheap, and un-encompassing word for all he felt then, dizzying and fortifying all at once.

But then the doctor had gone, and Rothwakes was still not out of there, and as much as Lawrence wanted to force his way in, he knew he had to wait. He didn't even know if Bobby was up for visitors, let alone *him,* but he couldn't just leave all the same. He'd leave her for tonight, if she didn't want to see him, that was fine, because they had all the time in the world now. To speak, to talk, to…build a future.

If she'll have me.

Lawrence stood back as Rothwakes approached the

looming solicitors, looking as if he'd just been asked to personally clean all the chamber pots in the kingdom.

Frowning, he dared take half a step forward, to better hear what was being said.

'Unless Hayes takes umbrage with her staying the night here, that is a moot point, Matthews.'

All eyes turned to him, and he stared between them all, not understanding.

'Why should I take umbrage with Bobby staying at the inn?'

'Only two planned stops were to have indoor accommodations. Otherwise, the riders were to be on their own in the wild, so to speak,' Watkins offered hesitantly.

'None of that matters anymore,' Lawrence said dumbly.

'His Lordship will not forfeit,' Matthews said gravely, and Lawrence's eyes widened in surprise. What the Devil was the little baron thinking? 'And Miss Kingsley, though severely injured, is not *incapacitated*, it would seem. As it stands, tomorrow's race will decide the winner, unless you make an issue of the assistance given to Miss Kingsley, and her stay at the inn this evening. The circumstances surrounding her injury are... murky, in terms of the contract, therefore it would be left to your discretion.'

'You're making her race it?' Lawrence asked Rothwakes, aghast, and the little baron's fists clenched around his crutches.

'She refuses to let me forfeit,' he gritted out, and anger rose with Lawrence's breast.

The woman is...too stubborn for her own good.

'We'll delay it,' Lawrence offered, raising his hand when the solicitors made to speak. 'Considering the circumstances—murky, as you say—that shouldn't be excluded, but if I must I will forfeit and bloody delay it, I don't give a damn!'

'Tell her that,' Rothwakes sneered, lumbering over, even as Lawrence rushed to meet him, ready to pummel the idiot into the ground.

He'd not had the chance with the others downstairs—they'd been long gone, taken by the magistrate by the time the doctor had arrived and kicked him out of Bobby's room.

'For the best,' Barnes had muttered, and Lawrence hadn't been able to deny it. For all his talk of words and fists, pens and swords... Violence was all his heart asked for. He also hadn't been able to stop himself hugging the man, thanking him for saving the most precious being in his life. A being who now insisted on endangering herself.

Infuriating woman.

'If you care for her at all,' Rothwakes hissed, shaking his head in distaste at having to do this. 'You'll ask her to end it here.'

'As if she would listen to me,' Lawrence scoffed. Honestly, had someone else bashed this man on the head? Apparently, he'd completely lost his wits. 'You're her friend, her family. She ran this race for you. To save *you.*'

'You think I don't know that?' Rothwakes explained, earning an eye-raising from the solicitors. Clenching his jaw, he continued, at a slightly lower tone. 'I tried. I told her I didn't care about the estate, any of it. Still, she's determined to finish this, even if it kills her. I think she might listen to you, because for some unknown reason, she holds you in high esteem. I don't care if you have to get down on your knees and beg. If you feel *anything* for her, you'll put an end to this madness.'

With that, Rothwakes strode off down the corridor—well, limped and hopped—rage, desperation, giving him speed, and the solicitors followed suit, all heading downstairs for a likely needed drink.

Lawrence took a breath and pondered Rothwakes' words.

He *did* care for Bobby. He loved her, actually, and was more than happy to admit that now. He was terrified of what could happen if she competed tomorrow.

I could lose her.

But with all they'd been though... Could *he* convince her not to race?

I doubt it.

She was stubborn, to an unbelievable degree, and he didn't think anything he said would work.

Still, I have to try.

If he thought she wouldn't murder him, he would forfeit himself.

Only she would.

And then she would still finish the race.

Having taken a few minutes to properly collect himself, and try to make a plan, which he hadn't truly succeeded at doing—though he had to agree that perhaps kneeling and begging were solid options—Lawrence finally shook his head, raking his fingers through his hair, centring himself before he opened the door to her room, and strode in.

She looked...horrendous.

The dim light of the fire and candles cast her thankfully minor cuts and bruises in a harrowing light, and even though she was the same as she'd been hours before—injuries notwithstanding—she seemed smaller, more fragile, propped up in the mass of pillows and covers in the small bed.

Not that he'd ever tell her she looked fragile.

'Looks worse than it is,' Bobby said, not weakly, but with exhaustion in her voice she couldn't hide. He glanced up from the brace and sling on her arm to find her sparkling onyx gaze on his, one eye slightly narrower thanks to the puffy flesh on the cheek below it. 'I feel absolutely splendid.'

'That would be the laudanum,' he said, offering her what he thought was a congenial *we're-in-this-together* smile.

'Didn't want any of that,' she told him, and he shook his head as he reached her bedside, folding into the chair set there. 'Clouds the mind, and I'll sleep all night. I am thinking about asking Julian for some brandy, though. If he ever comes back. He promised me willow bark tea. I didn't start it this time Lawrence,' she said quickly, the need for him to know so blatant, it twisted his heart. 'They wanted to hurt Arion.'

'I know,' he reassured her, and she nodded. Taking a deep breath, he steeled himself for all the rest he had to do, to say. 'Rothwakes said you still intend to race tomorrow,' he continued flatly, not bothering to play nice, and offer her a moment's more respite.

'Why does that seem to be so unfathomable to everyone?'

'Because you can barely sit up in bed! How precisely do you intend to race two miles tomorrow? And lest you forget, tomorrow's race is bareback. The pain alone—'

'Is mine to bear, and mine to manage!' Bobby shouted, and Lawrence winced. 'How can you come in here, and ask me all this? You know I have to finish this!'

'Why? Rothwakes doesn't care about the estate, and if you do then *I* don't care,' he exclaimed. 'I'll pay his bloody debts, and give you the money for your farm, and we can just forget about this insanity!'

'You still don't understand,' she sighed, tears falling again, *Goddammit*. 'I have to finish this. For myself. Yes, I knew I could help Julian save Rothwakes, *yes*, I wanted to, to repay his family, and secure a future for myself. But in the end, none of that has been what it's been about. I think you know that. So you can't ask me to quit.'

'I have to ask you to quit,' Lawrence whispered, for fear of his voice breaking. This was nowhere near how he'd imagined this, but if it stopped her... 'I love you, Bobby. And I know there are a plethora of reasons I shouldn't. I've been so foolish, denying what I felt, calling it different names up till now. The truth is, at this point, I don't care if you don't love me back. You've given me so much already, taught me so much. But whatever you feel, I can't just stand by, and watch you put your life on the line without telling you *nothing* is worth that. I can't risk losing you because you won't quit.'

'You told me to be myself, Lawrence,' she said quietly, after a long moment, her gaze hardened—the surprise of his confession melting away. Though in the end it hadn't been so great—so perhaps she'd known it already. 'To do that, believe me when I say I have to finish this. Or I'll always wonder. Regret it. I'll never have the chance again, to show myself what I'm capable of. So, if you truly love me, you'll race me tomorrow. And you'll race harder, and better, than you ever have in your life. You'll respect my decision, and give me the goddamn courtesy of treating me like a fully formed person, who can make their own choices. Whether or not you agree with them.'

Everything within him rebelled.

The hurt of her seeming rejection of his confession, was buried, to be excavated and dealt with later.

Long after never.

What had he hoped by saying the words, telling her of his feelings? That she would say, *Yes, Lawrence, I'll quit, and I love you too, let us live happily ever after*? He hadn't even offered her anything past a declaration—no vows, no promises, not that he didn't wish to make any—so that possibility was already unlikely. Only, he had thought it might change something.

Unharden her heart perhaps.

Examine it all later.

For now, he needed to push past everything he'd been bred to be. A gentleman, a man by society's precepts, one who made decisions for those less able to.

The poor.

The uneducated.

Children.

The weaker sex.

It was all hogwash—he'd always known that. He wasn't anyone's better, and dictating another's life was immoral. Wrong, in so many ways. Yet in that moment, he felt as if he had to physically push it all away, comforting as it was to think he *should* be heavy-handed, in this matter at least.

Make the decision for her.

Do what *he* thought best for her.

Put his own desire—*to see her safe*—before any of hers.

But he did push it all away, all those immoral, yet

somehow, primal, urges, and nodded before rising to his feet.

'I'll race you tomorrow, Bobby,' he declared, not coldly, but starkly perhaps. Her eyes drifted closed, and she nodded in gratitude. 'I'll give you no quarter, no concession, as you ask.'

'Thank you,' she breathed.

A summary bow, and he was striding right back out of the room before he could rethink his decision.

If there are gods and angels, I pray one of you at least keep her safe for me tomorrow.

Chapter Twenty-Five

What a perfect day for a race, Bobby thought, taking a deep inhale of the briny air, letting the warmth of the sun, the freshness of the early morning breeze, seep through her skin, and give her strength. The sky had only just turned from the pale blue-grey laced with a yellow tinge of dawn, to the bright blue, peppered with gold-kissed white clouds—but there was no mistaking the promise of the day for what it was.

The perfect day for a race.

The perfect day...for many things.

Like winning a race, she thought, smiling to herself as she pushed away the grimmer possibilities. If she was going to do this, she needed to have a clear mind, and a clear heart.

No doubts. No fear.

In truth, she had no fear. Fear of failure, perhaps. Fear of... Many things.

But in this moment? She had no fear of death. No fear of injury.

'Not with you carrying me, my friend,' she said, turning away from the sky, back to Arion.

Laying her forehead against his, she closed her eyes,

and visualised the route they had walked before she'd come to stand here, at the starting line, with him.

Before the entire village, and people from miles away, had gathered to line the path they would race, all the way down to the beach. She didn't need to see that part to know. So many people...

Breathe.

She did, running the fingers of her good hand down the lines of Arion's jaw. As heart-warming as it was that they should all be here, waving fanions or flowers, and shouting encouragement—some insults, but those were quickly erased by more boisterous supporters— she wouldn't get through this if she thought too hard about any of it. Not them, and certainly not the nigh on blinding pain she felt radiating from her shoulder down to the tips of her fingers still. Not the crisp, itchy pain of her smarting face, or the throbbing of her wrist. Achy, dull, sharp; it felt as if every type of pain in the book was present and accounted for.

Even the pain of hope. So alive, a raging wildfire in her heart. What Lawrence had said to her last night... There were no words which could express how alive, how full of joy, and hope they had made her feel. There had been no promises of a future, but just saying what he had...she knew what it had taken him. She'd wanted to leap up with what little strength she had, and hold him close, and tell him she loved him too, but...if she did...

If she had done that, she might've let herself be swayed. To abandon one dream, one need, for another. Instead, she'd locked his declaration safely in her heart, and asked him to do the same, if only for a time, until she could go to him, fulfilled by the completion of this task, so very integral to who she was now.

Foolish, perhaps—who knew if he'd still feel the same after all this, if indeed he intended to offer a future of something more than what they'd had—but she couldn't do anything else. All she could hope for, was a chance to speak to him when this all was over. To find out…what they could have. All she could hope for, was for him to be waiting, love still in his heart as it was in hers, on the other side of all this. For now, however…

Focus on all this.

If she thought about anything but the race, and Arion, she wouldn't stand a chance.

'Just you and me, my friend,' she breathed. 'We can do this. I trust you to help me finish this.'

A neigh, and a nudge of his nose were her answer.

'Riders!' Watkins called.

Opening her eyes, she looked into Arion's for a moment, and nodded.

Gritting her teeth, she grabbed a handful of his mane, prepared to swing up, but before she could, Arion knelt down for her, the crowd gasping and clapping.

'Thank you, my friend,' she whispered, climbing up onto his back.

He rose, and adjusted with her, stepping back and forth, before stilling. Closing her eyes for a moment, she drew in another breath, pushing away the pain her mounting—however easier than it might've been thanks to Arion—had caused.

You can do this.

'Be careful, Bobby,' Julian said grimly, and she opened her eyes to find him at her left side. 'By God, come back to me in one piece please.'

She nodded, emotion clogging her throat.

Reluctantly, he stepped away, disappearing into the crowd where he would find the cart bringing him down to the finish line. She dared to glance to her right, where Lawrence was already atop Beowulf, outfitted as she was in merely a shirt and trousers. He raised a brow, and met her eyes, displeasure, and concern in his gaze that somehow bolstered her determination. He inclined his head, then stared ahead, his jaw ticking.

There was much to be said when this was all over— but for now, she would finish this.

Glancing ahead at the ever-rising sun, casting fire over the village, Bobby focused on the two miles before them.

'Riders—on my mark!'

'Carry me, Arion,' she whispered.

'Three!'

'Carry me like the wind.'

'Two!'

'Show them how we fly.'

'One! Race!' Watkins cried, waving his handkerchief and slipping into the crowd.

Arion bolted ahead, not even needing the nudge of her thighs to know it was time.

She could feel Lawrence and Beowulf beside them, but if she paid them any more attention than that, she would be lost.

This, this is what you live for.

On they galloped, through the cobbled streets, everything a blur, save for her and Arion, steady and sure below her despite the treacherous ground. They slowed just enough at corners, then sped up in the straight lines.

Every bump, every step, sent fire and pain radiating up her arm, and she breathed through it, matching Arion's breaths as she clung tight to him, leaning in, moving with him so that she was nearly his second skin.

There was only them. His strength, fuelling her, as

he truly did fly on. Houses, people, the sky, everything, blurred together in a strange new type of picture.

And then, they reached the descent to the beach.

A rising sun still low on the horizon greeted them, rays of luminescence showing them the way. The wind whipped over and through them, as Arion's hooves met the new terrain, as sure as ever, even as he kicked up sand towards her. She led him to the waterline, finding the perfect spot, where the waves left the sand thick, damp, and slightly more compact. The sea greeted them both with coolness, the dancing rainbow of water celebrating their arrival.

It was the purest feeling she'd ever had before. Everything washed away.

It was…transcendental. Ascending to a higher plane of existence. There was no pain—no future, no past— merely the strange union between two creatures, united as one in this endeavour. A flash of black to her left momentarily tore her from the peaceful state, but without any urging, Arion surged forward. Grinning, Bobby leaned in even more, letting him show everyone what he was truly capable of.

Together, they sailed across the beach, Bobby's eyes glued to the ever-approaching finish line. Her heart beat until it was merely one beat—with the thrill, with hope, with gratitude, with unutterable joy—even as her breathing was as laboured, but steady, as Arion's.

And then, they were past it.

Vaguely, she heard cries, and shouts, and *huzzahs*, but she couldn't quite believe it. Couldn't quite hear it—so wrapped up in the moment as she was.

She let Arion slow at his own pace—there was no doubt he knew what to do. And before she could stop herself, she was crying. Tears, just, pouring out of her, with every pant of unbelieving breath. Tears of relief, of happiness, of pain, of sorrow, yes, a little too. Grief, for the ending of such a journey.

We did it.

'You did it, my friend,' she sobbed, leaning down so she could hug his neck.

He trotted along the waves for a time, until she finally felt ready to turn him back around. Steeling herself for what would meet her, though nothing could quite prepare her for the madness of the crowd cheering for her—for them. She spotted angry, disappointed faces too, but mostly jubilant ones. Even Matthews was clapping. And Julian, he looked so very proud.

Sliding off Arion, knowing he would follow her, or find some space if he needed, she went over, and hugged Julian as hard as she could.

A bad idea, she realised, wincing as he released her.

He tried to say something, but found he couldn't. Though he'd never admit it, she saw the tears in his eyes—and all he meant to say. Nodding, he patted her on the shoulder, and handed her off to Watkins, who took her good hand, and raised it high, to another round of whistling, *whooping* and clapping. Flowers were strewn at her feet, then Matthews was before her, shaking her hand heartily, and declaring her the winner, and she was passed along from person to person, until the crowd stopped.

They just…stopped, and froze, and Bobby knew who she would find when she turned.

And yes, there he was, with Beowulf, looking more magnificent than ever, and making her heart hurt despite all the joy which filled it.

For we have now reached the end.

She might've won the race, won a future, but some-how, it didn't feel quite as complete as it should.

Because he will perhaps, not be part of it.

Lawrence hadn't known there were degrees to being spellbinding, and hypnotic, and fascinating. He had thought Bobby had been all that before…and he was certain she had been. Only, the effect she'd had on him what seemed so long ago now, paled in comparison to how she affected him now.

Racing with her this morning, seeing her in her ele-ment—an Amazon, Selena, a fae, a nymph, all rolled into one… He felt, joy, and pride, and privilege, and ex-hilaration. He hadn't been able to watch her as much as he might've liked—he was focused on the race himself, on doing as he'd promised her, and giving it his all—but in the end, when he'd failed to overtake her on the beach, and Arion had surged forth as though he was one of those horses born of the sea itself…

He'd been able to watch her then. It was a miracle, an incredible, unbelievable sight, not in its nature, but in its unquantifiable, humbling beauty. The grace, the power of them both, charging across the sands in dawn's fiery light… The love in his heart grew to a degree it became unbearable, as if the entirety of the world couldn't con-tain it, much less him.

After all, he was nothing more than a mere mortal man.

And she was the most incredible being to walk this earth. He was certain of it. He didn't deserve to ask for her love, but by God, seeing her now… He couldn't *not*. Tired, in pain, he could tell, but jubilant, shining brighter than the sun itself.

The world stopped when he appeared, having given

her some time to enjoy what she was due. Applause, congratulations, *success*. She had more than earned it, and he wanted her to enjoy it all. Still, his feet eventually carried him forward, and the crowd parted for him, growing quieter, as if terrified of what he might say or do.

As if I could begrudge this woman her win.

He let Beowulf go, as she had Arion, sure the two would go and find somewhere to cool down together.

The bright summer sun sparkled in Bobby's dark hair, brightening her eyes to a lush brown, though he was displeased to see doubt lingering in them. Hesitation. He quirked his head enquiringly as he approached, everyone thankfully giving them a wide berth, even Rothwakes, though Lawrence admittedly came very, *very*, close to Bobby.

His eyes flitted across her face, all he could see, the rest of her hazy, fading into the glorious picture, but so long as he held her gaze, she wasn't lost to it. Returned to it, and lost to him.

Please give me hope.

He'd tried not to think on his declaration last night—its clumsy timing, all left unsaid. He tried not to think on it all for fear he would break his promise to her, but now the race was over, and he couldn't just walk away without doing this…

Properly.

'That was… You were…' Damnation, where had his voice, his eloquence gone? 'Incredible. Magnificent.'

'You raced me with all you had,' she smiled, tears welling in her eyes.

'I did promise I would.'

'Lawrence, I…'

'I shouldn't have leveraged my feelings to make you

quit,' he said before she could send him away, or he could lose his tongue just staring at her again.

'You didn't,' she frowned, and relief helped him catch his breath. 'At least that wasn't how it felt.'

'I… I realised my feelings about twenty miles out of Maidstone,' he admitted, watching her for any sign she didn't wish to hear him out. 'I couldn't wait to find you, to tell you, and then you were hurt, and I was so scared, Bobby.'

His voice broke, and she closed her eyes for a moment, centring herself, and he did too.

Finally she met his gaze again, and though he just wanted to kiss her, and hold her, and take her away somewhere they could be alone, he knew he had to get through this. If he didn't…

She might slip through his fingers.

'I don't know if you feel the same, but if you do… Don't let this be our ending. Whatever you want your life to be, it can be. Let me walk beside you. However you wish. Come visit me—we are neighbours after all,' he pointed out, and she laughed, a wet, choked laugh, but a laugh nonetheless. 'Come live with me, fight with me, I don't care, as long as you're with me. Start your farm wherever you wish, I will follow you if you'll let me. Marry me, if you decide you want that. I never saw marriage in my future, but then, it wouldn't be business with you. It would be a love match, for me at least, and that sounds rather nice. What I'm trying to say, ever so clumsily, is that I love you. I'll never… I'll never ask you to be anyone but yourself. Never ask for you to sacrifice who you are for me. I will do whatever it takes to share a life, and build a future with you. If that is something you might want.'

'I love you too,' Bobby whispered, and his eyes were

round as saucers, he knew it, but he didn't care. Someone, somewhere up high, had smiled on him. Because this woman loved him, and he her. 'I should've... I couldn't tell you last night, but it's the truth. And I think, I'd rather like a life with you. If you think you wouldn't mind having me as your viscountess. Not sure how good I will be at it, but I will give it my all.'

'You'll be perfect, just as you are.'

Grinning, heart full, he leaned down, and kissed her, letting all he felt pour into his kiss. He was mindful of her injuries, setting one hand carefully on her hip, kissing her slowly, gently, but deeply, and passionately, until she put her good arm around his neck and pulled him closer.

Then, he lost himself in what the lady demanded—no quarter.

He heard the crowd cheering and whistling, but he didn't care. Even when he broke their kiss, his eyes remained locked on hers, their foreheads still touching.

Until Rothwakes came back.

'I suppose you'll be wanting to take Arion with you,' he muttered angrily, and both Lawrence and Bobby started, turning to look at him. 'Oh, I'm not happy about this, do not think I am even remotely happy,' the little baron told them, trying to be menacing even as his crutches sank into the sand. 'But I won't stand in your way,' he added begrudgingly, fixing Lawrence with a stare that any man would've been a fool not to heed. 'In case you didn't guess as much, if you hurt her in any way—and I mean if you hurt her feelings by telling her she looks sickly in green, which by the way she does *not*—I will murder you, and use you to fertilise the rosebushes at Rothwakes.'

'Noted,' Lawrence agreed, offering the man his hand.

Rothwakes took it, making sure the message was in fact well taken to heart, before a smirk appeared on his lips.

'And if you think you can renege on any part of the bet, you are sorely mistaken.'

'I wouldn't dream of it.'

'Arion is yours by the way, Bobby,' Rothwakes told her. 'Always has been.'

'Thank you,' she breathed, leaning in to try and hug him, a difficult task considering both their conditions.

Rothwakes, aided by his men, wandered off, telling the crowd to '*leave the happy couple be*', and that drinks would be on him back at the inn.

Appreciative, though he knew they would have to face the well-wishers, and journalists at some point—not that he would ever deny Bobby a proper chance to revel in, and capitalise on, her success—Lawrence led Bobby to the waterline, where Arion and Beowulf waited.

'I should like to travel,' he told her, as they gazed out at the sea. 'This race has ignited my hunger for exploration.'

'Travelling sounds good,' she smiled. Lawrence took her good hand in his, and they walked along the shoreline; with one whistle, Arion and Beowulf followed. 'I think I should like to have a picnic, to celebrate our engagement. A small something.'

'A picnic sounds delightful.'

They walked together for a while, sharing their desires for the future, great and small.

Finally, Lawrence picked her up, and brought her back to the inn to rest for a while—despite what the woman declared she was up to. They napped for a time, nestled together, and then, they descended, to enjoy the celebration raging below.

And for the first time in his life, Lawrence had fun at a party.

Epilogue

Hayes Manor,
December 1838

'You'll wear a path in the otherwise plush carpet, and Fenwick will have your head for it,' Bobby said, leaning against the doorframe of the front drawing room—the one with the best vantage on the full length of the drive. She'd been watching her husband pace the floor for a while now, waiting for him to notice her, but he hadn't, until she spoke.

Husband.

Three months they'd been husband and wife now—having married in the nearby village in a perfectly casual, and simple affair—and still she found the word foreign in her mind and on her tongue. Oh, she liked it, very much; treasured it, cherished it, found quiet honour and beauty in being a wife, having a husband, but nonetheless it felt almost unreal. These past months overall felt incredibly unreal, in their extraordinary majesty and thrill.

Days of pleasure, of fun, of healing—body and heart—of happiness. Of hot summer days riding—

including with little Maureen in Hyde Park; of chilly autumn ones nestled together by the fire. Days full of mending fences—literally and metaphorically, as Rothwakes and Julian buried their old enmity just enough to be in the same room together for more than a few minutes—and days of planning for the future.

Lawrence with his railway—which would now pass through the northern part of his estate, over farmlands which were tired, and less prosperous, the farmers themselves being consulted before the decision was made, and happy to work on greener pastures, so to speak.

Bobby, with finding a farm nearby—close enough to her husband, and to Julian, so that no one need be uprooted—then building it up until it was ready to welcome horses young and old, ill or able, for peace or to be trained and sold. Their short experience with Maureen had also given her the urge to start a riding school for those who wouldn't normally have access to such skills—perhaps even in London. All in all, her dream wasn't much yet, the bare bones, but it was promising, and she had already garnered much interest. Apparently, the woman who'd won the four-hundred-mile race across England was in demand.

The subject of children had been discussed again, and it had been agreed that neither had a particular desire to raise any, but that they would see what life brought them. For now, they were happy just the two of them—horses, dogs, cats, and various other strays notwithstanding—and they were as careful as they could be when in engaging in rather passionate and frequent marital congress as society liked to call it. When christening every room of the manor, and the townhouse, as they liked to call it.

Julian, meanwhile, was busy with the success of Rothwakes' stables—Bobby not alone in having benefited from the publicity of the race—and his efforts to reinvigorate the estate, and ensure they never came so close to catastrophe again. She helped sometimes, though she argued she was merely making sure her replacements weren't making a complete muck of things. Julian and Bobby had had long talks, and though their friendship wasn't what it had once been, it was coming close to. There was something…different about Julian, which remained even after the estate was solvent and steady, and Bobby hoped that in time, he would open himself to her.

In time.

So yes, everything in her life was *good*. It turned out the viscountess Lawrence wanted and needed was in fact the viscountess she could be. Honest, open, suffering no fools, always ready to host a dinner party in the orchard, or sack races by the pond. Even sartorially she hadn't changed much—keeping to her trousers, suits, and shirts most of the time, though she did wear dresses every so often, for her own pleasure. Society had some things to say about the odd little viscountess—but then quickly grew bored, entertained by greater scandals, and eventually, they too, became enamoured with Lady Hayes.

Lady Hayes who turned out in the end to be all of Bobby, and Miss Kingsley, wrapped into one. The reconciliation of all the parts which made her up, finally, in harmony.

And love, as it turned out, at least that which she shared with Lawrence—commitment, being tethered in law, in heart, and soul to another—though still utterly terrifying some days, was worth it.

Some of her anger and general combativeness faded, as she settled, and learned how to worry less about other people. They had plans to travel the Continent—and beyond—next year, but for now at least, they had merely enjoyed the beginning of their life together, in their homes. A life, made of all her relationship with Lawrence had been full with already.

Ease.
Simplicity.
Love.
Rightness.
Adventure.
Pleasure.

Whirling around, Lawrence returned the bright smile she gave him as she returned to the matter at hand, though she couldn't exactly miss the tightness of it—of all of him—nor the anxiousness pulsing off him in jittery waves.

She supposed it was entirely justified, considering.

'They won't even have docked yet, so unless they have a magic flying apparatus, it will be hours still until they arrive.'

'I know, I just…'

'What do you say we go for a ride, husband,' she offered, stepping into the room, and to him. 'A crisp, cold day, with little frost or snow on the ground…'

He nodded as she slid her hands to his shoulders, and he kissed her sweetly as his own went to her waist.

'Fenwick and Mrs Llewelyn have everything under control here,' she reminded him, hugging him tightly. She liked this—being able to touch him, kiss him, whenever she felt like it, and she thought he rather liked it too, considering how often he indulged, polite company notwithstanding. 'All will be fine, you'll see.'

'I feel a bit foolish now the day has come,' he admitted softly, toying with the end of her queue, wrapping and unwrapping it in his fingers. 'I wonder what purpose this all serves.'

'To meet new people,' Bobby offered, leaning back to look him in the eye, still holding him tight. 'To make peace with that part of your past. Because you want to,' she grinned.

'Quite right,' he agreed. 'It will be nice to have some company for Christmas, if only to distract me from the fact Rothwakes will be wandering around these halls.'

Lawrence mock shuddered and she swatted his arm.

He liked to pretend he still hated Julian, but Bobby knew it was all for show. Julian was special to her, and therefore, to Lawrence. They might never be great friends, but neither of them ever wished to cause Bobby harm, so they…endured each other.

And as for those other people who would be joining them…

Milicent's daughter, Emily, now ten years old, and the couple who had taken her in. Lawrence had expressed a desire to do more for the girl, and Bobby had suggested he write to the parents, see what their thoughts might be. It emerged that they had in fact told Emily of her true mother, and that all the little girl needed was a chance to know something of Milicent. They had been asking for miniatures, or stories, but instead Lawrence sent them an invitation to visit. He failed to see the logic in his own gesture—but made it anyway—though Bobby reassured him that he should merely listen to his heart. No matter his relationship with Millicent, he could give this little girl pieces of her past—and Bobby for one knew how precious that could be. Besides, who knew what would happen.

So here they were, waiting for a not so imminent arrival.

'I have a new game I wish to play,' Bobby said, narrowing her eyes. 'We shall race to the old ash tree on Greenbrook Farm, and if I win, you cannot say anything disparaging about Julian for at least... A day,' she said, thinking anything more would prove impossible—bet or no bet.

Lawrence pretended to stumble back, half cradling her, a hand flying to cover his heart.

'I best not lose then,' he chuckled. 'And what if I win?'

'Your choice.'

'I get my coat back. *And* you have to decide the menus with Mrs Llewelyn for a week.'

'Evil, evil man,' Bobby hissed. The infamous coat she'd *borrowed* during the race...he could have back—she would merely steal it again. But the menus... Typically, that was his job—because apparently Mrs Llewelyn didn't care much for Bobby's *stew, stew, rabbit* requests. 'I suppose I have some serious skin in the game too, then.'

Waggling her brows, she released him, and sprinted off, Lawrence on her heels, the two of them giggling and laughing like unruly children.

In the end, technically Lawrence won, though she felt she did too when he took her up against the old ash tree while Beowulf and Arion made themselves scarce.

But then, she'd already won the greatest prize one could ever ask for.

Love.

* * * * *

If you enjoyed this story, why not check out Lotte R. James' Gentlemen of Mystery miniseries?

The Housekeeper of Thornhallow Hall
The Marquess of Yew Park House
The Gentleman of Holly Street

Get 3 FREE REWARDS!

We'll send you 2 FREE Books plus a FREE Mystery Gift.

FREE
Value Over
$20

Both the **Harlequin® Historical** and **Harlequin® Romance** series feature compelling novels filled with emotion and simmering romance.

YES! Please send me 2 FREE novels from the Harlequin Historical or Harlequin Romance series and my FREE Mystery Gift (gift is worth about $10 retail). After receiving them, if I don't wish to receive any more books, I can return the shipping statement marked "cancel." If I don't cancel, I will receive 6 brand-new Harlequin Historical books every month and be billed just $6.19 each in the U.S. or $6.74 each in Canada, a savings of at least 11% off the cover price, or 4 brand-new Harlequin Romance Larger-Print books every month and be billed just $6.09 each in the U.S. or $6.24 each in Canada, a savings of at least 13% off the cover price. It's quite a bargain! Shipping and handling is just 50¢ per book in the U.S. and $1.25 per book in Canada.* I understand that accepting the 2 free books and gift places me under no obligation to buy anything. I can always return a shipment and cancel at any time by calling the number below. The free books and gift are mine to keep no matter what I decide.

Choose one: ☐ **Harlequin Historical**
(246/349 BPA GRNX)

☐ **Harlequin Romance Larger-Print**
(119/319 BPA GRNX)

☐ **Or Try Both!**
(246/349 & 119/319 BPA GRRD)

Name (please print)

Address   Apt. #

City   State/Province   Zip/Postal Code

Email: Please check this box ☐ if you would like to receive newsletters and promotional emails from Harlequin Enterprises ULC and its affiliates. You can unsubscribe anytime.

Mail to the Harlequin Reader Service:
IN U.S.A.: P.O. Box 1341, Buffalo, NY 14240-8531
IN CANADA: P.O. Box 603, Fort Erie, Ontario L2A 5X3

Want to try 2 free books from another series! Call 1-800-873-8635 or visit www.ReaderService.com.

*Terms and prices subject to change without notice. Prices do not include sales taxes, which will be charged (if applicable) based on your state or country of residence. Canadian residents will be charged applicable taxes. Offer not valid in Quebec. This offer is limited to one order per household. Books received may not be as shown. Not valid for current subscribers to the Harlequin Historical or Harlequin Romance series. All orders subject to approval. Credit or debit balances in a customer's account(s) may be offset by any other outstanding balance owed by or to the customer. Please allow 4 to 6 weeks for delivery. Offer available while quantities last.

Your Privacy—Your information is being collected by Harlequin Enterprises ULC, operating as Harlequin Reader Service. For a complete summary of the information we collect, how we use this information and to whom it is disclosed, please visit our privacy notice located at corporate.harlequin.com/privacy-notice. From time to time we may also exchange your personal information with reputable third parties. If you wish to opt out of this sharing of your personal information, please visit readerservice.com/consumerschoice or call 1-800-873-8635. **Notice to California Residents**—Under California law, you have specific rights to control and access your data. For more information on these rights and how to exercise them, visit corporate.harlequin.com/california-privacy.

HHHRLP23